Show Up Dead

by Lisa Shiroff

Tasfil Publishing LLC

New Jersey, USA

ISBN: 0986258008

ISBN-13: 978-0986258008

Other books by this author:

Hitting the Sauce
Revenge Café

Short Stories by this author:

What You Tell Yourself
What Others Tell You
An Original Story

It's redundant, I know, but I dedicate this one

to my husband, Glenn.

It's because of you that I met Philadelphia.

I love you.

Table of Contents

Show Up Dead

Chapter 1: Best Interest

I'm pretty sure my eyes had been open for several minutes before I realized I could see. I remember darkness. Then light. Then blurred masses of color. Eventually the colors became distinguishable and detailed enough that I knew I was staring at a highly polished, mahogany ball-and-claw foot of a table leg. The points of the claws were painted with red lacquer. The table leg was standing on a Persian rug. The same Persian rug my face appeared to be resting on.

It was Mr. Wooley's Persian rug, which made sense since I was pretty sure I had gone into Mr. Wooley's house that morning.

The good news was that it didn't seem as if I was alone. A woman's stilted voice pierced the air, someone was tapping my cheek, and I sensed movement around me.

I rolled onto my back and found a man hovering over me, his blond head only about a foot above mine. Even though his face was upside down from my perspective, it was still quite pleasing to look at. His sapphire blue eyes peered at me with such intensity, I wondered if I were asleep and dreaming. Traditionally, I'd never been the kind of girl with charming knights at the ready for her rescue. Though I never thought it would be a detriment.

"Are you okay?" he asked. The unimaginative question disappointed me.

"I don't know." I leaned up on one elbow. "What happened?"

"I was hoping you could tell me," my handsome hero replied. He glanced up as another man, a dark-haired one who wasn't all that delicious to look at, knelt opposite him and took my free hand.

Looking around me, I confirmed I was in Mr. Wooley's townhouse, as were several of Philadelphia's finest men in blue. They were keeping company with a few other sundry people whose presence, I learned later, was useful whenever a dead body was found.

"Are you in any pain?" asked the man holding my hand. It turns out he was in an EMT uniform and was actually taking my pulse.

"I don't think so," I said. "I—"

"Peri!" shrieked Mr. Wooley's daughter. She ran across the room and dropped to the floor, bursting into my personal space before I was ready to deal with her. I fell back against my blue-eyed guardian angel. He righted me.

"What's going on?" I asked.

"My father!" Jacqueline's breath shot in and out. She shoved the EMT away then gripped my arms as if she were preparing to throw me over a balcony. "He's dead!"

"What?" I pulled my face back. She leaned in closer. My blond defender put his hand on her shoulder as if to shove her back.

She released her hold on me and flung her long wavy brown hair over her shoulder. "My father." She placed the back of her hand on her forehead. "He has passed."

"Is this . . . are you rehearsing?" I asked. I still wasn't sure whether I were awake or not. If I was, the only thing that could rationally explain the situation was if Jacqueline–pronounced with a soft *Zha* at the beginning and a long *eeeeen* at the end–was holding an acting workshop in her father's home. She did that periodically. She called them *impromptu performances*. Anyone who happened to be in the vicinity would either be forced into a nonspeaking role or expected to provide thunderous applause, complete with *encore!* calls, at the end.

"What have you done to him?" Jacqueline clasped her hands in prayer position. Her eyes pleaded with mine.

"To who?" I asked.

"I need to look at her." The EMT bent in front of Jacqueline to shine a light in my face. "Your vitals check out okay. Do you think you can stand?"

I nodded.

"It wouldn't hurt to get evaluated at the hospital," he added.

"I don't like hospitals," I said.

The EMT smirked as he stood. "I'm done here," he called out before walking away.

Jacqueline had disappeared, leaving me alone with my mystery man.

"I have a few questions for you if you're ready," he said as he helped me up.

We stood before the never-used wingback chair in Mr. Wooley's dining room. In the chair sat Mr. Wooley. A team of people separated him from me. They appeared to be inspecting him at a very close range.

"Oh my God." I pressed my fingertips against my temples almost able to remember why I was in Mr. Wooley's townhouse.

"Do you need the EMT again?" the man asked.

"No. I'm, I think I'm okay." My face scrunched as I looked at him. "Did I already ask what happened?"

"You did." He nodded. "Where did you come from?"

I inhaled deeply while I thought about his question.

"The back door." I pointed to the rear of the townhouse. Mr. Wooley's home stretched a half block. The front door opened to the street, the back to a narrow alley. "Yes, that's right," I continued. "I parked behind the townhouse . . . I knocked." I tucked my hair behind my ear. "Mr. Wooley didn't answer. He was expecting me. So I waited. Then I just came in. He lets me do that. I just like to knock first. Anyway, I had flowers for him."

"Are you the one who brought the funeral flowers?" His eyes took on a steely quality, somewhat akin to how my accountant's look when he challenges my claims for deductible expenses.

"Yes." My voice cracked. Stark memories from the morning emerged from the fog in my brain. "Is Mr. Wooley really dead?" I asked, although I knew the answer.

"The body of Shelby Wooley was found by his daughter this morning. She notified the police then waited for us at the front of his home. When she brought us to him, you were lying on the floor next to him. How did you get here and why are you here?"

"Like I said, I knocked—"

"I got that. How did you get in? Do you have a key?"

"I do, but I didn't use it. The door was unlocked."

"I see. So you came in. Then what happened?"

"I put the flowers on the counter and called out for Mr. Wooley. He didn't answer. So I went to look for him. That's when I saw the wax figure. I mean, I thought it was the wax figure. Then I, I . . . touched . . . his cheek and it . . ." My ears rang. "I think I need to . . ." was all I got out.

I awoke in the man's arms as he dragged me to a sofa at the front of the house. Mr. Wooley was out of sight.

"Do you need water?" he asked.

"Please."

He left me for a few minutes and returned with a glass of water. The EMT was on his heels.

"Thank you." I accepted the glass. "I feel silly. I haven't fainted in years."

The EMT took my pulse again. "Do you think it's possible someone hit you over the head earlier?" he asked.

I reached around to feel the back of my skull. "I'm not tender anywhere. I'm sure I fainted."

"Do you have a history of fainting?"

"Yeah. I used to do it a lot as a kid."

He looked into my eyes again. "I think you're okay. It would still be a good idea to get looked at by someone at the hospital."

"It's not necessary," I insisted. "Really. I'm allergic to hospitals." I sipped the water. "Actually, I'm allergic to their bills. They give me hives. Make me hyperventilate.

"I hear that's a common side effect," he said as he left.

"Sure you feel better?" mystery man asked.

"No, but I'm conscious so I guess I must be."

"Good. I have to ask you a couple more questions. I am Detective Collin Beatty. This is," he tilted his head toward a man who had just joined us, "my partner, Detective Micah Jameson."

"Hello," I said.

Detective Jameson nodded.

"And you are?" Beatty asked.

"I'm Peri Milano."

"Why are you here, Peri?" Jameson asked.

"I was bringing flowers for Mr. Wooley."

"The ones in the kitchen with the ribbon that says *In Sympathy*," Jameson said, or maybe asked.

"Yes," I offered in case it was a question.

The men exchanged a glance.

"How did you know Shelby Wooley was dead?" Beatty asked.

"I didn't." I set the glass on a coffee table, suddenly aware of how bad the situation looked for me. "I'm organizing a funeral-themed party for him. He is very particular about the details. I brought the flowers to get his approval on the red tips of the callas. The florist has been having a tough time getting the right shade of red dye."

"Who is the florist?" Beatty asked.

"Pearl Slack at Custom Floral Designs." I gave them poor Pearl's number. She'd found this event to be more of an artistic challenge than she was prepared for. I had a feeling her stress level would see a cliff-dive once she realized the pseudo-funeral was off.

"Why did you come through the back door?" Jameson asked.

"I always do when I'm bringing props. Mr. Wooley wants everything to be a surprise. No one is supposed to know all the details. Not even Jacqueline." I glanced toward the back of the house, to where Jacqueline stood speaking with someone. Her head was tilted. She held a hand over her heart.

Together, the men grilled me over the events of the day, about my relationship with Mr. Wooley, and then took my full contact information. I answered their questions all the while straining my ears to hear what the others in the house were saying. It seemed they were under the impression Mr. Wooley was put in the chair after he had passed away.

Eventually they sent me on my not-so-merry way, advising me it would be in my best interest to stay in town.

Chapter 2: Cookies

Outside in the back alley, I sat behind the steering wheel of my ancient Ford Explorer while I called my mother. The woman was a bit of a nutcase, though she never failed to have some kind of help or advice. Granted it wasn't always useful, nor was it ever offered with a cookie, still, she did her best to act like a normal mom and she was the only mom I had.

"I touched a dead body," I said when she picked up.

"Really? Why?" she asked.

"I thought it was a wax figure."

"How did it feel?"

"Spongy." I dropped my head back to rest on the car seat.

"What part did you touch?"

"The cheek."

"Butt or face?"

"Yuck!" I straightened to look out the front window. It was late April, but being in the back alley, there were no blooming flowers, nothing cheery, to be seen. "Why would I touch a dead butt?"

"Why would you touch a dead face?"

"Like I said, I thought it was a wax figure. I touched the face."

"Was it grimacing?"

"Uh . . . I don't know. Why?"

"Just wondering how dead it was."

"Oh God." I sighed. "Why did I call you?"

"Maybe that was the wrong choice of words. I was just wondering if you could tell if rigor mortis had set in. It begins with the face before stiffening up the rest of the body. Then it all reverses. What most people don't know is that the body gets soft again."

"Do I want to know how you know that?"

"*Criminal Minds.*"

"Who?"

"A TV show."

"Oh." I think I sighed again. "Do you have any cookies?"

"Of course not. I do have some delicious grain-free muffins. I made them with almond meal for a change instead of almond flour. How's *that* for living dangerously?"

"You're on the edge, Ma."

"Want some?"

"I don't think so." I wanted bright flowers. Bright flowers and cookies made with wheat gluten and sugar.

"You sure? They have walnuts and coconut flakes," she sang.

"Sounds tempting," I lied. "I have too much to do today."

"Don't get so busy you don't allow yourself to grieve."

"I wasn't that close to him, Ma. I'll be okay."

"That's what everyone says before they self-destruct in unresolved grief."

"I'm fine, Ma."

"Then why did you call me?"

"I can't remember." We clicked off.

I wanted to go home, climb into bed, and pull the covers over my head. Maybe even do it with a plate of cookies. You can always wash cookie crumbs out of bed sheets.

I looked at my to-do list on the passenger seat. It reminded me I was a girl of few luxuries, most notably of the time-off variety. As the owner of a one-woman business, I had to plan and organize far in advance for any downtime. As tempting as it was to ignore the outside world by going home, I had another client to meet first.

I started the truck, put it in gear and headed toward the east side of town. I had to make two pit stops along the way: one for a large black coffee with a chunk of plain biscotti on the side, the other for a nasal decongestant to relieve my stuffy head. Inside Pearl's shop is a flower that always gives me grief. The symptoms have a rhythm: shortly after I walk into her store my eyes burn and my nose runs. As soon as I leave, the burning stops and my nose clogs up. I never seemed to have allergies anywhere else in the world except in that shop. The obvious thing to do would be to find another florist. Unfortunately, she was the best of the best. My clients expected the best of the best.

Fortified and medicated, I arrived at a high rise on the Delaware River. A guard at the gated entry took my name before clearing my entry. Within a few minutes, I was several stories up meeting Brittany Johanssen to discuss her son's birthday party. She was a new client. This would be my first event for her, so I had no idea what to expect.

The Johanssen's apartment faced north. Looking out the windows of their great room, to my left was a gorgeous view of Philadelphia, to the right, the Delaware River. We were so high up that Camden, New Jersey actually looked pretty on the other side of the water.

Mrs. Johanssen invited me to sit in a white leather chair. She and her son, Aidan, sat across from me on a matching white leather sofa. Little Aidan was cute: a towheaded, blue-eyed imp playing a game on his iPad. He squatted on his sneaker-clad feet, heels firmly planted in the cushion below his rear.

"So how old will you be?" I asked him. Really I was more interested in how often their housecleaner had to scrub that leather and what did she use?

"He'll be six, but that's just between us," Mrs. Johanssen answered for him.

"I don't understand." I perched on the edge of my chair reminding myself he wasn't my son. If she didn't have a problem with his dirty shoes on the white leather, I shouldn't either. Really, I shouldn't, I thought as I forced myself to look at her.

"His birthday is the beginning of July," she said, making eye contact with me, briefly, before returning her attention to her manicure. "If we had put him in Kindergarten last fall, he would have been one of the youngest in the classroom. We didn't think he was ready, so we delayed his entrance into school."

"I see." My son, Ezra, was born in August. His preschool teachers had tried to talk me into holding him back because boys supposedly weren't ready for school when they were a "young five." I had to go against their well wishes back then. I couldn't afford another year of full-day day care.

"By holding him back," Mrs. Johanssen continued, "his age will serve him instead of being a hindrance. It will give him an edge."

"Right."

"But we don't want other kids to think he's a flunkie."

"Of course not." I felt my eyebrows lift.

"So we're going with not mentioning his age at all. If anyone asks, we're saying it's his fifth birthday party." She gave me a benign smile. "We didn't hold a party when he was three, so we'll be telling the truth if we say it that way."

I nodded, slowly. "So, do you have a theme in mind? Is there a special place where you want to have it?"

"Unfortunately, I think Atlantic City is our best option," Mrs. Johanssen said. "I'm hoping you could do some magic to make it happen here in Philly. I've been told you can micromanage miracles."

"Micromanage?"

"Yes, so I'm sure it won't be a problem for you. Of course, if you can't find a place here, you'll have to rent a bus or arrange limos to transport the kids to the shore. If you do that, then I suppose you'll have to find some kind of entertainment for them while they're travelling."

"Why are you thinking AC? Do you want a boardwalk theme?"

"I hate the boardwalk!" Aidan shouted. He jumped—literally jumped—jumped in his *dirty sneakered feet*—on the sofa to ensure I got the point.

"Oh, so is it beach-themed?" I clenched my jaw.

"No," his mother said. "Aidan wants an MMA party. They have cages for it in AC."

"MMA?" I held my breath for a count of three. "As in mixed martial arts?" I managed to ask, instead of scolding both child and mother while he, *in his dirty sneakers*, continued to jump on the white leather sofa with iPad in hand.

"Exactly!" Mrs. Johanssen clasped her hands together. "Aidan just loves wrestling. He wants an ultimate fighting party."

I pretended to make another note as I struggled to switch gears mentally. I needed to think about the potential ramifications of such a party. As people continually tried to top each other with their events, I'd started bumping up against legal issues. Recently, my cousin Melissa had suggested I start dating attorneys to get free legal advice. She was joking at the time, but I was beginning to think the idea had merit.

"You're not expecting the kids to fight, are you?" I asked.

"Yeah!" Aidan threw the iPad on the white tile floor as he jumped over the back of the sofa. He began kicking and punching the air.

"Can you do that?" Mrs. Johanssen asked. "With proper protection, of course," she added over Aidan's grunts. We paused to watch as he threw an imagined adversary to the ground and pummeled him.

"I will do my best." I smiled at her, or maybe I grimaced.

"Good! I'll e-mail you the people we want to definitely come as well as those you should invite anyway."

"Got it."

"I'd like to have it the last Saturday in June. What else? Oh, yes. I promised the hubby I wouldn't go over fifteen, tops."

She meant fifteen thousand dollars. Roughly what my son's high school guidance counselor told me I should expect to pay for each semester Ezra would be in college, if he didn't get a scholarship. Working for me was the fact that Ez had a genius-level IQ, which clearly he didn't get from his father. Yes, that meant I had made the right decision by not holding him back in preschool. In fact, he wound up skipping sixth grade. If I'd been psychic, I would have pulled him out of preschool a year earlier and invested that tuition in his meager college fund.

Of course, getting into a state school on a scholarship was pretty much guaranteed for him. Unfortunately, Ezra had his sights set on the physics programs either at the University of California or Harvard. Both places attract geniuses on such a grand scale that we can't take scholarships for granted.

In other words, I didn't balk at the idea of throwing a fifteen-grand party for a non-five-year-old. Some of my clients have me on a monthly retainer; Mrs. Johanssen was not one of them. For my services, I'd charge her twenty percent of the cost of the party. Perhaps that would at least be enough for a semester's worth of textbooks.

I left Mrs. Johanssen's building and drove across the Ben Franklin Bridge, admiring how clean it looked in the afternoon sun as I entered New Jersey. Next on my list was a visit to a small boutique in Cherry Hill where I was to purchase eight identical evening gowns.

As I had explained to the detectives earlier in the day, I'm not just a party planner. In fact, I never call myself that. On my business card it says I'm a *Lifestyle Manager,* a title I invented. I used to have a website that pretty much depicted me as a cross between a personal assistant and a concierge for the rich and less-than-famous Philadelphia elite. I took the website down when word of mouth proved more efficient at spreading my reputation.

Mostly, my services are requested for relatively sane and useful reasons. I still organize parties. I also find hard-to-get tickets to major events, make dinner reservations, coordinate meetings, and plan and reserve vacations. On the day-to-day level, I follow through on routine expectations ensuring my clients have peace of mind (without them ever needing to make a phone call) that their dog walkers, plant waterers, and house cleaners are done with their assignments on time; that their clothes are sent to the cleaners, picked up and repaired if necessary; that their friends and relatives receive cards or gifts for birthdays and anniversaries; that their daughters have flowers waiting for them after every dance recital and that their sons get the preferred time slots for little-league baseball lessons. None of them ever has to wait for repair techs or deliveries. Few of them do their own grocery shopping. They all rely on the fact that I know every popular restaurant manager by name and that I have an "in" with ticketing agencies.

Often, my job is routine and redundant. Sometimes, it borders on obscure and weird. Mostly, it's fun. Oh, and it pays well, particularly well for a high school dropout, thirty-one-year-old single mom of a diabetic fifteen-year-old son (please don't do the math).

With the organizational skills of a data processing program, the discretion of the CIA, and the creativity of an Ikea research and design engineer (that's how one of my clients described me in a thank-you card), I am the go-to for whatever whim my customers fancy to have fulfilled, and whatever method they needed for their madness.

Case in point: I went to Jersey that day on a mission to ensure no other woman in the Philadelphia region would wear the same dress as one of my clients to a major gala at the Kimmel Center the following month. That particular client had worn a dress identical to the hostess at two other events earlier in the year. She didn't want to risk it happening again. So she asked if I could do a little research to see who was selling it within a fifty-mile radius, then buy each one. After the gala, I would put them all up for sale at a consignment shop, tags attached, of course, on her behalf.

I returned home to my end-unit row house in northeast Philly just after lunchtime. The urge to hide in my bed had passed. The urge to eat cookies remained. I also wanted a shower. Every time I thought about how I touched Mr. Wooley's dead cheek, my ick factor raised. Despite doing everything in my power not to think about him, I did anyway. Too frequently, all morning.

I took a quick shower and changed into jeans and a big T-shirt before heading back downstairs to the dining room, which doubles as my office. According to my to-do list, I had plenty of time to bake something before I tackled anything else on it. Unfortunately, I didn't have much in the kitchen to cook with. I wound up using the last egg and what was left of the butter to make a small batch of chocolate-chip-Bailey's cookies.

While they baked, I did a background check on a potential nanny for a client. Called a Woodle breeder (a cross between a Poodle and a Wheaton Terrier) to see when he was expecting his next litter of puppies for another client. Then made three follow-up calls to some slackers who were overdue with their RSVPs for yet a different client's daughter's bat mitzvah.

While the cookies cooled, I ran a stack of envelopes through my printer to address them for graduation announcements. When the printing was done, the cookies were cool. So I took a break.

I moved into the living room where I sat on the floor to drink a fresh cup of coffee while I finally ate my favorite stress reliever.

Mrs. Johanssen called before I took my first bite.

"I just sent you the invite list. Did you get it?" she asked through the speaker of my cell.

I tapped on my phone to peek at my e-mail.

"Yes, it just came in."

"Good. I wanted to double-check. Sometimes e-mail doesn't work, you know."

"Right. You're safe." I clicked off and ate a cookie. The second I dunked in the coffee. By the time I finished the third, I was almost feeling like myself again. After cleaning up my dishes, I returned to the living room floor to let the TV keep me company while I stuffed the graduation announcements into their envelopes.

A talk show had been interrupted with breaking news.

Jessica Williamson, a perky, tough-looking reporter, whose blond hair I greatly admired, was standing across the street from Mr. Wooley's townhouse.

"It's been suggested the eccentric millionaire's untimely death was the result of foul play," she said. "The police have confirmed there was no sign of forced entry into the premises, nor apparently is there evidence to suggest Wooley struggled against an adversary. However, they are investigating as if—"

"My father was murdered!" Jacqueline suddenly filled the camera's view. She gripped tight to Jessica's microphone. With a toss of her head, she flicked her hair back. "I don't know how I'll ever heal from this, this tragedy." Her free hand clutched at her throat. "I won't rest until the murderer is put behind bars."

I pointed the remote at the television again and clicked it off.

For some reason, I never thought about *how* Mr. Wooley had died that morning. To think he'd been murdered was unsettling to say the least. Now I understood why the detectives had questioned me the way they did. Obviously, my showing up with funeral flowers for a dead man would be suspicious. But that didn't bother me.

What did bother me was the fact that only a handful of people knew Mr. Wooley was in Philadelphia this week. I knew them all. And that meant: I probably knew the murderer.

Chapter 3: Something Wrong

I called my mom again as I finished stuffing the envelopes. This time I didn't call with the vain hope of getting support or an offering of a sweet treat. One of my mother's many favorite pastimes was watching TV crime shows. I knew she'd get a kick out of learning her daughter had been at the scene of a murder.

Unfortunately, her line went to voice mail.

I sealed and applied custom-made stamps to the envelopes. Back at my computer, I cleared out my e-mails and updated my to-do list. I would mail the invitations on my way to my next appointment.

Promptly at four thirty, I met a furniture delivery crew at a high-rise next to Washington Square. They'd brought a replacement sofa for the faded one up in the Hoskinson's penthouse. I went in the main entrance of the building, spoke with Stephen, the concierge, then walked down a back hallway to open the freight entrance door. The door was surprisingly resistant. I had to jostle and force it into place while the delivery men waited for me, holding the sofa in their hands, on the other side.

"You dropped your phone." The delivery man, whose nametag read *JT,* said when I finally got the door opened. He nodded toward my feet.

I looked down. My phone lay in its solid black case on the sidewalk by my feet. Apparently I hadn't tucked it into my pocket well enough and it fell out when I struggled with the door. Just glancing down, I could clearly see how the old crack that had crossed just the top left corner of the touch screen was now joined by several more. The face of my cell looked like it was covered by a dense spider web struggling to hold the phone together.

"Thanks," I half-groaned. "You'd think the way I treat this thing that I had something against it."

"Well, if that's the way you are, we better stay on your good side," JT's partner, whose nametag also read *JT,* said.

"That's right." I grinned at them with narrowed eyes. "I'm tougher than I look."

As soon as the couch made it safely into the building, I grabbed the phone. I shoved it as deep as it would go into my back pocket before running to beat the men to the elevator. I hit the up button then retrieved a key from a side pocket of my purse. Once the elevator landed, I went inside, stuck the key into the hole for the penthouse floor and held the *doors open* button.

JT Number One leaned in and eyed the car.

"This ain't no freight elevator," he said. "I hope no one gets mad at us."

"What do you mean?" I asked.

"People in buildings this nice don't like to be put out none by us workin' folk. My supervisor gets a call that I'm in the wrong place, I'll—"

"Oh no! You don't have to worry about that. Trust me," I assured him. "This is a private elevator."

"Private, huh?" he whistled. "Man, some people got the *life.*"

They brought the sofa in and stood it on its end. Within a few minutes, the elevator eased to a stop and the doors opened onto the foyer of the Hoskinson's unit. I led the men down a short hall. We turned in to the living room where I was surprised to find Carolyn Hoskinson. She held tight to a glass of wine as she stared out over the tree tops in Washington Square.

"M—Carolyn," I called, remembering at the last second she wanted me to use her first name. "I thought you were heading over to Atlantic City for the weekend. Is everything okay?"

She turned slowly. Her eyes slid to the men then back to me.

"Of course it is," she said after she visibly pulled herself together.

"I had a headache so I told Gerard to go without me. The last place I want to be tonight is in a casino full of loud noise."

"I understand. I'll have these guys out in a flash," I assured her. In the center of the room, I touched the sofa that was to be replaced. "This is the one. You'll only need a second or two, right, gentlemen?"

"Whatever you want. I don't want my face lookin' like that phone of yours," JT Number Two laughed.

Carolyn left the room while the men switched out the sofas. I found her in the kitchen pouring another glass of wine.

"We're about finished," I said, eyeing up the nearly empty bottle. I knew wine only made headaches worse, however the look on her face suggested a headache was not really at the root of her suffering, so I kept mum. "Anything else I can do for you?"

Carolyn didn't answer right away. She fixed her eyes on me, as if determining whether she did have another need.

"All done out here," JT Number One said. "We're ready to head down."

"Great." I looked at him over my shoulder then turned back to Carolyn. "I'll see them out. Let me know how the new sofa works out, okay?"

"I will. And yes, Peri. I think I do have something else for you. I just need to think a little about it first. Will you be around tomorrow?"

"Absolutely."

"I'll call you then."

Outside I signed off on the delivery papers and gave each man a tip before heading toward my Explorer.

My cell phone rang from within my purse, which was odd since I thought I'd put it in my back pocket.

I dug it out. Just one crack ran across the upper left corner.

My cousin Ed was calling. Ed owned a bunch of neighborhood bars, including the one in my neighborhood. He'd been relying on me to work as a substitute bartender there since I was twenty-one. In fact, I had worked for him the night before, so I had a feeling he was calling to see if I could come in again that night.

I wasn't sure if I wanted to do it. While I appreciated the tips I could get on a Friday night, I had promised Ezra that the kids on his high school Invent Team could come over that evening, both boys and girls. Even though they were all super-bright kids intent on finishing the invention they were creating to represent their school at a competition, I wasn't completely comfortable leaving them alone for a very late night. Ezra may have inherited his smartness from my side of the family, but he was also living proof as to why boys and girls at the height of hormonal stupidness should not be left alone too much.

The phone decided for me. It quit ringing before I could make up my mind about working for Ed. I tossed it back in my purse then reached around to my pocket. So very glad I wasn't going to have to replace the screen on *that* cell, I gingerly scrolled through the contacts. There was nothing under *I* for *in case of emergency*, something I had forced my son to do. Nothing was under *home* either. I searched from *A* to *Z* until I found *mom*.

I clicked *call*.

"Ricky!" A woman answered. "Are you that lazy? You couldn't just walk down the stairs to talk to me?"

"I think Ricky lost his phone," I said. "I found it."

"Are you kidding me? He didn't say anything when he came in. I bet he doesn't even know." The woman must have moved her phone away from her face because I could hear her calling for Ricky to get his ass downstairs. "Would you believe this is the fourth phone he's lost this year?"

I climbed into my Ford. "How old is he?"

"Sixteen."

"Yeah, I believe it. My son's fifteen. He's the same way. Constantly losing things."

"So it's normal?"

"I think so." I started the engine.

"I'm glad to hear that. Still, I don't think he should get it back right away. Do you mind keeping it for a few days, as a kind of punishment?"

"I don't mind. Like I said, I have a son. I understand consequences."

"Thanks. He's a good kid, just so irresponsible. These phones are expensive!"

Her voice had such a bark to it, I felt sorry for poor Ricky.

"I understand your frustration," I said. "But think about it. When you were sixteen, could you keep track of a tiny piece of equipment?"

"I don't know. I'd like to think I could."

"Well I know I couldn't," I said. "I couldn't even keep track of my virginity."

The woman burst out laughing. "Thank you! I needed a laugh. And thanks for calling. That was kind of you." Her voice softened. "You're the first one ever to call. How can we get the phone?"

I gave her my street address and cell number. We agreed he could come get it on Sunday morning.

"Thank you, again," the woman said. "It's not every day when you hear about good deeds being done in this city."

I hung up, taking for granted that some good deeds actually do go unpunished.

My cell rang again as I pulled into the alley behind my row house. It stopped before I had a chance to park. I dug it out of my purse after I shut off the engine. Ed had called a second time. I returned the call.

"Yo, Peri!" he shouted at the other end of the line. He wasn't really shouting. Ed is a tried-and-true Philly boy, as much as any man could be a Philly boy, which meant he spoke loudly when he was on the phone. "You seen Mel lately?"

"As in today? No."

"Heard from her?"

"Nope." I stepped out of my truck and went around to the rear. "Is something wrong?"

"She's not picking up her goddamned phone. I can't find her anywhere."

"It's near the end of the month, Ed. I'm sure she's just busy doing office stuff." I removed the dresses from Jersey. With them draped over one shoulder, I shut the rear hatch with a grunt.

"I get that. What I don't get, is why she's not busy someplace where I can freaking find her. Look, if you hear from her before I do, tell her to call me."

We clicked off. I headed up the rear steps to my house, opened the backdoor of my home and nearly walked into the refrigerator door. My kitchen is a little on the small side.

"Hello," I said to the appliance. The door shut. Instead of seeing Ezra standing there, it was Melissa, Ed's wife.

"Hey there." She stepped aside to let me walk past.

"Ed's looking for you. You need to give him a call."

"I can't. I'm not speaking to him." She opened the refrigerator door again. "Do you realize you have absolutely nothing to eat?"

"I was planning on ordering in tonight. Ezra has a gang of kids coming over," I yelled from the dining room. I set the dresses on the table.

"What are those for?" Mel asked from the doorway.

I explained.

"These are nice." She ran her finger along the zigzag of sequins running down the length. "Any in my size?"

"You going somewhere where you need a dress like that?"

"No plans right now. A girl can dream, though, right?"

"Right." I smirked at her. "You never know."

I went to the front room, my living room. Near the door, I turned around to yell up the stairs. "Yo! Ez!"

No answer.

Back in the kitchen, I noticed Melissa was in denial about my state of provisions. She stood before the reopened fridge with hands on hips, staring into the cold, blank space.

I opened the door to the basement. "Yo! Ez!" I yelled and waited.

"I'll be up in a sec!" he yelled back.

"Seriously, you have nothing," Melissa slammed the door shut.

"Sorry. I haven't had time to grocery shop. What's in your fridge at home?"

"About the same." She flopped onto a chair at the table. "Where are you ordering from?"

"Your husband's place."

"Do you have to?"

"Did I mention I have a bunch of teens coming over? I'm feeding them all. I can't afford full retail price just so you can avoid your husband."

"Hey Ma," Ezra came through the basement door. I forced him

into a quick hug. "Some police guys were here looking for you." He pulled a business card from his jeans pocket. "Here. This one said he'd like you to call him. Are you in trouble?"

"What?" I took the card from him. It was Detective Beatty's. "No. Ugh, one of my clients passed away this morning. I think the police might suspect murder."

"Really?" Melissa shot her head toward me. "Who?"

"Shelby Wooley. He—"

"I just heard about that," she said.

"Who was he?" Ezra asked. He opened the refrigerator and stared inside. "Don't we have anything to eat?"

"There are a couple cookies in the jar."

"Hey! Why didn't you tell me that?" Melissa nearly trounced my son diving for the cookie jar.

"There's only three," Ezra said. "You can have them, Mel."

"Thanks, kid. I'm starving." She took the cookie jar to the table.

"When are your friends coming?" I asked.

"They're here now."

"Really?" Melissa asked him, wiping crumbs from her mouth. "That's the quietest bunch of teens ever."

"We're concentrating," Ezra answered.

I handed him the menu. "Take this down. Get everyone's orders. I'll call it in."

He disappeared down the stairs.

I sat at the table across from Mel, then immediately stood again. "Wine? I may not have food, but I know I have some wine."

"Sure." She finished another cookie. "So, tell me, are the rumors true?"

"What rumors?" I took two glasses from the cabinet.

"About that Wooley man."

"Again, what rumors?" I pulled out a half-full bottle of white wine from the refrigerator.

"It's been all over the TV. They've been interviewing all his neighbors and friends. Some people are saying he hasn't been seen in public for a year, that he's some kind of crazy recluse. Others are saying that he's been out of the country. Everyone's saying he's weird. And his daughter! Whew! She's a nutcase. She's been on every channel doing this 'woe is me' bit, flicking her hair, covering her eyes with her hands. If it weren't for the fact that her father was dead, she'd be funny."

I handed her a glass of wine. "Mr. Wooley was a bit eccentric." I slipped into my former chair with my own glass of wine on the table. "He'd been keeping a low profile because, well, because of some medical reasons."

"Oh, that's boring."

I took another drink to keep from saying anything else.

Ezra bounded into the kitchen again. "Here you go." He handed me the menu with another slip of paper. "That's what we want."

"Okay. I'll call it in. You guys can all walk over to pick it up."

"Sure." He grinned. "You know, you don't have to try so hard to keep us busy. Honest. We're working on our project. That's all."

"I trust you."

"No you don't."

"I do too. I just don't trust your hormones."

"Ma, have you seen the girls down there?" he whispered, nodding toward the open basement door. "You can trust my hormones around them."

He retreated down the stairs once more. I called in the food, adding an extra pizza for Mel and me. A few minutes later I made Ezra check his blood sugar then eat five jelly beans from our emergency stash before he set out with the other kids to walk the four blocks to pick up our order.

Parents of diabetics tend to be paranoid about low blood sugar, much to the annoyance of our children. However, until they become paranoid about it, someone needs to be. When he'd tested his blood, his sugar count was seventy-two, which is fine, but bordering on low. The walk to and from Ed's First Pub could have put him in the dangerously too low category. The jelly beans, having one carbohydrate of sugar in them each, would be enough to keep him in healthy range.

Mel and I eyed up the girls as they left the house.

"Jeesh," she said. "He sure was right about the babes, huh?"

I laughed and took a drink. The doorbell rang before I could respond.

Detectives Beatty and Jameson had returned.

Chapter 4: About Mr. Wooley

"I'm sorry," I said when I opened the main door. I kept the screen door shut. "I didn't realize you wanted me to call back tonight. I figured I could wait until normal business hours on Monday."

"We don't work normal business hours," Beatty said. "May we come in?"

"Um, sure." I opened the screen door and pressed hard against the frame while they squeezed by me. Inside, Beatty sat on the armchair in the living room without me offering it to him. Jameson similarly sat on the sofa.

"We just have a few more questions," Jameson said.

"Everything all right?" Mel stood in the doorway that separated the living from the dining room.

"Everything's fine." I sat on the sofa at the opposite end of Jameson. "These are the detectives I met this morning at Mr. Wooley's house."

"You didn't tell me you were at his house this morning!" Melissa sat on the sofa arm next to me. "Why were you there? Ooo, did you see him?"

"Excuse me," Beatty said. "We really don't need much of your time."

"Oh, sorry. I was just wondering why you need to talk to Peri about him," Mel said.

"I'm sure they're just doing their job," I offered.

"They said on the news you think he was murdered," she continued. "You don't think Peri killed him, do you? Cause let me tell you something, Peri takes *care* of everyone. She doesn't kill them."

"Mel, thanks for the support," I said to her. "I think if they came to accuse me of murdering Mr. Wooley, they'd probably be arresting me right now instead of just sitting here." I looked first at Jameson then at Beatty. "Right?"

Beatty grinned. "Right."

"She's a little on the protective side." I patted her arm then turned to them. "So what do you need to know?"

"First," Beatty said, "You said you were planning a funeral-themed party for him. Why did he want a funeral-themed party?"

I glanced at Melissa. Her eyes popped over her wineglass.

"Didn't you ask his daughter?" I responded.

"We're asking you now," Jameson said.

"Right." I peeped at Mel again before continuing. "He was starting a new, um, a new chapter in his life," I said slowly. "And he thought having a funeral for his old . . . his old self . . . would be appropriate."

"What about his old self was to die?" Jameson asked.

"Can I get my glass of wine?"

"How about your girlfriend gets it for you?" Beatty pointed his chin toward Melissa.

"Sure." She stood. "Wait a minute. What do you mean by *girlfriend?*"

"Um." His cheeks colored.

"You're not a very good detective," she snapped. "Peri's my best friend, that's it. I'm married to her shit-for-brains cousin. Who happens to be a male." She left the room.

"I'm sorry," he called after her.

"It's okay," I said. "Though that was kind of funny."

"The boy who answered the door earlier, is he her son?" Beatty asked.

"No. He's mine." I made eye contact and waited for the shocked look I usually get from people before their faces shift into either pity or disgust. "I'm a young mom."

"Got it." He nodded; his face blank.

"Why are you asking about him?"

"Just making pleasant conversation." He gave me a lopsided grin that I wasn't sure was genuine. "So let's get back to business. What was the change in Wooley's life?"

I ran my fingers through my hair. "Look, I have a reputation for keeping my clients' business and personal lives in confidentiality. I'm not sure how—"

"Here you go," Mel said, handing me my wine. She sat next to me on the arm of the sofa again.

"Even priests and psychologists tell the police confidential information at times." Jameson said.

"I realize that. I just . . ." I sipped before turning to my cousin's wife. "Mel, I swear to God if you blab any of this to anyone, I'll kill you."

Melissa burst out laughing. "Do you realize you just threatened me in front of the police?"

"What?" I laughed too. "No, no, no!" I said to the detectives. "I didn't mean it. It was a figure of speech. Hand to God! Honest!" I put my empty hand over my heart and held up the glass-holding one.

Beatty smiled. "I got it. Just watch your step."

"Whew, right." I took another sip. "So Mr. Wooley—"

Bang! Ezra and his troops pounded through the front door.

"Hey Mel, next time warn me," he said as they paraded by on their way to the kitchen. "Eddy knows you're here now. Sorry Ma, I didn't know you were keeping it from him. He's mad at you for not telling him."

"Call Ed, now," I said to Melissa. "And make sure he knows I didn't know you were here when I spoke to him, okay?"

"Okay," she dragged out of the room.

"Ez!" I shouted. "It's thirty-five carbs a slice!"

"I know Ma!" he shouted back.

I sighed. "Can we talk outside?" I asked the detectives. "I don't think my kid and his friends should hear this."

We went out to the front stoop, shutting the main door behind us. Because my home is at the end of a long string of row houses, I didn't just have a stoop. I had a cemented area that was large enough that it might have actually qualified the space as a porch. I sat on the swing. Jameson remained standing. Beatty sat next to me.

"So about Wooley's funeral," Beatty started.

"About Mr. Wooley's funeral," I echoed, meeting his eyes. It was early dusk and the porch light was on, so we could clearly see each other. I still found him very attractive. So attractive, I wished we were sitting out there for a completely different reason. Without, of course, the chaperone. "Okay, so, Mr. Wooley was about to have a transgender procedure," I blurted.

"He was going to become a she?" Jameson confirmed.

"Yes. Before he could undergo any medical treatments, his doctors insisted he spend at least a year living as a woman to be sure that's what he truly wanted."

"Was he about to start doing that?" Beatty asked.

"No. He had just finished it." I paused to drink. "See, Mr. Wooley is a very eccentric man. He likes to surprise . . . I mean, he used to like to surprise people. He decided to spend that first year living like a woman without anyone he knew knowing. Then he wanted to have a huge coming out party when he started the hormones."

"How was that possible?" Beatty asked.

"He pretended to be on an extended world tour collecting art. He was very active in the art community so people believed it. Also, he really was out of town quite a bit. Regardless, whether he was travelling or home, he dressed in women's clothes, makeup, the whole nine yards. He could be very theatrical."

"Like his daughter?" Jameson asked.

"She gets it honestly. Anyway, part of my job was to arrange bogus e-mails and photographs to be sent on his behalf to keep people from enquiring any further. Only a few of his closest friends knew what was really going on with him. The year would have ended at the end of this month. Next month, on the eighteenth, we were to have a major coming out party. It was going to be like nothing anyone had ever done before. At that party, Shelby Wooley was supposed to be laid to rest while Shelley Wooley would be introduced to the world. We had invited everyone in the art and socialite scene in Philly to a 'surprise event' in his honor to be held at the museum."

"The main art museum?" Beatty asked.

"Yes. The plan was for them to enter the room we rented and realize they were at a funeral, an overly elaborate, albeit very obvious funeral. I had commissioned a sculptor to create a wax replica of him that we would display in a casket."

"Which is what you thought you saw at Wooley's house." Jameson said.

"Right. I even have chanting monks lined up. Oh!" I sat up straight on the glider. "I just realized I have a bunch of stuff to cancel. I should have been doing that today. I need to get my phone." I stood.

"Why?" Beatty asked. "I'm sure the monks work standard business hours. You can call them Monday."

"Actually, they work twenty-four-seven. But that's not it. I have to send myself an e-mail. That's what I do when I want to make sure I remember to take care of something. So when I sit down at my desk, I see it and don't forget."

He pulled out his cell phone. "What's your e-mail address?"

I gave it to him as I returned to my place beside him on the glider.

"I just sent it," he said. "What's the name of the artist you hired to make the sculpture?"

I gave them Edvard Blunko's name.

"Go on," Jameson said. "Anything else you can tell us?"

"I think that's it. Was he really murdered?"

"We don't know what happened yet." Beatty tucked his phone into his jacket. "His daughter hadn't mentioned anything about the party you were planning nor anything about the transgender procedures. Are you sure that's—"

"Are you serious? She knew all about it. Maybe she just didn't want tell you. She wasn't thrilled with the idea. Anyway, I can give you his doctor's contact information. You can follow up with him. He knew about the party, too."

"Who is it?" Beatty pulled out a small notebook and a pen.

"He was under the care of Dr. Joaquin Valdez for the transgender stuff. His regular doctor, his primary physician is, was, Maxim Ivanov. He's another who knew all about what was going on. They were both invited to the mock funeral, too."

"I'd like to see the full list of invitees."

"Sure. I have it on my computer."

"I'll send you another e-mail to remind you to send it to me." He grinned as he pulled out his phone again. I stood.

"We're not quite done," Jameson said.

I sat.

"Where were you yesterday evening?" he asked.

"I was sub-bartending for my cousin Ed at Ed's First Pub. I was there until midnight last night then came straight home."

"Was your son here when you came home?"

"Yes, in bed and I didn't wake him."

"I see. What about earlier in the day?"

"If you'd like, I can send you my itinerary." I sipped my wine.

"We don't want an itinerary." Jameson cocked his head to the side. "We want what you remember fresh, now. You can send the itinerary to Beatty when you send the other information if you remember anything else."

"Well, after Ezra left for school, I spent the morning with my mom at Adler's fabrics. I dropped her off around noon. Then had lunch at the Franklin Fountain—"

"The ice cream place?" Beatty asked.

"Yes."

"You had ice cream for lunch?"

"Yes."

"I see." He sucked on his upper lip as if he couldn't decide what to say next. So I filled them in on the rest of my day as best I could from my memory.

"Very good," Beatty said as he flipped the notepad shut. "I'm done. What about you?" he looked at his partner.

"I think that might be all we need to ask for now. But—"

"Yo, Peri!" Ed yelled from the street. He half-jogged up the sidewalk, pointing his thumb toward Melissa's car parked at the curb. "So my wife's been here the whole time I was looking for her?"

"I swear to God I didn't know until after I hung up from you," I said. "I told her to call you."

"She still here?" He climbed the steps to the stoop.

"I think so. Go on in."

"Thanks." He opened the screen door. "Hey!" he said over my head to Beatty before going in. "You seeing my cousin?"

"I—"Beatty started.

"It's okay. Just let me warn ya now. You hurt her and you're dead. Got it?" Ed pushed open the main door, going inside before anyone could respond.

"So your family takes murder lightly, huh?" Jameson asked.

"Nah." I stared into my empty wineglass. "We're all just over protective."

Chapter 5: Second Guessed

"**W**as your client who died Shelby Wooley?" my mother asked Saturday morning when she finally returned my call.

"Yes, Ma." I emulated Mel from the night before by staring at the empty inside of my refrigerator as I spoke to her.

"Why didn't you tell me that yesterday?"

"I tried. You took forever to return my call."

"I've been busy. Had I known you were in the middle of a murder investigation, I would have made the time."

"I'm not sure I'm in the middle of an investigation. I'm more like on the periphery," I teased.

"Still. You got all the luck."

"How lucky could I be to touch a dead body?" I shut the fridge door and opened the freezer.

"You might have a point. I feel terrible, though."

"From jealousy?" I moved a bag of peas aside just in case something, granted a very small something, tasty lay under it. I should have known better—I've never found a four-leaf clover either. I did find a carton of ice cream near the back. I decided since it listed milk and eggs in the ingredients, ice cream could qualify as a nutritious breakfast. However, since I have a teenage son in the house, it was empty.

"I'm only a little jealous," Ma said. "Actually, I'm very sad that the world will now be without Shelby Wooley. I mean, I guess it would have happened eventually. It just seems too soon. He was such a good guy."

"How do you know?" I threw away the ice cream carton.

"I knew him."

"Really? How?"

"It was some time ago. We were on an advisory panel for the horticultural society together. He was very kind and understanding. In fact, he had my back during some trying times."

"I don't remember this at all. When? What trying times?"

"Oh, it was the year Ezra became diabetic. When was that?"

"Four years ago. Oh, now I remember you being on that panel. For the flower show, right?"

"Yes. You had your hands full so I didn't want to upset you with anything else."

"How could a flower show be trying?"

"The situation was quite intense. You have no idea how diva-ish floral designers can be. Temperamental artists can be rather catty."

"You're right. I have no idea." I rummaged through the cupboards.

"Well, Shelby appreciated my creative nature. He stood up for me quite a bit, though in the end no one listened to us at all. It's a shame really. We could have turned that show into something major."

"It is something major, Ma. A quarter of a million people attend that show every year."

"Maybe it would have been a quarter-million-and-one that year. Who knows? Anyway, tell me about it."

"About what?" I gave up on the cupboards.

"The scene yesterday."

"I already did. He was spongy."

"No, I mean, tell me everything. Everything you remember. This could be my first chance to crack a real mystery."

I sat at the kitchen table and rehashed the events at Mr. Wooley's as I drank my one cup of coffee. I didn't even have enough beans to make two cups.

"Hmmm," she said when I was done. "So you say he had a line on his neck?"

"Yeah. Like it was dividing the front from the back. The back part was darker than the front. I think I remember wondering if the artist had painted it to look like a shadow."

"That sounds like the line of lividity."

"The what?"

"That means he died on his back, then was moved to the chair."

"I think I heard someone there say something similar. How do you know?"

"I have all the *Homicide* shows memorized. How was the smell?"

"I don't know. I had just left a florist and couldn't breathe."

"You know, if you'd take chromium with bromelain and a little vitamin C, you wouldn't have any allergies."

"I do know. You keep telling me."

"I will continue to tell you until you start listening."

"I know that, too." I drained my cup. "I gotta go get bagels or something now, Ma. We have nothing to eat in this house."

"Bagels! The bane of your existence. What kind of person eats bagels?"

"All kinds. In fact, millions and millions of people do it every day."

"There's little to be gained in following trends, poopsie."

I clicked off and wrote a note to Ezra telling him I'd be back with bagels and coffee. I returned around ten o'clock to find my sweet teenager still in bed.

"Yo, Ez!" I shouted up the stairs.

"Urh?"

"Come on bud. You gotta get up. I need your help."

"Is there a monetary reward?"

"If there needs to be." I sighed. "I'll even go grocery shopping."

"You should have started with that," he said as he lumbered down the stairs.

While I was out getting bagels, Carolyn had called to ask if I could meet her for lunch at the Capital Grille near her building. Of course I could, even though that meant I'd need to shower and dress myself up a little. The yoga pants, T-shirt and backward Phillies cap I'd worn to the bagel place just wouldn't cut it at the Grille. Before joining Carolyn though, I had to meet with Ezra's father, which meant I didn't have time to do much about the MMA facilities.

"So you'll take care of this for me?" I asked.

"Easy stuff, Ma." Ezra sat in front of my computer. I had asked him to map out all the MMA studios in the city, beginning with whichever was closest to the Capital Grille and ending with the one closest to our home, put it into a document and e-mail it to me.

"Great, I really appreciate it." I approached him from behind to kiss the top of his head. "Any requests from the market?"

"Food! Please. And lots of it." He turned around in his chair. "What are you wearing?"

"A suit. A very expensive suit." I straightened my back, running my hands down the lapels. "One of my clients gave it to me. Do you like it?"

"Not really."

"What? Why?"

"You look like an old woman in it."

"I do not. I can't. It's by a high-end designer."

"A high-end designer for old ladies maybe." He laughed.

"Just e-mail me the results, would ya?" I went out the backdoor and climbed into my Ford. I knew Ezra was right. I had second guessed the suit the minute I put it on. I'd just never worn such an expensive piece of clothing before. I had to wear it at least once. Even if it did make me look old.

Ezra's dad Todd was sometimes a really nice guy. Sometimes, he was a complete ass. Often, he was just not very smart. What he was was musically gifted, or so he says. Not appreciated in the United States, he was currently either a pop star or a variety act in Japan. I wasn't clear on the details, although I was leaning toward variety act. He'd been in New York City the previous week on business. Now he wanted to spend some time with Ezra. I hadn't mentioned anything to Ez. I knew the odds were against Todd of actually following through on his promise. I'd hate like hell seeing my kid disappointed by his father, again.

We had agreed to meet at the Thirtieth Street train station. I was early, so I took a minute to skim through e-mails on my phone. I sat on one of the pew-like benches as I read. Detective Beatty's reminders were there, as well as a message from Mrs. Johanssen asking me to confirm via e-mail that I got her e-mail, the one she had confirmed over the phone the day before. As I confirmed on my phone, another e-mail popped into my inbox. It was from Mr. Wooley.

My ears rang. I felt nauseous. I opened Mr. Wooley's e-mail anyway and learned it was really from Jacqueline. She wanted my street address and cell phone number. I replied and hit *send* just as Todd approached me.

"Hey," he said when I stood to let him peck my cheek with a *hello* kiss.

"You made it." I tucked my phone in my jacket pocket.

He opened his arms, palms up and stood with legs wide. Dressed like a rockabilly performer in skinny jeans, black Dr. Martens combat boots, leather jacket and a white V-neck T-shirt exposing the gold chains around his neck, he still looked boyishly cute: dimpled cheeks, close-cropped curly black hair contrasting with his green-gray eyes. The problem was he knew exactly how good he looked. "Babe, did you really doubt me?"

"Of course I did."

"You know, if you want to get bitchy, I'll tell you how old you look in that suit."

"This is . . . oh, never mind." There was something about Todd that, except for one stupid night of my life, had always tempted me to slap him. "So are you going to see Ezra?"

"I'd like to. Can I?"

"You can. Not because I want it to happen, but because he'll be delighted. He believes all the stories you tell him about your life." I pointed my finger at him. Actually, I poked him in the chest with it. "Listen to me now, Todd. I swear to God, if you do something to break his heart again, that's it from us."

"What do you mean, 'from us'?"

"I mean, I no longer cover with Christmas and birthday gifts when you forget. I won't come up with excuses for why you didn't show when you said you would. I won't e-mail you reminders to contact him to see how his big events go. And, I won't save it all up to tell him as part of a deathbed confession. He will know immediately what a slacker you are as a dad, and then the future will all be on you."

"Fair enough," he stood. "Can I see him today?"

"Yeah. I won't be home for a couple hours. That should give you plenty of time for some father-son bonding."

"Cool. I think I'm ready for this parenting business."

He strutted away leaving me wondering just what would be so terrible if I did smack him.

Carolyn cancelled on me. As soon as I got in my Explorer at the train station, she called to say she'd have to move it to the next day and that she'd call me back soon. The whole conversation was whispered on her end, as if she didn't want someone overhearing.

I checked my e-mail again. My son had followed through already with the list of MMA studios just as I had asked, except the last one was actually closest to the supermarket instead of home. I started my truck and headed toward the first place on the list.

Three studios later, I had to take a break. I was in the Fishtown section of the city, so I thought the Milk Crate Café would be perfect for a cup of coffee. Actually, I thought it the perfect place to get a croissant smeared with Nutella and peanut butter alongside a cup of coffee. I sat on a bar stool where I could look out the plate glass window while I enjoyed my snack. While a classic rock vinyl record played in the background, I glanced through my e-mails again, rereading the four in a row from Detective Beatty.

I called my mom.

"Hello, my sweet," she answered.

"Hi, Ma."

"You sound like something's troubling you. What happened?"

"Nothing." I cupped my hand over my mouth and phone to keep the other diners from hearing me. "Do you think I'm considered a suspect in Mr. Wooley's death?"

"Absolutely. Oh!" She paused. I didn't have the heart to interrupt. "That's even more incentive for me to be actively investigating this case. My baby girl was found at the scene of the crime. I have to work to clear you. Is that why you called?"

"No, not really. I—"

"Tell me again, exactly what happened yesterday?"

"I already did. Twice."

I know, but I wasn't taking notes, then. So tell me now."

I looked around me. No one seemed interested in what I was saying. "Well, I knocked on his backdoor."

"Wait! I'm still not taking notes. I need to find a notepad first. Let me call you back."

I hung up, got a refill of coffee and left. Out in the parking lot, I checked Ezra's list of studios. My next stop was just a short distance away, down Girard Avenue. Ma called back almost as I settled in the driver's seat. My truck's too old for a Blue Tooth device, so I had to put her on speaker with the cell in a cup holder in the center console.

"Now I'm ready, poopsie."

"You know, I really like the name Peri. I never changed it."

"It doesn't matter. You'll always be my poopsie."

I sighed.

"Anyway, you knocked on your Wool-man's door and . . ."

So I filled her in, again.

"Hmm . . . When you say detectives were there, were they in uniforms?"

"No."

"How do you know they were detectives?"

"They told me."

"Interesting."

"Why?"

"Usually, uniformed cops show up first. Then, if they think there's foul play, they call for detectives and a crime-scene team."

"How do you know?"

"*CSI.*"

"What?"

"It's a TV show. I have every episode memorized."

"I thought you only had *Homicide* memorized."

"You have no idea what's in this head! Ha!"

"I'm not sure I want to."

"So how long do you think you were unconscious?"

"I don't know. Maybe a minute."

"Were the police there before you fainted?"

"No. I think I was alone with him."

"Oh, that's not good."

"Why?"

"There's something hinky going on. Those detectives wouldn't have been there so soon, unless they already knew it was a murder. In which case, you *would* be their number-one suspect."

"I would?"

"Absolutely! You were found at the scene of the crime."

"So what do I do?"

"Nothing! I'm on the case. You think I'm going to let my one and only child go to jail for murder?"

"Thanks, Ma, but—"

"I will prove you're innocent. As long as you are, I mean. You're not the murderer are you?"

"Seriously? Of course not!"

"You are under a considerable amount of strain these days. I'm sure it would only take a minor incident to—"

"I didn't freaking kill him!"

"You know your father and I would still love you and support you no matter what, even if you are a murderer."

"That's what's wrong with my life, Ma." I turned in to the parking lot of It's Your Mission MMA. "I gotta go. I have to talk to someone."

"Don't talk to a policeman without an attorney present!" she yelled before I could hit the *speaker* icon to end the call.

I might have sighed again. Mel likes to tell me I do that too much. I think I only do it when I have good reason.

Inside *It's Your Mission MMA* I found myself walking behind a trim, sculpted, dark-haired and sweaty, twenty-something man named Mikey. He was shoeless, shirtless, and wearing only a pair of sweatpants that were so loose he kept tugging on the waist to keep them up. For the record, he wore tight, aqua colored briefs.

The gym housed fifteen or so other equally buff males working out and beating on each other. Although it was stifling in there, the locker-room stench was not noticeable. That was one of my requirements for the party, which is why I had wanted to visit the facilities in person.

My escort stopped and rapped on the frame of an open office door.

"Gabe, youse busy?" he asked someone inside the office. "There's a chick here who needs a cage for a day."

Good news. Apparently even in an old-woman suit, I was still a chick. I almost wished Todd had been there to hear it.

"Nah. We're done," someone replied. Two men exited the office. The one with a swollen eyebrow nodded at me as he passed. The other stopped in front of me.

"This is my brother, Gabe," Mikey said before heading toward the man with the bad eye.

"How can I help you?" Gabe asked. He, too, was barefoot but he wore a black T-shirt and long gym shorts. There was a definite family resemblance between him and Mikey. Like his sibling, he was a little on the tall side, maybe just over six feet. His hair was short, dark, and curly. And he had an olive complexion with very dark, deep-set eyes. Those eyes locked onto my blue ones, making me swallow.

"Hi, I'm Peri Milano." I handed him a business card.

He looked at the card.

"Lifestyle manager?" he asked with an uneven grin. "You're the first one with a card to come in here." His eyes swooped down my body before meeting mine again. "I'm always surprised by how uptight you people look during the day. It's like your costume, right?"

"I don't think I understand." I wasn't sure, but I had the feeling I was being insulted.

He smiled. "How can I help you?"

"I have a client interested in holding an MMA-themed birthday party. She was hoping to find a place with a cage to possibly have supervised fights. Would you be interested in leasing your gym for the day? And would you have trainers available? Or are you not interested in that sort of business?"

That last question is the kind I'd ask only when I didn't really want to work with someone. I figure if they're still interested after such a snotty remark, they'd probably make it worth my while.

He snorted a laugh.

"Sure, if someone's willing to pay, I'm always willing to do business." He turned to walk down the hall, nodding his head to encourage me to follow. The back of his T-shirt had angel wings in faded gray stretching from his shoulders to the small of his back. While thick, his hair was so short that I thought I could see a line of some sort crossing the back of his skull. I couldn't get close enough to figure out what it was—a dog had left his office and walked between us. Dogs don't usually like me. Or maybe I don't usually like dogs. I can never remember which.

"We only have fighting gear," he called over his shoulder. "You'll have to supply your own whips and chains or whatever it is you people like. Asking to use one of my trainers is a new one, though." He laughed again. "You'll have to pay big for that one probably. Unless the women are good looking. You'll still have to sign a waiver of some kind. I don't want to get sued if my people accidentally hurt someone. We're not used to that kind of thing."

I stopped walking. He must have heard my heels were no longer striking the cement floor because he stopped too. He turned to look at me. The dog sat and stared up at him.

"This party will be for five- and six-year-old children. Certainly we don't expect anyone to get hurt. And what on Earth do you mean: we'll have to supply our own whips and chains?"

"What do you mean children?"

"I'm looking for a place to hold a child's birthday party."

"Your card says you're a lifestyle manager."

"Yes."

"Doesn't that mean . . ." he sucked on his lips as if trying not to laugh. "Is that different from a lifestyler?"

"I don't know, what's a lifestyler?"

He gave up trying to withhold his laughter, letting it out with a pound of his fist on the painted cinderblock wall. "Whew!" He wiped a tear from his eye. "A lifestyler is someone who lives some kind of alternative lifestyle. We have people coming in all the time looking to rent a cage for the night so they can have—" He scratched his forehead, looking at me from under his hand. "Kinky sex. Like bondage. S&M. That kind of stuff."

"Oh my God!" I covered my mouth with my hand. "I've never heard that expression before. Are you sure that's what they're called?"

"Yeah. Like I said, they come in here a lot." His put his hands on his hips and smiled at me. "Now then, what is it *you* do?"

Chapter 6: A Bad Influence

At dinner I tried to convince Ezra to give MMA a chance. He's a slight kid taking advanced math and science courses at school with bigger, older kids in a tough neighborhood. It seemed to me he had a giant bull's eye on his back for bullies. So far there had only been a few minor skirmishes. I still often wondered if whether he could defend himself if ever the need arose.

"MMA?" he asked as he piled a second helping of spaghetti with Bolognese sauce onto his plate. "Is that why you wanted me to look those places up? You want me to go?"

I gritted my teeth while he portioned out the food onto his plate without measuring out exactly how much he was eating. He wears an insulin pump attached to his abdomen that will properly dose him after he punches in the number of carbohydrates he intended to eat. There's no way to be accurate with the carb count without properly measuring the food. He likes to guess the carbs then correct with another insulin dose later if, when he checks his blood, his sugar count is high. His way of dosing has a whole host of problems associated with it that he refuses to perceive as problems. It's another of those things that keep parents of diabetics in paranoid mode. When I serve him his food, I carefully weigh and measure everything out. I do the same while I cook. I could tell him exactly how many grams of carbohydrates were in his meal, if he would just freaking weigh and measure it.

"No." I let the MMA subject drop because we seldom sit together for a meal. So I chose not to ruin the evening by nagging at him with diabetes talk. "I'm planning a birthday party for a kid. Anyway, I don't know, just when I was there, I thought the guys were like you. On the skinny side. Maybe it'd be good for you to get some exercise."

"I get plenty, Ma. I walk to school, remember? And I walk back. It's not uphill both ways, but I think it counts."

"I just think—"

"It's funny that you want me to exercise. I mean, how many times have you had a breakdown after checking my meter and seeing I didn't test my blood before gym class?" He chewed. "You know what, though? Maybe you should try it. Maybe you'd be less stressed if you had something to punch every now and then."

"I am not stressed." I set down my fork and glared at him.

"It's killing you that I didn't weigh my spaghetti," he said while he chewed. "I can see it in your face. There's a vein popping out on your forehead."

"I am not stressed," I repeated as I rubbed my forehead. Maybe I was trying to erase proof of the contrary.

"Maybe stressed isn't the right word. Uptight?" He sipped his water. "That's how Dad described you today."

"Oh it is, is it?" Not that I cared what Todd thought about me. I just found it troubling that the same, ugly word had been applied to me twice, in one day. I couldn't be uptight, could I?

"Yeah. He wanted a soda. I explained that we never have any."

A knock on the back door prevented me from going into a rant against Todd as well as against high fructose corn syrup. They were both among the few things I happened to share my mother's opinion of. In fact, the jelly beans we always have in the house are made with organic sugar. They're one of my big financial splurges. All of that might explain why I growled when I opened the back door to find Ezra's father standing there with a six-pack of cola.

"Does that mean you're glad to see me?" Todd asked as he swaggered in without an invitation.

"Your timing couldn't be any better." I somehow managed to shut the door without slamming it. "Ez was just telling me you called me uptight."

"Oh, babe." He threw an arm around my shoulder. "I didn't mean it in a bad way. I just think you're growing up faster than me. That's all."

I pulled loose from him. "We have a kid who's only a few years away from being a legal adult. Don't you think we should be grown up by now?"

"Exactly my point." He set the cola on the table. "Where are your glasses?"

"I'll get you one, Dad." Ezra stood to open a cabinet.

I hated hearing Ezra call Todd *Dad*. I wouldn't have minded if Todd had ever acted like a father instead of a cool, older friend, though no one could deny their relationship. Ezra was as close to looking like a clone of Todd as possible. Maybe that was the trade-off for the brain genes.

"I didn't realize you were coming back tonight." I tried, I honestly did, to convince myself to be polite and offer him some dinner.

"I wanted to talk to you and Ezra about an idea I have." He eyed up Ezra's plate of spaghetti with Bolognese sauce. "Is that okay? Do you guys have plans tonight?"

"I'm going to the movies with my friend, Theo," Ezra said. "But we have a few minutes. Want some dinner?"

"Love some," Todd grinned at him. "Looks good."

"Yeah, Ma's a great cook," Ezra said. "When we have groceries." He grinned his father's grin at me as he prepared another plate of food.

I sighed as I returned to my chair.

"What's the idea?" I asked.

"My stint in Tokyo is about over." Todd accepted his plate. "Thanks bud. So I'm figuring out what my next move should be."

"And?" Suddenly I lost my appetite.

"My manager's working on a regular gig in New York. I think my real home should be in a studio somewhere. On the production side of things."

"And?" I asked again.

"And, so, well, that part doesn't really matter." Todd shoveled a forkful into his mouth and chewed. "What matters is I'm moving home in the summer."

"Home, as in Philly?" I asked the same time Ezra asked: "Here?"

"I think so. Either here or New York."

"Cool!" shouted Ezra. I remained silent as they fist-bumped.

"What's your idea?" I leaned back in my chair, arms crossed. I may have even jutted my jaw and glowered at Todd.

"My idea is that Ezra should come to Japan with me for the summer. For most of it anyway. Like he could come whenever school lets out then stay until he returns home with me."

"Really? That's freaking AWESOME!" Ezra ripped Todd out of his chair and slammed him with hug. "Oh my God! Thank you! That's so cool!"

Funny thing, I finally didn't want to smack Todd. I wanted to punch him, maybe pull a couple of the MMA moves I'd spied at the gym on him. Though as I stewed on it, I realized those moves weren't good enough. I needed to grab one of the gold chains around his neck and twist it tighter, tighter, and tighter until . . .

The doorbell rang.

"I'll get it." I escaped the room, possibly to distract myself from acting out the fantasy.

"It's probably Theo," Ezra said. "Wait 'til I tell him!" He ran past me to the front door.

It wasn't Theo. Jacqueline had pressed the doorbell. She wore a black pillbox hat with a veil that only covered her forehead, short black gloves, a black low-cut, form-fitting dress with padded shoulders and a thin belt. She came across as vintage 1940s. Very cute, but over the top.

"Oh Peri," she said with a breathy voice. "I was going through Father's belongings. I thought you should have something from him." She placed a hand over her heart. "He adored you so."

"Um, well, thank you Jacqueline. It wasn't necessary. I—"

"But I insist." She turned and waved at a man pushing two large boxes on a hand-truck. He approached the stoop and carried them up the steps. Jacqueline pushed past me into my tiny living room. "I suppose just anywhere would be fine for now, right Peri?"

"I guess so." I caught Ezra's eyes bulging at the sight of her curves. Todd's, too, from where he stood with plate in hand, eating in the doorway to the dining room. "What is it?"

"Just some antique dishware." Jacqueline waved her hand. "There. Now it's all yours." She came within a foot of kissing me on each cheek. "I'll be in touch soon to let you know about the funeral arrangements." She stopped in the doorway. "Oh, actually. Why don't you take care of all that? Do whatever you were doing for the party, just move it up to next Saturday."

She left without me even saying good-bye.

Todd ambled to the window to check her out as she walked down the front walk. "Who is that?"

"The daughter of a client. Her name's Jacqueline Wooley." I picked at the tape on the top box. "She's far out of your league. I'll introduce you anyway if you want. It'll be fun for me to watch."

"Do you have to talk like that in front of our son?" He laughed as he made himself at home on the sofa, placing his dinner on the coffee table where he continued to eat. The man must have been famished.

"What'd she bring?" Ezra asked.

I managed to pull the tape enough to rip the box open. Inside were several pieces of red Fiesta ware. "Like she said, antique china." I held a plate for him to see.

"How antique?" Ezra took the plate from me. He turned it over, looking as if he knew what he was doing.

"I don't know. Maybe 1930s?"

"Are you sure it's not new?"

"Trust me, the client who owned it only had original everything."

"Wow. Do you know it's probably radioactive?" Ezra smiled as if that were a good thing. "How cool is that?"

"I don't think very cool." I took the plate from him, put it back in the box then wiped my hands on my yoga pants as if that would clear them of any radioactivity. Todd stood to take it back out. I let him hold it as long as he wanted.

"What do you mean, radioactive?" he asked.

"The red they used to use for pottery way back when was made out of uranium oxide."

"What? How do you know, Ez?" I asked. The doorbell rang again.

"We talked about it when we were studying the periodic tables," Ezra let his friend, Theo, in.

"What are the period tables?" Todd asked.

"Remember that stuff about pottery being radioactive?" Ez asked Theo. He took the plate from Todd. "I think this is it."

"Radioactive plates!" Theo bobbed his head. "Cool."

"Yeah, cool." I took the plate away again. "Um . . ." I was so rattled I couldn't think what to say next. I took a deep breath and zeroed in on the easiest target. "Todd. You need to leave, now. I'm not at all happy with you. You'll be safer if you go. I might have to rip your face off if you don't let me process some things first."

He held up his hands as if I were pointing a gun at him. "Okay, okay." He walked backward toward the kitchen, leaving his dirty dish behind. "I get it. Just so you know, this is what I was talking about. You got that mature, uptight thing going on right now."

He was out of sight before I could throw a radioactive plate, Frisbee-style, into his neck. I turned to Ezra and his friend.

"Now, you two," I said. "What movie, time, and place? Who else is going? How are you getting there and who's picking you up?"

Ezra partially turned away from me and rolled his eyes at Theo. I knew he was thinking Todd was right.

"I just need to know," I said, trying to sound the opposite of an uptight, overly mature tyrant, and potential control freak, "if I need to be on call to drive you somewhere at a particular time or take anyone else home."

"It's the usual kids, Ma," Ezra said. "Theo walked over. We're going to his house. His mom is driving us all to the movie."

"Yeah," Theo offered. "She said he can stay over at our place if he wants."

"Can I?" Ezra asked.

"Of course." I bit my lip instead of adding *just text me when the movie's done, when you get there, a list of who else is staying at Theo's place, all your blood sugar numbers, how many carbs you're eating, and don't forget your toothbrush.*

Suddenly, I was left all alone with radioactive china and a bunch of dirty dishes. Ezra always cleaned up after himself. Todd was already a bad influence.

Chapter 7: She's Gone

Before I could get settled in and start feeling sorry for myself for being alone on a Saturday night, Ed called to see if I could work a partial shift at Ed's First Pub. I didn't even have to think about it. Partial shifts meant I didn't have to close, so I'd still get to bed at a decent time and Saturday nights were just as good as Fridays for tips.

I changed into jeans and an *Ed's First Pub* T-shirt and paused in front of the bathroom mirror to brush out my hair. I have blonde hair that's just a couple of inches past my shoulders. When I was younger, it had a nice, soft curl to it and lots of body. Something happened when I hit thirty. Within just one year the curl left. Now it's just slightly wavy. Kathy, my stylist at the salon down the street, said it was part of the aging process. Because she apparently has a sadistic streak, she warned me that I'll eventually need to start coloring my hair too, if I want to keep my color. According to her there are no natural blonds past the age of thirty. She promised that sometime in the very near future, I'll notice my roots are a mousey brown color.

After Kathy broke the news to me, I realized that I was getting older whether or not I wanted to. Some days I even thought I felt older. Today was one of them. I even thought it was showing on my face, though I didn't see that vein Ezra had mentioned. As I stood there critiquing my looks, I realized I might have hit that point where I shouldn't wear eye liner on the bottom rim of my eyes anymore. I'd once read in a magazine that under-the-eye liner ages a woman. Of course, being a too-young mother of a diabetic son ages a woman. I couldn't control that. Eyeliner was controllable.

I called my mother on the short drive to the pub.

"How's my poopsie?" she answered.

"Todd wants to take Ezra to Japan," I said.

"How very fun for Ezra."

"And dangerous."

"I don't think the crime rate is any worse there than here in Philly."

"That's not what I mean. What if he has a problem with his diabetes?"

"I'm sure they have endocrine doctors in Japan," she said. "Though that's not why you're really upset."

"Of course it is," I insisted.

"Of course it is not. You're upset because—oh no. One of my neighbors is pounding on the door."

"Mother, are you naked?"

"I gotta go take care of something. Your father's not home yet to do it." She clicked off. Which was probably for the best. My parents' neighbors were not pleased with my mom and dad at that point in time. Actually, they hadn't been pleased with them for about two years. Which is why I should have remembered to put *find online fabric store* on my to-do list for the day. I pulled in behind the pub and sat in the truck a few minutes while I sent myself an e-mail reminder for the next day.

I entered Ed's First Pub to a chorus shouting "Yo Peri!" I waved and shouted *hello* back to everyone as I ran to the rear of the room. Jenna, the other bartender on duty, gave me a hug. Then with the speed of an announcer reading the rules and regulations of a contest, she gave me a run down on who's on what tab and who's going to need a ride home while I put on an apron.

She took the south end of the bar while I covered the north. I settled into the pouring and mixing routine and gabbed with the patrons. I knew them all by name. The genius of Ed's business plan, as he loves to tell anyone who will listen, is that all seven of his pubs truly are neighborhood pubs; just about everyone who went to them lived within walking distance, hence they were very loyal patrons.

So everyone there that night lived in my neighborhood. Everyone, that is, except for Detective Collin Beatty, who popped by around ten thirty.

He took a seat near the cash register, in the north end of the bar.

"Imagine finding you here," he said.

"Actually, I think I'm supposed to be the one to say that to you." I slid a coaster to him. "What are you doing here?"

"I came for one of those." He pointed to a beer sign.

"From the tap or a bottle?"

"Bottle."

I pulled a cold one out, opened it, and set it down before him. "Seriously, why are you here?"

"A man can't come in for a good drink?" he asked.

"I'd believe that was the case if you had picked a decent brand. One you couldn't buy in any liquor store for a quarter of the price." I folded my arms in front of my chest. "Just tell me, are you here to check up on me?"

He grinned as he cheered me with his bottle.

"Hey Per!" someone shouted from the other side of the room. "Can you get the Phils on the TV?"

"Maybe," I turned away from Detective Beatty to hunt down the remote. "Are you sure they're playing this late?"

"They're in California."

I found the remote, changed the channel. Lou stopped me to order a Special Eddy for his new girlfriend, which meant that Lou was expecting to get lucky that night.

"What's a Special Eddy?" the detective asked as I fished out a large cocktail glass.

"White rum, orange curacao, dry vermouth, with passion fruit and pineapple juices." My phone vibrated in my jeans pocket to tell me I'd just received a text message. I pulled it out expecting to learn Ezra forgot his toothbrush. Instead, I read a message from Ed.

Wheres Mel?

With the glass still in one hand, I used my thumb on my phone hand to answer: *Idk.*

Wat u mean? She not there? was the immediate reply.

No. I typed. I waited for another response from him; after a few seconds of receiving none, I put the phone back in my pocket.

"I invented it," I explained to Detective Beatty as I mixed the drink. "My cousin, Ed—"

"The one who threatened me last night?"

"He didn't mean it, honest." I smirked as I shook my head. "Anyway, he liked it so much, he named it after himself."

He took a tiny sip of his beer, so tiny I'd have wagered he wasn't drinking, which I thought would suggest that he was on duty. "How's it taste?"

"Like the height of summer." I stuck a lemon wedge on the rim of the glass and tilted my head. "You interested?"

"Maybe." He winked.

I took the drink to Lou wondering if the detective was flirting with me. After all, my hair had still probably looked decent when I'd met him the day before and was in okay shape at the moment. I returned to his end of the bar.

"Looks like you're a single mom," he said.

"That I am."

"How old's your son?"

"Fifteen." I paused to deliberately stare into his eyes. "Why are you asking about my son?"

He shrugged. "Just curious." He took another sip of his beer. At least he tipped it up to his mouth. I had no idea if it was true that police officers don't drink when working on a case, but I had the feeling my mother would tell me it was so. "Is he familiar with your clients?"

"A few of them, not many. He had never met Mr. Wooley." I pressed my hands against the bar, leaning hard on them. "My son would never even *think* of murdering anyone. He's a good kid."

"I didn't say anything about anyone murdering someone."

"Right, well, tell me something." I reached for a towel to wipe the bar. Not because it was dirty. I just needed to *do* something. "Why were you at Mr. Wooley's house?"

"I'm a police detective." He shrugged. "You could say it's in my job description."

"Ha! I mean, why were you there so soon? Seems like you got there the same time as the uniformed officers. Were there no other crimes going on in Philly yesterday morning?"

He took another drink, that time I was pretty sure he did actually swallow beer. "None that needed my attention at the moment. Why are you asking?"

"Plainclothes cops don't arrive until after it's been determined a murder has occurred." I stood straight and conjured as much of an authoritative voice as I could. "You don't usually come running the second a nine-one-one call is made."

"What makes you think that?"

"SCT." I flicked the towel over my shoulder.

"What?"

I felt my spine crumble. "CTI?"

He stared at me, blank.

I threw my hands up in the air. "Okay! So my mom watches a lot of TV. The point is--"

I was interrupted by a raucous sound of male voices shouting "Yo! Eddy!" signifying my cousin, Ed, was in the building.

"Hey! Hey! How 'bout them Phils? Huh? Look they're up!" Ed pointed to the TV as his burly body made its way through the small crowd slapping him on the back. "Anyone seen my wife?" he asked when he approached the bar.

"I have. She's quite the looker," Derek said from his regular spot, a couple of stools down from Detective Beatty. "I mean, she's not as hot as my Kimmy. Still, you should keep your eye on her."

"Seriously, Peri." Ed stood across the bar from me. "Have you seen Melissa today?" He looked worried as he stared hard into my eyes. I almost didn't recognize his face. I don't think anyone had ever seen Ed worry before.

"No. I haven't been in the back since I got here," I said. "Maybe she's there."

"She wasn't here when I came in," Jenna said, coming from the south end. "Check the kitchen. I think Sorel was here first today."

Ed tore off to the back of the pub.

"That doesn't look good," Jenna said to me as he disappeared from our sight.

"Not at all," I agreed. Ed never disappeared. Ed liked being the center of attention.

"Something wrong?" Detective Beatty asked.

"I don't know. Ed's kind of weird tonight." There was a thump. I looked over. Derek's head had hit the bar. "*That* can't go on much longer." I nodded toward Derek. "Ever since his wife left him, he's been a wreck." Jenna and I went over to check on him.

"Hey Noel," I called out to a middle-aged man in sweatpants and a Sixers T-shirt. He sat at his table with his wife and her sister, whom I suspected he was sleeping with.

"Whatcha need, Per?" Noel kept his head pointed toward the television.

"Will you make sure Derek gets home okay?" I gently lifted Derek's head to reposition it so it rested on his forearm bent over the bar.

"Sure thing, babe," Noel said. "Soon as this inning's over."

"Thanks." I began wiping the bar again, this time to clean up the spilled beer oozing away from Derek.

"Your cousin was right. You do take good care of your people," Detective Beatty said as I approached him.

"Derek's a regular. He actually lives a couple blocks over from—"

"NO ONE MOVE!" Ed shouted. Every head in the bar, including Detective Beatty's and mine, swung around to stare at him. Ed stood outside the swinging doors separating the kitchen from the bar, holding Melissa's purse and cell phone. His face white, eyes wide.

"She's gone. She's just gone."

Chapter 8: Worry None

Detective Beatty immediately went into cop mode, insisting no one leave the bar while we waited for whoever was on duty in the area to make it over. I called my house. No one answered. Mel always answered my house phone when she was there, whether or not I was. She also never went anywhere without her purse and her cell phone. While I couldn't quite accept the idea that she had been abducted, I couldn't figure out any other reason for her complete absence.

Eventually, the police on duty arrived. Beatty briefed them on what had happened. They began the investigation by taking statements. I listened to everyone else in the bar, including Ed. No one had seen Mel all day. No one had heard from her either, except for Ed, when she had called him and left a voice mail at three thirty-three in the afternoon to let him know she had put some paperwork on his desk.

The police scanned her phone. She hadn't used it since that call to Ed. Nor had she used an app. The only time she had been on the Internet was to check her bank balance around four o'clock. At that point, Ed verified that her ATM card was missing from her wallet.

Although no one was willing to say it, it appeared to me that someone had come in the back door and taken Mel and her bank card away.

I was lightheaded when I gave my statement. Afterward, Beatty walked me to my Explorer parked behind the pub.

"Thanks," I said as we approached my SUV. "I appreciate your taking the time to see me out." I rooted in my purse for my keys. It seemed an impossible task. I had to take a break and lean against the truck with my eyes shut.

"You okay?" Detective Beatty touched my arm. "Are you going to faint again?"

"No." I shook my head and opened my eyes. "I think I'm okay. I felt a little off in the bar, but I think I'm fine now." I searched for my keys again. "Though it almost sounds like something I need to do for a long time. Just blank out until the world is normal again." I found the keys and removed them.

"Is the world ever normal?" he asked.

"Maybe 'normal' isn't the right word. How about . . . controllable?" I beeped my doors unlocked. "I usually have everything in my environment under control. My clients don't just up and die on me. Mel and Ed fight all the time, but she never just disappears without her phone and purse. And my son doesn't ever want to leave me."

"What?"

I opened the SUV door. "Nothing. I'm sorry. I think I just need to go home."

"It's okay." He held onto the door. "Will your son be home?"

I shook my head.

"Will you be all right alone?"

"Yeah. I'll be fine. I'm always fine." I sat in the driver's seat. "It's just been a trying couple of days. I think I forgot for a moment that I'm a strong person. I remember now. I can handle it all. I got it all under control. "

He nodded before shutting the door for me.

I buckled myself in and immediately dialed my mom. The call went to voice mail. I called my dad and got his voice mail, too. I tried their home phone, no one answered. By then, I had driven the four blocks to my row house.

Built sometime in the late 1930s, my home was the end unit of a long row of identical, attached houses. It had once been my grandmother's, the woman my pregnant self had moved in with when I was sixteen. Being at the end, I had a few more windows than the other residents who only had them in the front and back. I also had a tiny patch of lawn to the side where there was an equally tiny cherry tree with a bird feeder and the requisite statue of St. Francis, the patron saint of animals, that Gram had placed there long before I was even born. If she hadn't planned on feeding the birds, I'm sure she would have installed the Virgin Mother in her blue robe, because that's what you put in your yard in northeast Philly.

Once I moved in, I stayed permanently. Gram eventually left the house to me in her will. Now I was another feature of the neighborhood like everyone else. Just as with all the regulars in the bar, I knew every person in the area. I knew who was married to whom and who was in a relationship with whom. I knew where everyone worked, who was handy with a screwdriver, who had the answers to gardening questions and which kid left his bike in someone's yard. Most importantly, I knew the kind of people who shared my tiny corner of the world. I also knew none of them were capable of harming Melissa.

A stranger had intruded my territory.

Instead of going around the corner to enter the very dark alley, I parked in front of my house and thought about what that meant: a stranger was on my turf. A potentially dangerous stranger.

Perhaps a little too late, I questioned my judgment about not asking Beatty or one of the other men to see me home. But then I remembered I was Nora Potts' granddaughter. My heroine's motto was succinct: Worry none, prepare well, and pray should the need arise.

I had yet to master the not worrying part. However, I was a good preparer and a prayer when the need arose. I made the sign of the cross, stepped out of my truck, clicked the locks, and made a fist with my biggest key pointing out from between my forefinger and middle finger. I could blind a man with a fist like that. Armed, I ran up the walk to my stoop, swinging my head left and right, keeping an eye out for unusual shadows.

Perhaps because I'd been so focused on what might be outside of my home, I didn't notice the sliver of light that must have been shining through the slit in the front window drapes.

I did, however, notice how bright the living room was when I entered my house. The light surprised me. I am usually very conscientious about electricity. I keep that particular bill to a minimum. Ezra must have come home to get something he'd forgotten.

As I shut the door behind me, I noticed the light in the dining room was on, too. Once in there, I saw the light in the kitchen was on. I started preparing a rant to end all rants for my energy-wasting son.

In the kitchen, I changed my mind. Ezra hadn't been home. Someone else had stopped by. Someone had reheated the leftover spaghetti Bolognese from the refrigerator, eaten it with a glass of wine and left the dirty dishes in the sink. That someone also left a smudge of lipstick on the glass that looked amazingly similar to the Coral Bombshell color Melissa wore.

I went to the front of the house to call up the stairs.

"Melissa! You here?" I waited. After a few seconds of silence, I climbed halfway up, far enough so my head was above the landing. "Mel! Are you here?" I called through the railing.

All three upstairs doors were open. No sounds came from the darkness beyond them.

I returned to the kitchen and picked up the glass. The smear was definitely from her lipstick. I knew that color well. When she had learned the manufacturer discontinued it, Mel had panicked. She enlisted my help to track down the remaining stock. We'd managed to find forty-seven tubes, which she believed would give her long enough time to find a suitable replacement.

It was well after one in the morning. I figured I should call Ed anyway, or the police. Maybe even both. I pulled my cell from my purse and scrolled to Ed's name.

"Hey, Peri," Melissa said before I hit *call.*

I spun and saw her standing barefoot in the doorway to the dining room. Scratching her tousled head, Melissa wore nothing except one of Ezra's T-shirts and her underwear.

"My God! Mel!" I hugged her tight. "What the hell happened? Are you all right? We gotta call Ed to tell him you're here. He's having a breakdown."

"No," Melissa broke out of my hold. "You can't call him." She yanked the phone away and tucked it into the T-shirt, apparently forgetting she'd taken off her bra. It fell through, clattered to the floor and landed in front of the refrigerator. We both dove for it. Mel slammed into me. She knocked me sideways and flicked the phone completely under the fridge.

"What the hell is wrong with you?" I yelled as I climbed to my feet.

Melissa knelt on the floor, face in her hands, and sobbed. "I can't go back to him, not yet."

"What? So you left him? As in *left* him left him?" I sat next to her with a hand on her back. "Listen, he doesn't know. He thinks you just disappeared. He even called the cops."

She rubbed her eyes. "Was he actually worried?"

"Yes! He's nuts. I just got home. The police were at the bar. They might still be there."

"Wait." Melissa stood and went to the kitchen table. "What time did he call the cops?"

"I don't know." I took a wooden spoon out of a drawer and swished its handle under the refrigerator. After a couple of swipes in vain, I was able to knock the phone to the front of the fridge where I could pick it up. It was covered in dust bunnies. "Maybe around eleven?"

"Ha! He's such a shit! God, he's a real shit!" Melissa slammed her hand on the table. "Guess when the last time he actually saw me was. Or spoke to me."

"Three thirty-three today?" I dampened a paper towel to clean my phone.

"What?"

"You called him at—"

"Right. I left a voice mail for the bastard. The last time we spoke was at dinner. Dinner *last night* after we left *here*!" Melissa stood with such force she nearly knocked her chair over. With knuckles pressed against the table, she leered at me. "The last time my so-called concerned husband spoke to me was over twenty-four hours ago. And do you know why he suddenly realized I wasn't around?"

I shook my head.

"I set him up. He was expecting to find the sponsorship paperwork for the Mummer's parade on his desk in Pub Six on Monday afternoon. I made sure it was completed and ready for his signature at three o'clock today. I went back to the First Pub and called him to tell him it was on his desk. Then I started timing him to see how long it'd take for him to return my call to say *thanks,* or maybe just *hello.* After a while, I got bored, so I went for a walk. I walked all over this stupid city just waiting for him to call. Nothing. So I got tired of waiting. I went in the back door at the First Pub, left my stuff without speaking to anyone. I took my bank card, walked down to Roosevelt Boulevard, got some cash from an ATM and then hailed a cab to take me to the train station. I thought I'd take the Amtrak somewhere until I realized I didn't know where to go. I was hungry so I wound up having the cabbie drop me here instead."

"Why didn't you tell anyone at the bar where you were going?"

"Because they would tell *him!* I didn't want him to know yet. I wanted him to think for one stupid minute just about *me,* about what kind of person *I* am, about what his life would be like without me. And you know something? I was kind of hoping he'd find me here because it would be proof that he knew me. That he stopped to think about how every time I get mad at him, I come here. That would tell me he does know me, at least, a little bit. Not surprisingly, he failed!" She leered at me for another second before spinning around. "You know how he is on Saturdays. He makes his rounds at the pubs and has a drink at each one to look like he's a regular everywhere, right?" She turned back to look at me. "Well, he needs me to drive him. So that means he didn't even think of me, until he noticed I didn't show up at Ed's Sixth Pub to be his goddamned chauffeur." She added before she left the room.

"Mel, I'm sorry." I caught her arm in the living room at the bottom of the stairs. "I didn't realize you two were having problems."

"That's the thing, Peri, we're *not* having problems. That's how we freaking live. And I can't take it anymore." She tore up the stairs.

I followed and was relieved to find her in Ezra's room, not mine. Melissa lay face down on the twin bed, sobbing into the comets and planets displayed on the blue background of the pillow case.

"Mel," I sat on the edge of the bed, stroking the back of her head. "Okay, so you're not happy with him right now. I get it. Still, you gotta call let him know you're all right."

"Why?"

"Because . . . because he's worried. It's just the right thing to do."

"I want him to worry. He needs to worry about me just a little, Peri. Please. Let me have just this one night of him worrying. I'll call him tomorrow. I promise."

"It's already tomorrow."

"Then what difference will a couple hours make?"

Chapter 9: Being Controlled

My cell phone woke me around eight o'clock the next morning.

"I know it's indecent to call people before nine o'clock," Carolyn Hoskison said when I answered. "But Peri, I need your help."

"Sure, what is it?" I propped myself up on an elbow.

"It's nothing I can discuss right now," Carolyn whispered into the phone. "Besides, it's something I think you should see in person."

I fell back against my pillow and prayed she wouldn't want to see me until after noon. "Should I come see you later?"

"No. I need to come to you. Gerard came home from the shore yesterday to be with me. I want to show you something he can't see," Carolyn continued to whisper. "Can I come now? Where do you live?"

I talked her into waiting until nine thirty. I wanted to shower and get a little caffeine in my system first. Besides, Ricky-of-the-lost-phone was coming around nine o'clock. By the way Carolyn sounded, she was expecting a confidential, uninterrupted conversation.

Before I went downstairs, I placed a note beside Melissa's head, asking her to stay upstairs until I told her otherwise.

In the kitchen, I made the precious coffee then went into the dining room to check my e-mail while I waited for Ricky and Carolyn. Mrs. Johanssen had sent another e-mail. This one was asking if I'd ordered invitations yet. I replied that since we hadn't chosen the venue, I couldn't send out the invitations. I might have sighed while I wrote it.

I saw my reminder to look up online fabric stores. I also read a note from Detective Beatty saying he hoped I slept well.

I texted Ezra to remind him to check his blood and to text me his sugar count before he ate breakfast. Then I called my mom.

"Anything fun and exciting going on with you?" she asked.

"Not really. Well, not unless you count Melissa going missing last night."

"Did you look at your house?"

"I'm there now, Ma. And yes, that's where she is."

"See? I'm good at this detective business. I think I should go for my P.I. license."

"So life coach, hypnotist, Reiki master, and holistic nutritionist aren't enough for you? Do you have room on your business card to add *detective*?"

"I'd just have to have the font made smaller. I do think it's a natural outcropping of all my talents. I was just talking to your dad about it last night when we were watching an old *Hill Street Blues* rerun. He thinks I should go for it."

"Of course he does."

"Now, what were you calling for? Oh, yes! You want to discuss the case of the dead man, right? My warrior, Shelby Wooley."

"I don't think I'd ever call him a warrior, but, yes, I do. I mean, I kind of—"

"Ooo! Maybe I could be a psychic, too."

"Or psychotic," I semi-whispered as I took a sip of coffee. "Anyway, I'm really calling about that detective who questioned me—"

"Really? Why?"

"He was at the pub last night. Came in while I was bartending."

"I told you he thinks you're a suspect."

"Maybe. But he had a beer and actually drank it. And I think he flirted with me, too."

"Oh poopsie, don't get messed up with a police officer."

"I'm not getting messed up with a police officer, Ma. I was just wondering—"

"I mean they're good guys and all, it's just that you should never date one."

"I'm sure. They tend to have a short life span. Look, I—"

"Well there's that, too, I suppose, I never thought of *that*. What I meant was: they don't make good catches."

I reread Detective Beatty's short e-mail again: *I hope you slept well.*

"Now that I think about it," my mother continued, "you haven't dated in so long, I suppose it wouldn't hurt if you dabbled with a man in blue. I mean, if you can't get anyone else."

"It's not that I can't get anyone else. I'm a very busy person," I insisted.

"I know you are and you're very controlling. I'm sure it's difficult for you."

"I am NOT controlling!"

"Just find out if he has a hobby or some other outlet to deal with the stress of the job. Otherwise, he's probably an alcoholic or a drug addict. I mean, that's datable, too, I suppose. Oh, forget I even said anything. You just go enjoy yourself my beautiful girl!"

"Wait! Mom." *Click.* She hung up. I redialed.

"Something else, poopsie?" she asked.

"I'm not dating him. That wasn't why I brought him up. I was just wondering if he'd *do* that, flirt with me, if he really thought I was a suspect. What do you think?"

"Hmm . . . I don't suppose so. Unless he was trying to charm you into slipping up somehow. Regardless, you have nothing to worry about. I'm on the case, right? I'll save you."

"I feel so safe now." I sighed and clicked off the call. I keep telling myself I have to stop calling her. Except, whenever I try to cut back, I always miss her. I also keep telling myself that I have to stop expecting her to be someone else, because deep down I also know I'd miss her quirkiness. Still, every once in a while it would be so nice to have a normal mom.

Around nine-ten someone rang the doorbell.

Mel was coming down the stairs as I approached the front door.

"What are you doing?" I hissed in a whisper. "My client needs privacy. I'll let you know when the coast is clear." She retreated. I opened the door to find Carolyn Hoskinson's face pinched with concern. Behind her stood a confused-looking teen boy.

"Come in, come in," I took her by the hand and led her inside. "Hi," I said to the boy. "You must be Ricky."

He nodded.

"Just a minute." I picked up his phone from the coffee table. "I charged it for you overnight. So you have a full battery."

He looked at the cracked screen then looked past me, into the house.

"Is everything all right?" I asked him.

"Uh, yeah." He scratched the back of his shaggy head. "Um, who . . . Thanks a lot," he said then turned and ran down the steps. At the street he climbed into a tiny, convertible sports car with the top down. The young male driving greeted him with: *"Dude!* What took you so long?"

I shut the door and faced Carolyn. She held her face in her hands.

"What happened?" I asked.

She collapsed against me, hugging tightly. "I'm so glad you could see me," she said. "I—I don't know who else I could trust right now. You must help me."

I got Carolyn settled in the kitchen with a fresh cup of coffee for both of us then waited patiently for her to summon whatever she needed to summon to explain her situation

"I found this note." Carolyn reached into her purse. "It was folded up and taped to the outside of my mailbox. Thank God Gerard didn't get the mail."

She handed the paper to me. I unfolded it. Someone had made a letter look like it was written from words cut out of a magazine, like an old-fashioned ransom note. Only this message had been generated by a computer and printed. It read: *I know who U are, Carol. I know what U did. It's time to say ur sorry.*

"Oh, wow," was all I could say at first. I reread it a few more times. "What, um, what does it mean?" I finally asked although I was thinking: *what do you want from me?*

"It could mean so much," Carolyn held her head in both hands, elbows on the kitchen table. "Oh Peri, so very much."

"What did Mr. Hoskin—"

"Gerard cannot know!" Carolyn snapped her face up. "He cannot know. Not yet. Not until you find who wrote this and why."

"Me? Why me?" I leaned back in my chair, hand on my chest. "Your husband's a judge. Surely he's in a better position to figure this out."

"No!" Carolyn shouted. Acting like a frequent visitor to my kitchen, she got up and topped off her barely touched coffee. "Listen, there are a few things about me Gerard doesn't know. He knows more than most people in this town, but not everything. You, Peri, are the exception." She sat in her chair. "Out of all the people in Philadelphia, you know most of my secrets. I trust you with my true hair color. With what I do at my dermatologist's office." Carolyn put air quotes around the word *dermatologist.* "You know who I really like, who I must fake liking. You even know how I'm self-conscious about the shape of my ears. You know it all. Remember? I told you this when I insisted you call me by my first name."

"I do remember. I'm glad you trust me."

"I feel like you are my one, true friend in this town. You're the only one I can trust with this." Carolyn's eyes brimmed with tears.

"Oh, Carolyn, I appreciate it, I really do. And I like you, too. I consider you a friend who happens to employ me. I just don't know how I can help you with this."

"You can find out who wrote that note."

"How?"

"I don't know, Peri. How do you do anything? You have resources and more resources and more. You're amazing at what you do in this town. You can research better than any student at Drexel."

"But I'm not a detective." *Though I do know someone who wants to be one,* I thought.

"And that's a good thing. I can't let the police get involved." She reached over the table to place her hand on my arm. "Look, you only know everything about me since I became the wife of the Honorable Gerard Hoskinson. What you don't know is what no one knows. Gerard knows a little . . . ." She paused and took in a long, deep breath. "You might want to get one of your handy notepads right about now."

I retrieved a pen and pad from the dining room.

"I guess I should start with my real age," Carolyn said when I returned to the table. "I'm not thirty-three."

"You're thirty-seven," I said.

"How do you know?"

"I took care of renewing your driver's license, remember?"

"Oh yes, right." Carolyn smiled. "See? You do know my secrets."

"Right. So I also know your real name is Carol Lynn." I raised my eyebrows and tilted my head, waiting. "Anyway," I said after a few minutes of silence.

"Anyway, when I was younger, I went to college at a small, private school. I lived at home so I could keep my car."

Again, I waited, quietly.

"Actually, that's not the truth." Carolyn shook her head. She cast her eyes downward. "I do wish I was telling you this in the evening. I could use a glass of wine right about now."

"We don't have to hurry," I said. "Unless you do. Take your time."

"Thank you." She paused to sip her coffee. "Well, I attended college at Bryn Athyn."

"Never heard of it."

"It's a very small school. Not too far from Philadelphia, though. I enjoyed my time there. It was intimate. The people were very nice. It was the only school my parents approved because it was close to home and it's a religious school." She fingered her cup in its saucer, concentrating her eyes on it. "Well, the night I turned twenty-one, my friends helped me escape through my bedroom window. I went to a college party for the first time. I overdid it and got whipped by my father the next morning when I accidentally woke him as I stumbled in around five. Nine months later, I gave birth."

Carolyn took another sip.

I forced my mouth to shut and noted: *had baby at 21.*

"My parents made me give the child up for adoption. When I finished college, I ran away to Miami with a girlfriend who was moving there."

I wrote: *Moved to Miami after college.*

"I had never worked a day in my life, my degree was in art, which was worthless. The only job I could get at first was as a cashier at a supermarket. It was only part-time and didn't pay well. Eventually, a girl I had become friendly with talked me into becoming a stripper at a little club."

"A, a what?" Carolyn dressed as conservatively as Hillary Clinton. She never even showed cleavage while wearing a cocktail gown.

"A stripper. Of course, she called it exotic dancer. This is one of the things Gerard doesn't know. He knows about the baby and my parents." She took a long drink of the coffee. "You know, just talking about it with you is helping. I know I can count on you to help me. I think this is the first time I might come close to relaxing since I found that note Friday."

Note Friday.

"So, as I said, I worked as a stripper. The place was called *Heaven or Bust*. I went by the name Carly. The owner was a nasty, smarmy man named Jorje something. I can't remember. Frankly, I'm not sure he ever told us his full name." She ran her hands through her hair. "I'm not proud of this."

"I'm not judging you," I said. "I understand mistakes and poor judgment when you're young. Trust me. I understand."

Carolyn smiled. "Do you understand rebellion?"

"Oh God, yes."

"Thank you." She took a breath. "So, Jorje paid us an hourly wage, in cash, then he took half the tips my co-workers and I earned. One day, one of the girls left. A month or so later, she came back and told us how much she was making at a rival place. We girls banded together, stormed Jorje's office, and demanded better pay."

"Did he give it to you?"

"Of course not. He flat out refused. Our timing couldn't have been better. He was actually sitting at his desk with all this cash spread out in front of him. I guess he was making a deposit or something, I'm not sure. Well, he laughed at us. He called us *a bunch of worthless whores.*" Carolyn's eyes clenched shut. "He had made eye contact with me when he said it. That was exactly what my mother had called me when I told her I was pregnant and . . . and I don't know what came over me. I was so angry. I was sick and tired of being taken advantage of, of being told what to do, of being controlled by everyone else. I picked up his phone." She opened her eyes and looked at me. Tears seemed about to fall over the rims. "Do you remember those old-fashioned desk phones that used to be in a lot of offices? They were usually beige or black. The handset was connected by a coiled cord. Remember those?"

I nodded.

"They were heavy. Must have been made of metal at the base." She wiped her eyes and shrugged. "His was that beige color. As I looked at it, something came over me. It was like I was watching myself from outside my body. I picked up that phone and slammed it against the side of his head."

I caught my breath.

"I knocked him out. We girls divided the cash and ran."

"Wow."

Carolyn sniffed. "Right. Wow."

"Did he live?"

"I think so. That is, I never heard about his murder on the news." She frowned as she rummaged through her purse. "So Jorje is a possibility."

Chapter 10: Can't Easily Quit

I stood to get the box of tissues from the counter.

"Thank you," Carolyn said, taking one out.

I returned to the table. "Go on."

"Well, I couldn't go back to work for Jorje again, obviously, so when one of the other girls landed a job with a cruise ship as a cocktail waitress, she helped me get hired, too."

"That sounds exciting."

"It sounded that way to me too, back then. The company was a small outfit called Flamingo Cruises. It's not in business anymore."

I wrote.

"Our wages were horrific. Living quarters were probably better on the Mayflower. Though we had fun working on the deck. Money-wise, we lived hand to mouth. Then one day the head chef approached my friend and me. He'd heard us complaining about not being able to afford much of anything. He had a business partner in South America. They needed help with their import-export business. They offered us some extra cash on the side if we could help them."

"Let me guess," I said. "Illegal pharmaceuticals?"

"Right.

"Did you?"

"We did. We hid the stuff in our quarters and took it off ship in our bags in South Florida each time we returned to port. Back then, custom officials let the cruise employees come and go with ease, especially the pretty young things who'd flirt with them. So eventually, we'd safely made enough runs that we'd each saved enough money to quit the cruise ship. We figured we'd buy our own condos on some island paradise and maybe tend bar at a resort." Carolyn stood again to walk over to the sink to look out the window.

"And?" I asked after a few minutes.

"You can't easily quit the drug trafficking trade." Carolyn said, turning around.

"So what did you do?"

"Well, at the time it sounded smart. Maybe it was. My girlfriend suggested we turn the cruise line in for hiring illegal aliens and for smuggling. Both were true. We weren't even working for them with legitimate papers. My passport at the time said my name was *Carly Lin.*"

"What happened?"

"I took my share of the cash we'd squirreled away and put it in a bank in the British Virgin Islands. We made the call. The cruise ship went bust. I moved to Tortola, intent on starting my life anew."

"Holy cow." I updated my steno pad.

"By then," Carolyn continued, "I was twenty-six. I should have known better, but an older gentleman, one who had a son my age, was rather taken with me, as he said." She rubbed her forehead and sighed. "He was so nice. For the first time in my life, I thought I'd finally found someone who valued me as an individual. We dated. We married." She looked directly at me. "He wound up being an abusive alcoholic."

"Holy—no, I used that. I think I'm running out of expressions." I leaned back in my chair unable to take my eyes off Carolyn, a woman whom I had assumed lived a straitlaced, borderline boring life since the day she was born.

"Good thing I'm almost done." She smiled as she returned to the table. "One day he was in a particularly nasty mood. He swore up and down I was having an affair with our landscaper."

"Were you?"

"No! What kind of woman do you think I am?"

I didn't answer.

"Believe it or not, throughout the entire time, I never slept around."

"I'm sorry," I said, not believing her. "I really am."

"Don't be. It would make sense if I had, I guess." She crumpled in the chair. "It's awful. I'm in such a habit of living a lie. Telling the truth doesn't even occur to me sometimes. Actually, I never slept around because was I terrified of getting pregnant again, not because I was a good girl. I didn't have regular access to doctors for prevention I could trust until I married. My mother prevented me from using any drugs when I gave birth. She said I was to suffer the pain as much as possible as a consequence of my actions and hired a midwife from hell."

"Carolyn! Are you serious?"

"Unfortunately. The experience made me never want to give birth again."

"I can understand that. Again, I'm sorry." I shook my head. "Okay, you said you're almost done. What next?"

"He flew into a rage and beat me but good that day. I knew what would happen next. Every single time he'd hurt me, he'd feel guilty afterward and force me to have make-up sex. All throughout dinner I kept thinking about him wanting to climb on me. It made my skin crawl. So I crushed up a little Benadryl and stirred it into some chopped cherries to put on his ice cream for dessert. He was drunk and didn't notice if it tasted different. I just wanted him to pass out, that was all."

"Oh God," I said, guessing what was coming next.

"Yes, he died."

"Oh. My. God."

"Honest, it wasn't my fault." Carolyn leaned over the table. "You can look it up in the papers. It wasn't from the Benadryl. Well, it wasn't just from the Benadryl. He'd taken a bunch of medication that night. The Benadryl may have been the final push, although he might have died without it."

"Was there a police report?"

"Yes. I think they thought I killed him. They'd been called by the neighbors to our home so many times because of my screams and his yelling. They knew what kind of relationship we had. I think they felt it was justified, if I had intentionally done it. Anyway, they were very quick to rule it an accidental overdose."

Somewhat relieved, I settled back in my chair.

"However, because he'd left everything to me in his will," Carolyn continued, "his kids were much more suspicious. They tried to file suits. Things got ugly. I wound up liquidating everything and moving here. I'd always wanted to work at the art museum in Philly. So I started my life over as Carolyn Clark. Clark was my maiden name. I guess you could say I became the woman I was supposed to be. I volunteered at the museum and that's where I met Gerard. He knows I'm the widow of a British Virgin Islands man. He just doesn't know exactly how he died."

I put the pen down and looked over my notes. There appeared to be several people who could have it in for Carolyn. On the one hand, it might just be a matter of Internet searching to find them. On the other, I was pretty sure I wasn't equipped to be dealing with dangerous drug smugglers, slimy strip club operators, or angry West Indians.

"Peri, please help me discover who wrote this. Once I know, I'll tell Gerard if necessary. He loves me. My life is finally in a good place. I'm in love with a good man. I'm doing work at the museum that I enjoy. We're thinking about adopting children. Please, help me." Her eyes pleaded into mine. "Of course, since this is above and beyond anything you'd normally do for us, this will not be paid for by your retainer. I'll give you twenty-five-thousand dollars, cash, under the table if you want, from my own private funds, if you do this for me."

I didn't have to think about the answer. Suddenly I was perfectly equipped to handle dangerous drug smugglers, slimy strip club owners and angry West Indians.

"I'll get started on it right away."

Carolyn flew around the table and pulled me into a hug.

"Thank you! Oh thank you! Thank you! Thank you!" Tears streamed down the woman's face. "You have no idea what this means to me. Thank you."

I shut the front door behind Carolyn and leaned against it, stunned. I wanted to question my judgment for taking on the job. Yet each time I tried to analyze my way through it, twenty-five thousand reasons why I should skip making a judgment call intruded.

Sometimes money clouds one's perspective, I knew that. Then again, sometimes one can't simply ignore a large chunk of cash thrown in one's lap.

"Peri!" Melissa shrieked. "That's intense!"

"What do you mean?"

"That woman! What's her name?" Mel peaked through the front curtains.

"Were you listening?" I pulled her away from the window.

"Of course! That's some juicy story. Who is she?"

"Look, you can't tell anyone about this." We sat on the sofa. "Do you hear me? No one!"

"Okay. Okay." Melissa pretended to zip her lips shut. "Seriously, who is she?"

Usually my willingness to defend my clients' privacy rivaled that of a well-paid Hollywood attorney's. I'd just never been handed such a background story on a plate before. I needed help compartmentalizing my brain to get it to wrap around the conversation I'd just had. So I filled Melissa in on the details of who Carolyn was according to what people in Philadelphia believed: the wife of a judge, exhibit planner at the art museum, kindhearted philanthropist.

"So she's this well-respected citizen with baggage like that?" Melissa asked.

"Apparently so."

"That's insane! Can I see the note?"

In the kitchen, I picked the note up from the table and handed it to Melissa.

"Obviously it's from a young person," she said.

"What makes you think so?" I asked from the sink where I washed the coffee cups.

"They used a *U* instead of spelling the word. Same with *Ur.* I mean, they did it with a computer. Why go through the hassle of finding images to make some words then not spell the others right? Only a teen would do that."

I looked at the note over Melissa's shoulder.

"Maybe. Though why would a kid . . ." I ripped the note out of her hand. "It doesn't matter now. Right now, you have to call Ed."

"I'm not ready yet." Still wearing Ezra's T-shirt and now a pair of his socks, she looked vulnerable, but not so vulnerable that I couldn't give her a tongue-lashing.

"And that doesn't matter either. You have to call him."

"What am I to tell him?"

"That you're not lost, or kidnapped, or whatever." I threw my hands in the air.

"That's not what I mean." Melissa sat at the table. "What do I tell him about why I left?"

"Tell him what you told me last night." I poured the remaining coffee from the carafe into a travel mug.

"Last night I was upset because it took him so long to realize I wasn't there. But that's only part of it, Peri. You know what will happen?"

I shook my head.

"I'll tell him I don't like how we never spend time together. He'll make a promise to spend more time with me. And I'm sure he'll follow through on it for a while. Then eventually, he'll start treating me like just another employee. One he sleeps with on the weekends."

"Yikes, Mel." I sighed as I sat across from her at the table.

"Yeah, but you know what? I think I'm figuring it out." She sat up straight. "I think I need to quit working for him. I need to do something for me."

"Oh." I sat straighter, too. "Then tell him that. Tell him you just needed some time to think and now you know you need to quit working for him."

"Just like that?"

"Just like that."

She held my eyes. "I'm not sure I can. At least not now."

"Why not now?"

"I need to get up my nerve and strength. You know how persuasive Ed can be, right?"

I understood what Melissa meant. Ed always got what he wanted. He wasn't mean or tough. Nor did he use brute strength to get his way. He just assumed the world was his and somehow the world agreed with him, always. Whenever anyone challenged that assumption, he'd charm them into changing their minds.

"Yeah, I know how he can be."

"So I just need a little bit of time to completely figure it out. To line up some answers to throw back at him when he starts to wheedle at me. Okay?"

I sighed.

"That's the second time you've sighed within the last five minutes."

"By criticizing me you make me want to call Ed and say 'come and get her.'"

"Uncle!" She shook her head so hard the whole top of her body shimmied. "My mind is just not in a good place right now. It's hard to think clearly. Please. I need time before I call him."

I looked at her with half-open eyes. Perhaps I didn't want to be a complete witness to the bad decision I was about to make. "Okay. Just don't make me regret letting you slide." I glanced at the clock on the microwave. "Listen, I have to take care of something for a client. I should only be about an hour, maybe an hour and a half if traffic is heavy. Get yourself ready. When I get back, you're calling Ed." I stood to leave the room. My cell dinged with a text.

The message was from Ezra: *102, 62 carbs.* I texted back *thank you.*

"That's Ez," I said to Mel. "You should get dressed soon. You don't want him popping in with you sitting around in his T-shirt."

"Oh, he knows I'm wearing it. He came in last night when you were at the pub. He forgot his toothbrush. That's how I knew I could sleep in his bed and he found this giant shirt for me to sleep in. He's a good kid, you know."

"I know, Mel. But, uh, if you ever go missing again, you shouldn't be so obvious about it."

Chapter 11: Still Confused

I drove all the way out to my dream house in Ardmore, a charming little town at the northwest edge of Philly. It belonged to Marion Webster, who only pretended to hate her name whenever someone mentioned the dictionary with a similar, albeit not quite the same, moniker.

Marion had once told me her home was built in French Carriage house style. Yet it wasn't the house I loved so much as the yard, for which she had no name. She had close to an acre of lavishly landscaped grounds with a brick walk winding through it to the front door then out to the pool in the back.

I parked on the street instead of in the driveway when I arrived at her home. I wanted to take the time to appreciate the azaleas in bloom and to relish how full-on-green spring had become. The only time I ever thought I could use the word *enchanting* without sounding like a flake, was when I walked up that sidewalk in the springtime.

Inside the house, however, when Marion wasn't home, was an entirely different matter. I put the key in the lock, took a deep breath, turned it and pushed open the door.

"Kisses!" I hollered in the most pleasant voice I could muster as I punched in the alarm code. "Kisses! Hello kitty!"

Not a sound could be heard. Which meant the cat was in attack position. It must have been stalking me through the windows.

Kisses weighed in at just over twenty-seven pounds—of pure muscle. One of the very many previous vets had told Marion he believed she was part Bobcat. He further elaborated by saying Kisses had no business inside someone's home, let alone in his office. Marion had rescued Kisses when she was a tiny kitten found in a parking lot and now Kisses returned the favor by protecting Marion and her home with the fierceness of, well, of a bobcat.

I tiptoed to the kitchen to retrieve Kisses' food from the freezer (she ate a commercial, raw-meat cat food). I warmed it just enough in the microwave and had almost got the bowl set back on the floor when she pounced. Her claws had been removed years ago, thank heavens, though she still had fangs, that is teeth, which left permanent scars on my calf.

On the plus side, she kept my reflexes in good shape. I leaped to the countertop, literally. She glared up at my perch, making a whale-like growling sound and whipping her tail. Then she must have sniffed the raw meat in her bowl because she nosed over and ate, completely ignoring me. I sat cross legged on the counter, reading the note Marion had left for me.

Thank you so much for taking care of Kisses on such short notice. I know you're not a big fan of her. I just needed to get away for the weekend to breathe and gather myself. Please, if it's not too much trouble, when the funeral arrangements are made, would you have a sizeable floral arrangement created for Shel from me? I can't bear the thought of doing it.

That was how she referred to him: *Shel.* Marion was Mr. Wooley's sister. She was one of a handful of people who knew what his plans were. Thinking about that made me realize I had completely forgotten to tell Detective Beatty that only a few people knew he was in town. My mother would probably want to know, too.

I waited for Kisses to finish her meal. While she cleaned herself in a sunbeam, I washed her dish. We finished at the same time, which meant I dashed out of the house with her chasing me.

Out in my truck, I called my mom first.

"Can you talk?" I asked.

"Almost. I'm just saying good-bye to a client. Let me put you on hold." Which meant: *let me lay the phone down on my desk and deal with this customer while you listen.* Sometimes it was fun when she did that, like once I overheard a morning local TV weathercaster asking about burp prevention. Other times it wasn't, like when a hypnotherapy client cried and cried and cried for the ants to quit biting. Today it was simply someone asking about how much milk thistle he needed to tonify his liver.

"All right, whatcha need?" she asked when she picked up the receiver. "You and Detective Hot Hands in action yet?"

"Oh my God, no."

She laughed.

"And Detective Hot Hands, really?" I asked.

"Go on then, why did you call?"

"Did I tell you," I paused to count in my head. "Only nine people knew Mr. Wooley was in town the day he was murdered?"

"Ooooooo, this is good. Wait . . . Okay, I got a pencil. Who are they?"

"Well, me, of course," I said then I gave her the names of his doctors. "His chef, Julio McStravick. His—"

"Is that really his name?"

"Yep. Also, his . . ." I stumbled. I couldn't mention his housekeeper, Noreen Parkerson, to my mom. Noreen used to clean for my parents. Her job with them didn't end well and my mother would use this as an excuse to contact the woman, which could possibly lead to a lawsuit. "There's his daughter, Jacqueline," I said instead.

"My bet's on her."

"Why?"

"Easiest access. I'd say your detective man has his eye on her, too. They always suspect the close family members."

"Did I tell you she gave me his china?"

"What? No! Now how am I to prove you're innocent if you're holding out valuable information?"

"I don't know if it's valuable. I just think it's odd. She showed up yesterday with a bunch of china that she said he'd have wanted me to have."

"Really? That *is* odd."

"She's odd."

"How odd does one have to be to divvy up his belongings before the will is read?"

"I hadn't thought of that."

"See there? Good thing you got me. Now then, who else knew the old man was around?"

"Just for the record, he was younger than you. Anyway, his close friends Julian Westman and Alex Foster knew, as did his sister, Marion Webster."

"What's with those names?" my mother cackled.

"Coming from a woman named Honey, who willingly took on her husband's surname of Potts?" My phone clicked with call-waiting. I looked at the screen, saw my grandmother's name and ignored Melissa. "Marion's a client of mine. She is very distraught right now. I know very little about Julian Westman or Alex Foster."

"I know an Alex Foster. Wonder if it's the same one. I believe I saved his kidneys. I may have to check in on him and see how he's doing. He might owe me a favor. "

"You do that."

"I will. Now, who's the last one?"

"What?"

"That's only seven, people, eight counting you. You said nine."

"Oh, uh, I guess I miscounted."

"That's all right. I'll see you for dinner later, right?"

I didn't even try to hold in the groan. "Sure." I hung up.

I am confused as to why I'm still alive and walking on this planet despite my mom's cooking. Yes, I could honestly say I grew up well nourished. I could also honestly say the foodstuffs were rarely edible. And, as my son can attest because we have dinner with my parents every Sunday night, there is no evidence she's becoming a better cook.

I looked at Marion's house and realized I'd forgotten to re-set the alarm.

"Oh hell," I said aloud as I dialed her. Thankfully, she was able to reset the alarm remotely with an app on her phone. While I was on with her, Melissa called me again. Once I hung up from Marion, I rang my house. No answer. I hung up and turned on my Ford. Melissa called back as I put the truck in gear.

"Hey, did you just call?" she asked when I answered.

"Yes. I was returning your calls." I put the phone on speaker so I could talk hands free while I drove. "Are you all right?"

"Yeah. I'm good. Really good. Like never before good."

"That almost scares me."

"Me too. So anyway, I don't think I should use your phone to call Ed. I don't want him to know where I am."

"That's actually a good idea." I nodded out the front window. "Thanks. That way he won't be mad at me for harboring you, again."

"Right, there's that and, uh, I was also thinking that maybe I could stay here with you for a little while."

"What? No! You have to call him. You can't let him continue to think you're missing. That's just mean." I turned left onto Ardmore Drive.

"No, I mean, I know. I'll call him. I will. I'm just not ready to go back to him yet. Can I stay with you, for a little while longer? I won't tell him where I'll be. I promise."

Just say "no." Just say "no."

"Mel, I don't want to be in the middle of your marriage problems," I said instead. "Ed would kill me if he ever found out."

"I promise you, he won't. Besides, you need me. I can help you with Carolyn while you do all the other shit you need to do. I'll earn my keep."

I stared at the Sunday traffic ahead of me unable to figure out why there needed to be so many people out on the road. There always seemed to be more people out than necessary. More things in my way than I could easily handle. Maybe Mel had a point. Maybe I could sit her down in front of my computer and have her research everyone from Carolyn's past while I continue my regular work. I hated researching anyway.

"As long as you call Ed to tell him you're okay. Deal?" I asked.

"Deal. But I need a phone to call him. Can you pick up one of those disposable phones somewhere? You know what I'm talking about?"

"Yeah. I'll be home in about an hour and a half."

It was closer to two hours by the time I was heading down my street. I was hungry. I hoped Mel and Ezra hadn't eaten all the Bolognese sauce. I had visions of dunking chunky bread into that red deliciousness. I slowed as I neared the end of my street and stopped instead of driving around back.

Detective Beatty was heading up the stairs of my stoop.

I pounded the button to make the passenger-side window go down.

"Hey!" I shouted as soon as it cracked open a hair, just before he pressed the doorbell. He turned and waved. I parked and flew out of the truck. "What are you doing here?" I yelled as I ran-walked toward him.

He waited on the porch. "I thought I'd check on you, see how you're doing," he said.

"Oh, that's really nice." I sat on the glider, patting the space next to me. "I'm okay, though it was a rough night."

"I'm sure." He sat.

"You know, I was thinking about something this morning that I think I should tell you," I said. "It's about Mr. Wooley."

"What about him?"

"Well, you said Jacqueline never told you anything about the mock funeral, right?"

"Right."

"Did she tell you only nine people knew he was in Philly?"

"How do you know?"

"As I said, I was doing everything for him to keep his secret a secret. Jacqueline just moved back home about two months ago."

"Where did she move from?"

"She was trying to make it as a soap star in California."

"That explains a lot about her. She's always so . . . so . . ."

"Theatrical? Yes."

"Again, that explains so much about her. We were beginning to think she was mentally ill. She seems to talk to herself quite a bit."

"Right, well, to be fair, she's probably not talking to herself. She has a tendency to wander around repeating lines and acting out scenes from movies and plays."

"Oblivious of what anyone else in the vicinity is doing?"

I nodded. "She says she's 'rehearsing.'"

"I see." He pulled a pen and small notebook out of his pocket. "You were saying only a few people knew Wooley was in town. Do you know who they are?"

I gave him the same information I'd just given my mother except I added: "Also there's Noreen Parkerson, his housecleaner." He wrote everything down.

"Huh." He nodded, staring at his list. I got the feeling he'd come across at least one of those names before. "Thank you," he said before looking up at me. "I don't know if you've spoken to your cousin yet, so you may already know this: the Philly PD is considering his wife officially missing."

"What does that mean?" Keeping my eyes on his, I crinkled the top of the plastic bag I had in my hand, rolling it down a little further to make sure *EZ-Get Phones n More* was obscured.

"That means we're combing the city," he said. "We're reviewing all the surveillance cameras in the area, unfortunately there aren't that many around here. We're also doing the old-fashioned thing of pounding the pavement for witnesses, talking to cab drivers, and all that. We believe she's been abducted even though the photo taken at the ATM showed she was alone."

"Oh my God!" I nearly shouted. In fact, I said it so loudly, I scared a squirrel away from the bird feeder. "Ed must be freaking out!" I jumped up. "I need to call him or something."

"Yeah. Listen," Detective Beatty stood, too. "I'm not assigned to the case and I can't divulge any information while it's open, but if I hear anything that, you know, sounds hopeful, I'll do my best to let you know somehow."

I backed away from him, heading toward the door rear-end first, clutching the bag to my stomach. "Thank you," I said. "Seriously, I really need to call Ed now."

I entered my house and shrieked, "Aaaa!"

Chapter 12: On The Hunt

Melissa or Ezra, one of them, maybe both, had been very busy while I was out. I scanned the living room, mentally cataloguing the mess:

- One open box of cereal on the coffee table, with pieces scattered on the floor;
- One half-full bowl of milk next to the box;
- One used spoon, lying in a tiny puddle of milk beside the bowl;
- One magazine spread open on the floor, two advertising cards once housed within its pages were loose and scattered nearby;
- One wadded paper towel under the table;
- One of Ezra's socks, wrong-side out, on the other side of the table.

I picked up the sock and headed toward the kitchen, betting it was more Melissa than Ezra because he knew better.

In the kitchen I found:

- One open carton of milk beside the sink, lid missing, droplets splattered across the basin to the other side, where the bowl presumably had been filled;
- One coffee cup half-full of coffee with cream (milk) on the kitchen table;
- One wadded paper towel on the kitchen table and another *on*

top of the trash bin lid, not in the bin;

• Two of the chairs at the kitchen table not pushed in.

In addition to those atrocities, the coffeepot was still on, despite the fact that only dregs remained in the bottom of the carafe and now the room was filled with a horrid burnt-coffee odor. The overhead light was on. The over-the-sink light was on. The radio was on. And the dishwasher door was half open.

On the plus side, there was still plenty of Bolognese in the refrigerator.

However, even though I was starving, I channeled my inner Kisses and went on the hunt for Melissa.

She was upstairs on the floor of the bathroom, painting her toenails.

"Call. Ed. Now," I greeted her. "I'll be downstairs. In the kitchen. Cleaning." I turned and left the tiny room only to rotate and go back in. "Where the hell is the other sock?" I shook Ezra's sock in my fist.

Melissa looked around the bathroom. "Here. Sorry." She pulled it out from between the toilet and tub.

I took the sock and placed it with its mate in the hamper. Once again, I spun a circle instead of going back downstairs.

"Has Ezra been home?"

"Nope." Melissa twisted the lid onto the polish bottle.

I finally left the bathroom and typed a text to my son on my way downstairs.

U alright?

Melissa was on my heels when I entered the kitchen.

"Sorry about the mess, Peri," she said. "I was going to clean it up before you got home."

"Call Ed," was my answer. Ez's response dinged my phone. *Y. will cal ltr.*

"You sound upset," she said. "I said I'm sorry. I mean it."

"Just freaking call Ed!" meanwhile I typed: *whats Y mean?*

"But are you okay with me?" Mel asked.

"Melissa, I'm so hungry right now I'm about to bite off a chunk of your arm. You know I get testy when I'm hungry. And you know I can't stand it when people mess up my house. So right now I'm *not* okay with you. Maybe after I eat and you clean up after yourself, I will be." I ripped open the refrigerator door and pulled out the

Bolognese. "Do you have any idea the kind of trouble you've started?"

"What? What do you mean?" Melissa backed into a chair.

I popped the Bolognese into the microwave. Ezra answered $Y = yes$. I took a deep breath and felt myself calm down a hair.

"I was just speaking with Detective Beatty. You know, one of the cops who was here Friday night?" I took a remnant of an Italian loaf out of the breadbox.

"That cute blond one or the equally cute partner?"

"The blond. He—"

"Did he ask you out? I thought there was something in the way he looked at you after he realized you were straight. Did he hit on you?"

"He did. Kind of. I mean, it doesn't matter!" The microwave beeped while I yelled. "Do you know why?"

"Why?"

"Because instead of chatting pleasantly with him, maybe even inviting him in for a little coffee, I had to find you." I set my bowl and bread on the table and poured a glass of water. "I had to find you first to tell you to call Ed."

"That could have waited." Melissa picked at her fingernails.

"No, it couldn't. Do you realize Philadelphia's finest are all on the hunt for you? You're officially missing. You have to call Ed, now, and call off the hunt!"

"What do you mean 'officially missing'?"

"I mean," I started and paused. I wished I could force steam out of the top of my head so she'd be afraid of me. "The police are ripping this city apart, looking for you. Don't you think they have other things, real crimes, they should be focusing on? What if they don't have the extra resources and some little girl gets lost forever because they're stretched too thin looking for you?"

"I never thought—"

"What if they find you here? He said they'll be interviewing cab drivers! Then we'll both be in hot water. What if—"

"Okay! Okay. I'll call Ed." She stood. "You don't have to get pissy about it."

"Yes, I do!" I slammed my hand into my forehead, I suppose instead of hitting her. "How else can I inspire you to do the right thing?"

"Getting pissy doesn't inspire," she said with one hand on a hip. "It uninspires."

"That's not a word! Anyway, *you* made me pissy, so pissy is what you got. If you want me *un*pissy, then do the right freaking thing and call your husband." I glared at her.

"I am not responsible for your emotions, you know. It's not fair for you to blame them on me."

"Oh. My. God." I slammed my hand down on the table. "You've been talking to my mother, haven't you? Not responsible for my emotions? That's a Honey-ism if I ever heard one."

"She's right you know. I figured it all out today. I've been making Ed be responsible for my feelings. I'd convinced myself it was all his fault I was unhappy in my marriage. His fault I was unsatisfied with my job. His fault I felt ignored and unappreciated."

"From the sounds of it, he neglected you, took advantage of your work skills and driver's license. So yeah, I think he is responsible."

"I let him do it."

"He's a Goddamned bully! Isn't that what Gram always said about him? That he was a nice kind of bully?"

"Yes, and how did she teach us to handle bullies, huh? By finding our inner power and standing up to them. And if that didn't work, to get help. I never did either one. I'm ready to take step one now."

"Then why the hell haven't you called him?" I'm not sure if I was screaming or yelling.

"I was waiting on you!" She screamed or yelled back. "Where's the phone?"

I ate while Mel spoke to Ed over the disposable phone. She called him from upstairs so I wasn't sure what was said. When she came back down, her face was pale, her eyes red.

"That was the hardest conversation I ever had in my life." She gave me a weak smile as she opened the refrigerator door.

"What'd you tell him?" I asked.

"A lot of stuff. It all wound down to: I needed a break from him and my job to reevaluate my life." She shut the refrigerator door and turned around to look at me. "Did you just finish off the Bolognese sauce?"

"Yes."

She pressed her lips tight together in a semi-sneer.

"Why don't you warm up some pasta with a little garlic, oil and parmesan?" I suggested.

"Okay." She pulled out the tub of leftover pasta. It looked heavy in her hands.

"You want some help?" I asked.

"No. I got it." She dumped the pasta in a bowl and opened the microwave.

"Obviously, you don't." I took the bowl from her. "Sit down," I ordered. "I'll sauté it right."

"Thanks." She sat. "It's crazy. I had it all figured out until I spoke to him. Now I don't know what to do with myself."

"I can tell you."

"I would expect nothing less from you."

"You'll have lunch." I melted a little butter into olive oil in a pan while I smashed a couple of garlic cloves and removed their skins. "You'll eat, then you'll clean up the mess you made."

"And then what? How do I figure out what to do with my life?"

"I haven't a clue. Since you're such a disciple, why don't you ask my mother?" I dropped the garlic into the oil. The aroma instantly hit me in a most delightful way. "You can go with Ezra and me to my parents' place for dinner tonight."

"I'd love to, but Ed doesn't know I'm here. I don't want to risk him spotting me as I'm travelling through the neighborhood."

"Oh, that was good." I nodded to her. "And quick. I almost believed you."

She smirked. "Can you blame me? I'll always love Honey. It's just that I think I'm still recovering from the last time I ate with your parents. She force-fed me juiced cauliflower and habanero. She called it her special cavity cleanse."

"Cleans your colon and sinuses at the same time," I said in my best Honey Potts impression. We laughed. "You're forgiven. But, uh, where does Ed think you are?" I picked the garlic out of the oil with a fork.

"He thinks I took a thousand out of the bank and went to Florida on Amtrak."

"What?" I dumped the pasta into the garlic-infused oil and stirred. "You actually have that kind of cash in the bank all the time?"

"No. And we don't have it now. It doesn't matter, though. He never looks at the account." She sniffed the air. "That smells yummy."

"Better than anything you could do in a microwave." I poured the pasta into a bowl.

"Anyway," Mel continued. "That's all I could think of. Supposedly I'm staying at a condo that belongs to the parents of an old girlfriend from high school that I've just recently re-bonded with on Facebook."

"He bought that?"

"Sounded like it. The idiot forgot we went to high school together, have always known the same people and none of them have parents with vacant condos in Florida. Whatever." She waved a hand in the air as if dismissing the subject. "That was my most creative lie ever. I don't think I could come up with anything better." She slouched at the kitchen table, holding her head. "The crazy thing is my mind is completely blank now. Like it took everything I had to have that conversation with him. I honestly don't know what to do with myself now."

"I do. Let me show you how to use People Finder." I topped the pasta with shredded parmesan. "Eat first, then clean up the messes you made. Then you can get started on researching people from Carolyn's past." I set the bowl down in front of her

"We're both going to need some caffeine if either of us has a chance of staying awake tonight after our carb-laden lunch," I said as I put on another pot of coffee.

While it brewed and Mel ate, I wound up doing the cleaning. I had to keep moving. Something was up with my son. I could feel it in my bones, as my grandmother used to say.

I didn't think it was anything dangerous, like his health. I could just tell he wasn't being completely honest with me. He was withholding information.

Unfortunately, while my mother's intuition is never wrong, it's seldom detailed.

Chapter 13: Know Exactly

Once I got Melissa settled at the computer, I gave her a brief tutorial on People Finder before I went upstairs to change into black leggings and a black tank top over which I wore an open-weave red tunic. I was *not* going to look uptight for this visit to It's Your Mission MMA studios.

Coming down the stairs I couldn't take my son's text-only silence any longer. I called, under the pretense of forgetting what time I was supposed to pick him up.

"Oh, um, like, Dad called my cell early this morning," he said. "He wanted to take me to breakfast."

"Did he?" I was under the impression Todd was never awake early enough in the day to eat something called *breakfast.*

"Yeah. He, uh . . ." he paused. I could hear Todd asking him if I had a problem with them spending time together. "No, it's all good," Ezra said to him. "He picked me up from Theo's," he said to me.

"That was nice." I choked out the words as I sat at the bottom of the stairs to put on a pair of black, non-uptight high-heeled boots. In fact, they were so non-uptight, a streetwalker would have felt at home in them. "And what are you doing now?"

"Well, breakfast was at this awesome diner in Atlantic City. And—"

"You're at the Jersey shore? Your dad took you to the shore for breakfast?" Atlantic City is about an hour and a half from my home. It seemed to me that was a distance far enough away that Todd should have mentioned something to me about it first. Certainly, Ezra should have called beforehand so that I could remind him to take some emergency carbs with him.

"Yeah. The food was great. You'd have liked it. Anyway, we're hanging out on the boardwalk now. He has a friend playing a gig tonight somewhere here. We're meeting up with him beforehand for dinner."

"Have you forgotten it's Sunday? We eat dinner with Grandmom and Granddad on Sundays."

"I know. I called them. They're cool with things."

Cool with things? I may have stomped my feet a little when I stood. Cool with things was *so* a Todd-ism.

"Well." I pressed my palm against my forehead. "I guess that's good, then." Very good, in fact. This way I wouldn't have to ask my mother, in front of my son, if she had a handy list I could look over to see what could qualify homicide as justifiable. "What, uh, what time will you be home?"

"We're leaving after we eat. Dad wanted me to skip school tomorrow so I could stay overnight and see his friend play. I told him I couldn't because I have to do that presentation with my Invent Team."

"Glad he understands." I think I may have grunted the words out.

"I'll text you my numbers, I promise," he said, perhaps as a consolation prize. I knew Todd had no way of knowing whether or not Ezra was dosing correctly.

"Thank you. I'll see you tonight, honey." I clicked the call off and stared at the crack running across the upper left-hand corner. Good thing it was there. Otherwise, I might have forgotten how fragile the damn thing could be and let it slam against a wall, accidentally, of course.

Outside, I headed to It's Your Mission MMA in my truck. I'd decided to hold Aidan Johanssen's birthday party there and wanted to sign off on whatever forms were needed and to take some photographs of the place so I could plan decorations.

On the way, I dialed my mother, of course.

"When did Ezra call you?" I yelled into the speaker of my cell as I turned south on Roosevelt Boulevard.

"I don't know. At some point today, why?"

"Why didn't you tell me?"

"I didn't think about it."

"You think it's all right for him to spend the day in Atlantic City? With Todd? It's freaking TODD!" I slammed on my breaks to let an elderly woman walk across the street at a crosswalk. She waved and nodded as she slowly toddled past in her white sneakers, blue slacks and gray coat. She made me think of my grandmother. It hadn't quite been a year since her death and I still missed her like crazy. She would know exactly what to say to Todd to keep him under control.

"Yes, it's Todd." I heard my mother say. "It's also Ezra. He's the most responsible kid I know."

"Oh God, that makes it worse." I continued down the Boulevard. "You used to say that about me, too."

"Ha!" she laughed. "And I was right, poopsie! You better still be coming for dinner, though. Are you?"

"Yes, I'm coming." Otherwise, she'd track me down and get even with worse food, claiming she worried I wasn't eating right.

"Great! I did a little freeze-drying experiment. You're gonna get your seaweed fix tonight!"

I clicked off, totally forgiving Ezra for bailing on dinner.

This time when I entered the studio, Gabe was up front, shirtless and shiny. He must have just finished a class or a workout or someone had sprayed him with water. The man glistened with such perfection he looked like he was Photoshopped. He was so mesmerizing, I almost forgot why I was there.

"Hey, you're the non-lifestyler, right?" he dried his hands on a towel and extended one to me.

"Yes," I shook it. "Peri Milano. Do you have a minute?"

"Sure." He flicked the towel over his shoulder. "You wanna fight?"

"I'd love to, but that's not why I'm here." I reached into my purse for my planner. "I'd like to hold a birthday party here."

"Oh that, yeah." He tipped his head toward the back. "Let's go to my office."

He turned around and headed toward the rear of the building. The dog I'd seen before immediately fell into place beside him. I followed at a slight distance, checking out the people on the floor, though Gabe's backside was mighty distracting.

A couple of women were doing something with long heavy ropes, as if they were trying to whip them through the air. Some men sparred wearing head and chest protectors. Others were punching bags of various sorts. I slowed to a stop to watch a woman clutching the sides of a large, long bag as she slammed knee after knee into it.

"It's great exercise," Gabe said, startling me with his nearness.

"I'm sure. It also looks like it'd be a great stress reliever. Like maybe you could picture someone's face on that thing."

He laughed. "Let's get this birthday party scheduled. Then you can let loose on it."

About forty-five minutes later, I lay in a puddle of my own sweat on the floor. I was barefoot, in just my yoga pants and tank top, gasping so hard I wasn't sure if my lungs were on the verge of imploding or exploding.

"Man! You Italian girls sure have a fire in you." Gabe sat beside me extending a bottle of water in my direction.

"I'm not Italian." I forced myself to sit upright enough so I could drink without gagging. "I'm pretty much Irish and Scotch with a few unknowns thrown in."

"Your husband Italian?"

"I never married." I took a long swallow of the water. "I was in a weird place in my life once and legally changed my name."

"A weird place?" He cocked his head to the side. "One that made you want to be Italian?"

"I didn't even consider the ethnicity when I did it." I laughed. "I was trying to punish my parents. I couldn't come up with a better way to do it than to refuse their name. So I went from Peri Potts to Peri Milano. Milano is the namesake of my favorite kind of cookies."

"Yeah, that's weird." He nodded. "How did your parents take it?"

"The way they take everything. They thought it was the greatest idea I'd ever had and loved it." I blew out a long stream of air. "I have the most unconditionally accepting parents on the planet. I love it now. Back when I was a teen, though, I longed for restrictions, for boundaries, for someone else to make decisions for me." I shook my head. "I'm sorry! I don't know why I'm telling you this! Yikes. I must sound like a freak. TMI as my kid would say." I rolled over and pushed myself to stand.

He stood too, that's when I noticed the dog had been behind him. Gabe had been leaning against it.

"No worries," he said. "You sound interesting. So when are you coming back for another workout?"

Usually gym memberships were out of my budgetary reach. But Todd was going to be in town for the whole week.

"Do you have a trial membership kind of thing?"

"I have a pay-as-you-go kind of thing."

"Deal!"

I left with a schedule of classes, which I pretty much ignored, and a list of open gym times, which I quickly memorized. Open gym times were when I could go and pommel whatever I wanted to pommel for as long as I could pommel it.

At home, I took my second shower of the day, filled a bowl with yogurt, granola, berries, and whipped cream. I slipped into a chair in the dining room beside Mel, who was now wearing a pair of my jeans and one of my sweaters. She had been a quick learner with People Finder and had discovered my log-in information was the same for Intellius. Unfortunately, she'd only been researching people from high school against whom she still had a grudge.

"Do you have any idea how dangerous this information could be in the wrong hands?" she asked me.

"Yes, that's why they charge so much for it." I stirred my parfait.

"Why do you have it?"

"Research for clients."

"What kind"

"Anything from background checks for personal employees to referrals on potential tenants, to just finding correct mailing addresses."

"Cool." She raised her eyebrows and grinned. "You know a lot of private information about a lot of people, huh?"

I nodded. "But I don't know anything about Fiesta ware." I filled her in on the new, antique china I was now storing in the front closet. "They're pretty, so I wouldn't mind eating off of them. However, if they're only going to slowly kill us with radiation, I think maybe selling them online might be the best choice."

Mel clicked into Google's search engine and started typing while I filled up on yogurt.

"Turns out the kid is right," Mel said. "It is a little bit radioactive. Although, there's some disagreement over whether it's safe."

"You mean there's safe radiation?"

"I'm not sure . . ." She hunched over the monitor. "Maybe it's not a matter of safe versus not safe so much as how much exposure you get to it. Everyone agrees the more exposure, the more dangerous. I can't seem to find anyone saying how much you have to handle it before it becomes a problem."

"I'm not sure I care." I pointed my spoon at her. "I mean, if I had a choice between glowing in the dark just a little versus a lot, I think I would choose not at all."

"I guess you're right. Hmm. I would think there should be something definitive." She clicked on the screen. "Oh, wait. I'm on the EPA's website now. Says here, that they recommend consumers don't use radioactive glazed products for food or drink."

"Which means I should just sell those babies instead of letting them light up the kitchen."

"There's someone else saying they're fine for short-term use. They think you just shouldn't store food on them due to the potential for uranium to leak into it."

"Ebay it is." I scraped my spoon against the inside of my bowl.

"Did he eat off of them? That Wooley guy?" Melissa spun around in the desk chair to look at me.

I licked the back of the spoon before answering.

"Probably." I put the spoon and bowl down on the desk and sat up straight in my chair. "Actually, now that I think about it, I know he did. I remember seeing it one time. It was late in the evening and his personal chef had already left for the night."

"I'd like a personal chef."

"I thought I was your personal chef."

"Let me amend that. I'd like a personal chef who was good looking, spoke with an accent, and had an exotic name."

"I think I want one, too." I nodded. "Well anyway, Mr. Wooley had called to see if I could bring him some yogurt to settle his stomach. He was having a bad reaction to a medicine or something." I pulled my hair back and clasped it behind my head. "I took it to him. When I got there, he said he was feeling better so I put it in the refrigerator for him to have later. I opened the fridge door and was hit in the face with an awful smell. I guess he saw my face, or something, because he laughed and said 'that's the Stilton. You know, I think I'm well enough to have it now.'"

"Isn't that cheese?"

"Yes, a smelly, blue cheese from England. But here's the thing," I put my hand on her arm, "and it might mean something. The cheese was just sitting on the plate in the refrigerator. He said Jacqueline portioned out some for him every day. She'd put it in the fridge for him to have with a little port each night for a late-night snack. He joked about how she insisted he eat it on a red plate because she thought it looked pretty."

"Oh, whoa." Mel met my eyes. "Do you think she was slowly killing him with radioactivity?"

"I don't know. I mean, it might be a stretch to think she's that smart. Or does everyone know about the dangers of red plates?"

"We didn't." We stared at each other for a few minutes.

"Still. . ." Mel said.

"Still." I nodded. "Maybe I'll ask mom what she thinks."

"Why her?"

"She's on a kick to be a private detective now."

"Ha! Of course she is. It's been at least a year since her last career began."

I looked at my watch and sighed. "Well, wish me luck. I need to head over there now." I stood and picked up my bowl that I was pretty sure was not radioactive. "You'll get started on researching Carolyn's past?"

"Aye aye, sir!" Mel saluted me.

Chapter 14: As Suggested

I stashed a package of Milano cookies in the center console of my Ford before I left my tiny, barely blue-collar row home to drive down to the Center City Philly to my childhood home: a townhouse mansion on Delancey Place built in the mid1700s. Despite its frou-frou location, which seemed to suggest only well-heeled inhabitants with decorators on speed-dial lived there, my parents were not inclined to keep up with the Joneses.

My father, perpetually amused by my mother's antics, left the care and upkeep of the place to her, which subsequently made the National Historic Register take it off their list. Ma believes a house should reflect a person's personality, regardless of how quickly and strongly that person reacted to whims.

The subject of whims should explain why my mother decided one day that she no longer liked the drapes in the front window so she took them down. She had set them curbside to be taken by someone with an appreciation for mauve silk dupioni fabric. She was sure a stroke of brilliance would come along that would inspire her to replace them. That was two years ago. I'm guessing those strokes had been hitting others.

My mother didn't think that was a problem because, as she said, neither she nor my father regularly paraded naked through the living room at a time when children would most likely be passing by on their way to or from school. Unfortunately, they did it frequently at other times of the day. Being that the house abutted the street with no front yard to potentially obscure the view . . . well, it was causing a bit of a stir among the neighbors.

And all of that should explain why, when I parked on the other side of the street from their home, I could clearly see inside my parents' living room. So I knew before opening the front door that Detective Collin Beatty was not enjoying whatever freeze-dried seaweed treat ole Honey Potts had force-fed him.

"If it isn't my sweet Peri!" my father announced when I stumbled across the foyer. Apparently, my mother had had a recent whim to relocate the cement foo dog statuettes to a more prominent position.

"Hi, Dad," I kissed him hello.

He pulled me into a bear hug. "You're in for a treat!"

"I see you've met Detective Beatty," I said as I kissed my mother.

"Yes, Collin and I are fast friends now." She winked at me. "In fact, he's delighted to join us for dinner."

"I'm glad someone is," I murmured as I turned to him. It appeared he was unable to speak as he struggled to swallow whatever delicacy he had politely accepted. "What, uh, well, I certainly wasn't expecting to see you today."

"He had to follow up on you, you know," Ma said. She took him by the elbow and pulled him out of the chair. "Isn't that right, Col? That would be proper police procedure."

Col nodded, still unable to speak.

I followed them to the kitchen. Dad excused himself to run upstairs to change. He had been wearing a white button-down shirt and brown corduroy trousers, which I thought would have been fine to keep wearing. But he likes to dress for dinner. I prayed he and Ma hadn't been exploring Chinatown shops again. The man doesn't look good in fuchsia and gold jacquard.

Ma held tight to Beatty's arm chatting him up about all the changes they'd made to the house that "those people on the Historic Registry's board just aren't enlightened enough to accept as relevant," which included the now combined eat-in kitchen and dining room she'd had created. He remained mute.

She forced him into a chair and disappeared out the back door, probably to get some rare herb from her tiny greenhouse in the courtyard. I headed straight to the cupboard, removed a glass and filled it from the special water dispenser my mother had installed to alkalize the drinking water. I handed it and a paper towel to the detective.

"Here." I wrinkled my nose at him. "You can spit whatever it is into the napkin. No one will hold it against you."

He did as suggested. Gave me a curt nod and slugged back the entire glass of water in one long drink.

"Thank you!" He wiped his mouth with the back of his hand. "I think I've taken enough of your parents' time. I'll just see myself out."

"NO!" Ma shrieked, running into the kitchen. She dumped a handful of mushrooms, or maybe it was clumps of dirt, on the counter, before grabbing Beatty by the arm. She forced him into a chair at the table. "You said you would love to stay for dinner, remember? You must! We have so much to talk about. Isn't that right, Archie?" She batted her eyes at Dad who appeared wearing silk pajamas. They were cream colored, with a long-sleeved, button-down shirt complete with a pen pocket on the left side. The pants had a silken rope draw string, which hung almost to his knees. He must have recently purchased the set and hadn't had them laundered yet—the creases from being folded in a package were still evident.

It sounds crazy, but he actually looked rather handsome. He still has a full head of white, curly hair that seems to make his stark blue eyes even bluer. And he is very tan. My mom is a big believer in getting your daily requirements of vitamin D from the sun. She insists on my father and her spending time outdoors or under sunlamps to ensure they get enough. Somehow that night, the contrast of his hair, eyes, skin and jammies balanced together to create a pleasing effect. So much so that he took my mother's breath away.

She gazed lovingly at him for so long, I was certain she'd forgotten what she was talking about.

Of course my father, who has an IQ so close to 200 that the Guinness people keep pestering him to retest to determine whether he's the smartest man in the world, remembered verbatim.

"We always have so much to talk about," he said. "However, if the good public servant wants to leave—"

"I'm sure he's mistaken," my mother insisted. "He doesn't *want* to leave. Maybe he feels he's imposing. Do assure him he's not." She pointed her eyes and tilted her head toward me in one of the worst attempts ever to be nonchalant.

"On the other hand," Dad pointed a finger in the air, "if one promises to break bread, then . . . well one must follow through and break bread."

"Or kombu as the case may be," Ma added as she patted the detective on the head.

"And did I mention I have some of the finest privately brewed ales in the city?" Dad asked him.

Beatty looked at me. I nodded and mouthed "it's safe" as I took my place opposite him at the table.

"An ale would be good right now," he said. "Thank you."

"So that means you're not here on official business, right?" I teased him.

"Not anymore," Ma said as she busied herself at the stove. "The good detective is all done with business. We got through all the official questions early on in his visit. Isn't that right, Col?"

He drew his head back to allow her to set a large trivet in the center of the table. "Um, right."

"So he can partake of an ale with your father," she announced.

"Lucky him," I murmured.

"Are you partaking, too, Peri, my sweet?" Dad asked.

"Just water for me, thanks. I had a good workout earlier and don't want to get dehydrated."

"Great. Wine it is." He opened the door to the basement and headed down to where he keeps some very expensive wines and his favorite brews. I had always suspected he kept a stash of food down there, too. One that Mom didn't know about. She accepted beer and wine alcohols because she claimed fermentation had had a positive impact on human evolution that she has never clearly explained to me.

I stared at her back while she chopped the mushrooms/clumps of dirt at the counter and only casually wondered what was going through Beatty's head. As a very young girl, I idolized my mother. She was absolutely gorgeous, so different and eccentric, though I didn't know the word back then, that all the little girls around me idolized her, too. She was like a beautiful, exotic animal no one had ever seen before.

As a teen, I was embarrassed to admit I even knew her. Throughout my twenties, I managed to learn to appreciate the true strength of character she had, though she still drove me nuts, and I apologized for her whenever I met someone who had experienced her. Now, sharing the back view of her with Beatty, I realized how much I loved the nutbag that she was and I was only mildly curious about how he perceived her.

She stood at the stove, stirring the brown clumpy stuff into a large Dutch oven. She is extraordinarily skinny, muscular, yet shapely though she is in her early sixties. She's tan (of course) and has waist-length, thin dreadlocks that, at that moment, were piled high on her head. I had never seen her without dreadlocks in real life. Though I knew somewhere in the house was a photo album that held a black-and-white photograph from her first communion, where her wavy flaxen hair seemed to glow around her chubby face.

Today she wore black yoga pants, which unlike mine, were probably used for yoga, and a lavender sports bra that was clearly visible under her sheer, dark purple caftan top.

I glanced at Beatty's face. His expression was inscrutable, though I thought it bordered on fear.

Eventually Ma placed the lid on the Dutch oven and carried it to us.

Beatty's eyes darted around the table then took in the kitchen. I could tell he was trying to keep the panic at bay as it sunk in that the only foodstuffs we'd be eating for dinner were in that mysterious Dutch oven. The one where it was very possible she had just stirred dirt.

"We'll wait for Archie to come back before I serve, sound good?"

"Sure, Ma." I leaned back in my chair and grinned, possibly mischievously, at Beatty.

He cleared his throat. "I hear your cousin's wife is safe," he said to me.

"Yes. We're all very relieved."

"I'm still surprised she wasn't hiding out at Peri's," Ma said as she set a stack of bowls on the table.

"Why would she do that?" Beatty asked, staring at me.

"Oh, that's always where Mel goes when she has a fight with Ed. All my girls are creatures of habit."

He frowned. "She's your niece, right?""

"Niece-in-law, I guess. She's Archie's brother's son's wife." Ma placed spoons at each setting on the table. "I don't consider her that, though. She's like another daughter to me. She and Peri have been best friends all their lives. Poor thing comes from alcoholic parents and when Peri moved out to live with her grandmother, Mel moved in here with us. So—"

"You know, Ma, I don't think Detective Beatty really cares to hear about all that."

She paused and put her hands on her hips. "Which is really Peri's way of saying she's embarrassed by the conversation, Collin." She put her hand on her chin, paused, then visibly remembered what she was doing. "So we'll change the topic. Can you tell me about toxicity analysis?"

"Excuse me?" he said.

"I'm talking specifically about autopsies. Do they just do an overall panel to search for all known toxins or do they start with the most likely one?"

"Well—"

"Granted, I guess they would need to know what would be the most likely at the moment."

"It would—"

"And you would have to really suspect a toxin to be at play to begin with, right? Now then, last night, Archie and I were watching . . . here he is!" My father entered the room. "Voila!" Ma lifted the lid of the Dutch oven, smiling first at me then at Detective Beatty. "I know I promised you freeze-dried seaweed, Peri poopsie, and I hope you're not disappointed. I just couldn't get it to hold together. It kept crumbling. So I had to do a little magic and turn it into a stew."

She ladled out a thick liquid that was such a dark green it was almost black.

"What else is in it, Ma?" I peered into my bowl unable to detect any of the solid pieces she'd just stirred in to the dark goo. It was as if they never even existed.

"Well, there's a variety of seaweed. I used the freeze-dried disappointment, some straight kombu and a little sea plant that I pureed. And then I cooked it all together in a soy-based broth." She put the ladle down to place her hand on Beatty's shoulder. "Now don't you worry, Collie, Peri's boobs are safe."

I did what Ezra would call a face-palm while she ladled out a bowl of ooziness for her Collie.

"I know many people are concerned about the phytoestrogens in soy," she continued. "Some believe they have the potential to cause breast cancer. However, I have written several papers debunking that myth." She gave him another ladleful. "I also loaded the stew with garlic and mushrooms, too, so it will strengthen your immune system. And who doesn't need that these days?"

She finished doling out the stew while my father poured the ale into a couple of tumblers. He poured two glasses of wine, winking at me as he set mine beside my alkalized water. Before he took his seat across from my mother, he kissed her cheek because they are still madly in love.

Perhaps not surprisingly, the stew tasted like the ocean, which at first I found tolerable. Judging by Detective Beatty's face, he was of a similar inclination.

"When you said you've written papers, does that mean you're a professor?" he asked my mother.

"Oh heavens no," Ma waved her hand in the air. "That would be Archie. He's a professor Emeritus at Temple."

"I also practice Gestalt therapy from my home office," Dad added.

"I do have enough degrees that I suppose I could be one, though." Ma frowned. I could tell she was wondering if maybe she should pursue the idea. She shook her head and continued. "Anyway, I do all kinds of research and write educational information for my clients. I'm a nutritionist, among other things."

"What are the other things?" he grinned at me.

"Nothing exciting enough to discuss now," she said. "What *is* exciting, though, is I'm aspiring to become a private detective. Could I ask you a few questions I have about police procedure and deductive reasoning? And can you explain the math behind lividity to me?"

The meal was spent with my father nodding and gazing lovingly at my mother, with her grilling the detective, and with my gag reflex barely under control. After about the third spoonful of the stew, although it tasted almost tolerable, there was something about the texture that my body was doing everything it could to repel. Eventually, I had to excuse myself to the powder room.

I stayed in only long enough to make my tongue stop twitching, which I didn't think was all that long. Apparently, everyone else thought I'd been gone enough to travel to Cleveland.

"I was beginning to worry about you, poopsie," Ma said.

"I'm sorry. I just felt a little off. I'm fine now." I sat in my former chair and tried not to look at the stew in my bowl.

"Do you think you might faint, again?" Beatty leaned over the table toward me.

"No." I laughed. "I don't faint that often. Honest. In fact, until Friday, I hadn't fainted since I was a kid."

"You fainted?" my father asked. "When?"

"It's nothing, Dad. Just, on Friday morning, when I found Mr. Wooley . . ." I waved my hand in the air.

"Oh, so you were under pressure?" he asked.

"Yes."

"Peri does have a tendency to escape reality when she feels she might not be able to handle it," Dad explained to Beatty.

"I do not."

"Sure you do, love. And that's fine. Everyone needs a good escape, now and then. You always manage to come back when you need to."

"I do not escape!" I stood. "Do you remember what it was like when Ezra was in the hospital? I was conscious the whole freaking time."

"It depends on how you define conscious," Dad leaned back in his chair. "As I recall, you were in constant motion cleaning his room, rearranging the supplies, telling the nurses how they could be more efficient—"

"It was quite obvious that they hadn't revisited their procedures in some time."

"Poopsie, sit your heiny back down," Ma took my hand. "Your father was just pointing out how you handle life to the handsome detective. It's nothing bad."

I squinted at her as I tried to devise a comeback.

"Why don't I help you clean up?" the handsome detective suggested to me.

I followed his lead and took my goo-laden bowl to the sink.

My mother went into a long discourse on the health benefits of seaweed as we cleaned.

"The downside to seaweed is you have to be careful about the source," she said as she shut the dishwasher door. "That whole nuclear oopsie thing they had in Japan resulted in the contamination of quite a bit of it. Which is ironic because if you were ever in fear of radiation poisoning, I would tell you to eat some kelp or kombu because they are terrific sources of iodine and, well, we all know how good iodine is for our thyroids." She wiped her hands on a towel and frowned. "Now then, where was I?"

"I don't know." I put my arm around her shoulder. "It's funny you should mention radiation. Detective Beatty. Did Mr. Wooley die from radiation poisoning?"

The question caught him off guard. He choked on his ale.

"I don't think he can answer that, Peri," Ma said. "Everyone knows he's not at liberty to discuss the case until it's solved. Particularly not with a prime suspect. Not that I think he thinks you're really a suspect, but he does have to go by the book on occasion. Even if it is after swigging down an ale or two. Right, Col baby?" She chucked him on the arm.

"I think so." He wiped his mouth. "Why do you ask Peri?"

I told them both about the red plates while Ma polished her stove. She likes to keep it shiny.

"I'm not sure if it means anything," Detective Beatty said when I was done. "I do find it interesting."

"I do, too." My mother glared at me.

I turned my face away from the detective and mouthed *what*?

She mouthed back something I couldn't understand.

I whispered, "what?"

"She said you were supposed to tell her first to give her a head start," Beatty explained.

"Ooo, you're good!" Ma exclaimed and pecked him on the cheek with a kiss. "I can learn so much from you." She looped one arm in his, another in mine and led us down the hall toward the front of the house. My father was nowhere in sight. "I think it's getting late and the hubby and I want some quality time alone." She stepped over the foo dogs and stopped before the front door. "Isn't that right Arch?" she yelled.

"Of course," yelled Dad from the powder room.

"But Ma, I wanted to sit in front of a computer with you to look at fabric online."

"That will have to wait for another day," she insisted. She opened the door and deposited us out on the stoop.

Chapter 15: Order

"**T**hey are rather eccentric," Detective Beatty said as he walked me across the street.

"Your observation skills are a gift." I pulled my keys out of my purse and beeped the lock. "So why exactly did you come here today?"

"You mother was right. I was following up on what you said about shopping with her on Thursday morning."

I pointed to the windows across the street, to where we could see my mom apparently ballroom dancing with herself. Looked like Dad was still on the john.

"And then you stayed because?" I asked.

He gave me a lopsided grin. "Official questions were over so I thought I'd have a little fun."

I opened the door of my Ford, sat in the seat, paused to make sure he could see me frown at him, then shut the door.

As Detective Beatty walked to his car, I texted Ezra. *You just missed a seaweed delight.*

Lol came his immediate response. *on way home. wont tell u wot I ate. Dont want 2 make u feel bad. bs wz 84. carbs 97.*

Todd must have fed him quite the meal. Ninety-seven carbs? What the hell?

Instead of calling either of them, I called Todd's grandfather.

"Hi there, kid," Mick answered.

"Hi, yourself, old man. Would you like a couple of cookies?"

"Always."

So I headed to my second weekly stop. Ezra and I always had dessert with Mick after dinner with my parents.

In fact, it was Mick who had introduced me to Milano cookies and unintentionally planted the seed for me to move in with my grandmother. When I discovered I was pregnant at sixteen, from the only day in my entire life that Todd and I got along, Mick adopted me as family. He came by my house every week to check on me. He always asked if there was anything he could do for me. And he always brought a store-bought treat: Milano cookies.

My mother tolerated the hermetically sealed goodies because she adored Mick. What she didn't realize was the more cookies he brought, the more time I spent with him. The more time I spent with him, the more I thought about spending time with my grandmother, my father's mother, who actually baked cookies as well as ate normal, homemade foods. And the more I thought about *that*, the more I thought it would be a great place for me to live and raise my kid.

He was standing outside of his low-rise condo building on Second Street, waiting for me, when I arrived. I picked him up. We drove a block or two until I could find a street-side place to park.

He hugged me when we got out of the Explorer.

"Where's the boy?" he asked.

"He's uh, he's . . ." I pretended to look for something in my purse.

"So Todd's in town, huh?" Mick looped his arm in mine and led me toward Christ Church Burial Ground.

"Yeah." We walked silently until we stopped at the locked gates of the cemetery. Mick reached into his pocket for his keys and undid the latch.

"He doing okay?" he asked, holding the gate for me.

"Seems to be."

"He being good to Ezra?"

"I think so."

He nodded. I think he nodded. Since it was evening and a little dark, I couldn't tell for sure. I just knew Mick well enough to know he nods a lot. He locked the gate behind us then took two folding chairs out from the information booth kiosk. We set up camp in our favorite spot: on the bricks beside Ben Franklin's tomb.

"Did I tell you I decided not to retire?" he asked after I handed him a cookie.

"No, you didn't. What made you change your mind?"

"I took three days in a row off. After the first day, I had nothing better to do than come here to make sure the other attendants were doing a good job."

I laughed. He remained quiet, probably nodding.

"So, um, about Todd," I started and stopped. I may have eaten a cookie instead of continuing.

"About Todd," Mick repeated a few minutes later.

"He, uh, well, he told Ez and me that he's thinking of moving back home."

"Home country or—"

"Home as in Philly. Maybe." I paused. "Or maybe New York. He's not sure."

"That could be good for Ezra," Mick said after a few quiet moments.

"It could. Possibly good for you, too."

"Possibly." I knew Todd's estrangement from his grandfather was killing Mick. They hadn't spoken in four years, not since Ezra had landed in the ICU when he was first diagnosed as a diabetic. I still wasn't sure why. I had repeatedly asked them both. Each time Todd answered saying it was none of my business. Mick always said it didn't matter.

I knew it was possible that they were both right. I just didn't want to give Todd the benefit of the doubt and I knew it was hurting Mick, so I was hell-bent on fixing things between them.

"How are your parents?" Mick asked.

"Oh, they're just fine and dandy." I swallowed a mouthful of cookie.

"Why are you angry with them?" he asked.

"I didn't say that."

"You did too. Just not with words."

"I'm fine with my parents."

"If you were fine with your parents, you would have tackled me just now for changing the subject off of Todd. You would be trying to force me into setting up a dinner date with him. You're not acting like your usual self. What's wrong?"

"Nothing's wrong."

"Then why did you let me change the subject?"

"My dad," I sighed. "Thinks I'm crazy."

"No he doesn't."

"Oh, he does. He just told me he thinks I hide from reality by cleaning, organizing, and fixing things, particularly for other people."

"Well, you can be a bit of a control freak."

"I am not!"

"It's okay, Really."

"I am not!" I slapped my thigh.

"Look, Peri. You know what I just found out?"

"What?"

"All my life I've been counting things when I'm not doing something. I count my breaths. I count my steps. Everything. Back in the seventies, when I was a hippie, I thought I was meditating all the time because I did that, you know? It cleared my head, made me feel calm and at ease. That's what meditation is supposed to do, right? Calm your mind."

"I guess so."

"Well, on my first day off last week, I was at the doctor's getting a physical. While he was listening to me breathe, I guess he saw my lips move and thought I was talking to him. He said, 'excuse me?' I explained I was counting my breaths." He took another cookie out of the bag in my hand. "Well, next thing I know, he's doing this full interview and I leave with a list of recommended therapists to talk to about what he's calling OCD: Obsessive Compulsive Disorder. He even suggested I get a medication for it."

"Wow. So what are you going to do?"

"Nothing."

"What? You have a disorder. You have to get it under control. You—"

"You're missing my point, sweetheart."

"Maybe you didn't explain it well enough, doll face."

He laughed. "That's how I manage my life. I count anything I can count. So in a way, you could say that's how I stay sane—by being a little crazy, OCD. I didn't think it was a bad thing before I went to the doctor but when I left with that suggestion for therapy and drugs, I started to doubt myself. So I asked your dad out for a beer last night to get a second opinion."

"What'd he say?"

"He agreed. He said that it sounded like OCD to him, too. Then he said since it wasn't interfering with me living my life and it actually gave me peace, he didn't think I needed therapy for it. Nor should I be taking any drugs for it."

"So what are you going to do?" Though really, I was thinking about my father. Yes, he was on the faculty of a prestigious university, and yes, he made lots of money as a therapist, but I didn't think either one of those facts meant he always knew what he was talking about. After all, another doctor wanted Mick medicated.

"Nothing."

"Mick, your doctor told you, you have a problem."

"My doctor *thinks* I have a problem. So what? I don't think so."

"You can't just ignore your doctor's advice!"

"See that? You're doing it again. You're trying to find a problem to fix. You're trying to control something instead of asking why I'm telling you all this."

"Ugh!" I snorted a sigh. "You're making me nuts, but I'll play your game. Why are you telling me all this?"

"Because I don't think you got your dad's point."

"And you do?"

"Did he tell you that you need to get help?"

"No."

"So why are you mad at him for pointing out a character trait about you?"

I took the last two cookies out of the package and handed one to Mick. He probably nodded his *thanks*. I ate the other one. He was quiet while I chewed.

"Ezra thinks I'm overprotective and controlling. I always thought that was normal parental behavior. Yet lately, people keep saying things that . . . like twice in one day, I was told I was uptight. Mel thinks I get pissy when things aren't in order. One client told another that I was a good micromanager. I'm not liking the implications of all that."

"Because?"

"Because . . ." I pulled my purse onto my lap to search for spare change. "Because what if they're right?"

"Then I don't think you should be mad at your parents about it."

I used my cell phone to light the pile of coins in my hand. Mick picked out a penny. I took one for myself and let the rest drop into my purse. We stood and folded the chairs in silence.

"Stay safe, Ben," I said, tossing my penny onto the tomb.

"Behave yourself," added Mick with his.

Chapter 16: That Easy

My plan for Monday, which I'd originally scheduled to be a day off to rest and do laundry, was still to rest and do laundry, as well as to make all the arrangements for Mr. Wooley's funeral. Mel was going to continue her research into the people from Carolyn's past. She had been able to verify the owner of *Heaven or Bust* was a man named Jorje Garcia and that he was still in business in Miami, currently running a topless doughnut shop called *Holes are Us*.

She found his home address and phone number then, in a move that surprised and impressed me, as well as frightened me a little, she took down the names and phone numbers of his two ex-wives and his neighbors. She figured if she couldn't confirm he'd been in town at work, she'd create a bogus reason to call them to see if he'd been seen lately.

Before either of us got going on anything, Carolyn called. She'd received another note first thing that morning, tucked under the windshield wiper of her car. She brought it to my house immediately. Ezra passed her on his way down the porch steps heading to school.

"I can't stay," she said at the door. "I just don't want to keep these things. It's better if you have them." She shoved the paper into my hand, kissed me on the cheek then ran down the stoop apparently to somewhere important.

"You can come out," I opened the closet door where Mel was squished in with the radioactive china.

"What's it say?" she asked.

"How could you not recognize me? I hate you. I hate you and will make you pay." I handed her the note. This one was just typed. The sender didn't bother to make it look like graffiti.

"So this means he's seen her since Friday," Mel said.

"That's what it looks like." I went to the kitchen to get some coffee and my phone. Mel followed me.

At the table, I called Carolyn's cell.

"I only have a few minutes," she said. "I'm on my way to the art museum. We have an emergency meeting to discuss how to honor Shelby Wooley. He was such a huge patron."

"Oh, you know, I was going to call over there today. I need to cancel the hold on the room. Also, his daughter asked me to handle all the funeral arrangements. I'll let you all know the details. I'm sure the whole board would want to go."

"Absolutely. Oh Peri, I feel so selfish! I didn't even think about how you're doing. I'd forgotten Shelby was one of your clients. How are you?"

"I'm holding up okay," I said. "Thanks. I'm calling because I really need to ask about that note."

She was quiet.

"It seems like the person who left it saw you recently."

"I know. I've been racking my brain! It's impossible. I haven't been anywhere to be seen."

"Are you sure?"

"Yes! I stayed home all Friday night. Gerard came home Saturday morning. We had no plans. Remember? We were supposed to be at the shore. Since he thought I wasn't feeling well, we ordered in lunch and dinner. We lounged around all day. Yesterday, I went to your house and that's it."

"Really?"

"Yes."

"Hmm. Okay. Well, yeah. Okay. I guess that's it then."

"I'm at the museum now. Please let us know when the arrangements are made for Shelby."

I hung up. "She says the only place she's been is my house," I told

Mel.

"She's lying."

"Could be. She did tell me she was good at that."

I remained sitting at the table to call Jacqueline. Before I could reschedule the faux funeral arrangements for the real ordeal the following Saturday, I needed to know what funeral home Mr. Wooley would want to use. Melissa made me put the call on speaker so she could listen in.

"In angst and horrific grief, I regret to inform you I cannot answer your call," Jacqueline's voice mail message said. "Please, if you would be so kind, do leave a message. I cannot promise when I will be in a strong enough emotional state to respond. I shall do my best to recover soon for your sake. However, if this is in response to an audition I attended, I'll have my agent contact you immediately."

I looked at Mel. She had her knuckles squished into her mouth in an obvious attempt not to laugh out loud.

"I hate to bother you in your time of mourning, Jacqueline," I said unable to continue without giggling. "Please call me back," I squeaked out before punching the call off.

Mel and I burst at the same time.

"Oh my God!" She grabbed my arm. "We need to video her. Put her online. She'll go viral. We'll get a sitcom deal from her and be rich!"

"If only it were that easy." I sipped my coffee. "Now, what do I do? I can't make any real funeral arrangements until I know where he'd like to have it."

"I don't know, but . . . ." Mel poured the last of the coffee into a cup. "Jeesh. Has anyone ever told you you drink a lot of coffee?"

"Only my mother."

"She might actually have a point there." She sat across from me at the table. I stood to clean the carafe and prepare it for another pot so I could just push the *on* button the next time I wanted more.

"Yeah, you might listen to your mom on maybe that one thing," Mel said as she watched me. "Is she still dead set on getting to the bottom of the murder?"

"Yeah." I turned to lean against the counter to speak with her. "I think so. She feels it's her duty, since she thinks I'm a suspect. Though she might just be trying to fix me up with that police detective at this point."

"How is that possible?"

I filled her in on dinner.

"I don't know, Per. I kind of think if anyone is able to sit through a whole meal made by Honey Potts, they're immediately family. Kinda like how you're stuck with me. You might have to marry him now."

"At least he's good looking." I cheered her with my cup.

"I'll take his partner."

"You'll go back to Ed."

"You're not always right, you know. Anyway, do you think you're a suspect?"

"Not really. I mean, all my alibis must have checked out. Besides, I had no motive. I think Beatty was going through the motions of following up on me because he had to. I guess I won't know his complete intentions until the murderer is found, right?"

My cell rang on the table. Mel picked it up and looked at the screen.

"And that might be now," she said, handing the phone to me. "It says Phila PD on your screen."

I answered.

"Peri!" screamed a familiar, female voice. "Oh thank God, you're there!"

"Hi, uh, Jacqueline." I felt my upper lip curl when I looked at Mel. "Why are you—where are you calling from?"

"I'm *in* JAIL!" I heard a thump on the other end, a shuffle sound, then a man saying *you have to hold the phone, ma'am.* A few seconds later, Jacqueline's voice was back on the line. "They arrested me. ME! You have to come get me out."

"Why? Do you need bail money?"

"I need out of here!"

"Right, of course. I'm sorry. I was just confused as to why you were calling me."

"I only get one phone call, Peri, please don't mess this up."

"One call? This is your one call? You called me on your one call?"

"I don't understand why Daddy thought you were so smart. Honestly, Peri! Yes, this is my one phone call. Now you must take care of this mess."

"I don't even know what the mess is!"

"I JUST TOLD YOU THE MESS!" she screamed. "They arrested me!"

"For what?" It was one of those times when hindsight told me I should have been putting two and two together.

"They actually think I killed Daddy! They think I poisoned him! They barged into my condo this morning and charged me with murder. Murder! They said they knew right away I was guilty by the way I overacted when I found Daddy's body. Me! Overacted! They're as unperceptive and dimwitted as my last producer. They wouldn't recognize acting if they were at a performance at the Palace Theater. I performed there, you know. I spent an entire summer in London and actually stood on that stage to raucous applause. I—"

"I'm sorry, Jacqueline. What is it you need from me?"

"You have to get me out of here! I can't survive here. Have you any idea how low the thread count is on their sheets?"

"Nope. Never thought about it before."

"How can you be flip right now? You're not taking your responsibility for me seriously, are you?"

"What?"

"Daddy wanted you to make sure I'm well cared for. And let me tell you Peri, I'm not well cared for in this place."

"I don't understand, Jacqueline. I think you should call an attorney or something."

"Peri." Her voice grew stern. "I know you're not this dense. I called you so you would call Daddy's attorney."

"I, well of course I'll call Mr. Bernard for you. I guess you only get one phone call, right? I'll do that now." I hung up and immediately hit the coffeepot's *on* button.

"So is she going to be your client now?" Mel asked as I looked up the phone number to Bernard and Bernard law offices. "Is it normal to inherit clients?"

"I might have to move out of Philly," I answered.

I was patched through to Mervin Bernard immediately.

"You are on my list, Peri," he said.

"I hope it's a good list."

"You are always on my personal good list. Today you are on my business list to contact. Since you got to me first, I suppose this means you've heard of your new responsibility?"

"I'm not sure. Are you talking about Jacqueline Wooley being in jail?"

"She's what?"

"She was arrested for her father's murder."

"Oh good Lord."

"She used her one phone call to have me call you."

"I'm so sorry for you."

"What do you mean?"

"I'll take care of Jacqueline now. In the meantime, you might want to come to my office as soon as possible."

"Really? Why? Is there something else?"

"There is. I'm not sure how much you're going to like it."

I prepared well for the Bernard and Bernard offices: I put the dry ingredients needed for a mug cake into a small plastic, lidded bowl and oil, milk and butter in another. I grabbed some peanut butter and a bag of chocolate chips from the pantry and packed everything into a thermal-insulated lunch bag.

Within minutes, I parked in a lot in Center City where I had to walk three blocks to the glass and cement building that housed the law offices. On the way, I passed the storefront of Custom Floral arrangements and stepped inside.

Pearl's assistant, a heavily tattooed man named, or rather called, Madder, greeted me. He came around the design consultation counter and picked me up in a semipainful bear hug.

"Is Pearl in?" I shook out my limbs, perhaps in an effort to make sure nothing was broken.

"Not yet. Don't know when to expect her. She's been in a weird way since last week."

"Do I wanna know what you mean by 'weird way'?" I asked.

He pulled up a stool and patted the seat. "Sit your tushy down, doll, while I serve you," he said in his best Pearl imitation. Then in a melodious tone he added: "Just a vibe I'm picking up on her. Like her soul experienced something it can't process."

He sat on the other side of the counter.

"Like her soul . . . Are you back on the books, Mad?"

"Hey, there's more than one kind of addict, man. As far as I'm concerned, an addiction to self-help books is the healthiest kind."

I laughed. "I guess so."

"Besides, I can't afford therapy with an actual therapist. And while I did learn the art of flower arranging in prison, I can't say there was anything else there that would make me want to go back. I need my books."

"You know what? My dad's a shrink. I don't know why I didn't suggest him before. Here." While I may not be sure whether my father's a good therapist, I was sure he'd work *pro bono* if a client couldn't afford the bills. I pulled one of his business cards out of my purse, hesitated, then pulled one of my mother's out, too. She tends to get a little jealous when she thinks there's favoritism going on. "Take this one, too. My mom does all sorts of stuff. Tell them I sent you. Between the two of them, you'll get more help for whatever is ailing you than you probably need, and they'll be happy to do it for free since you're a friend of mine."

"Coolness," Madder nodded as he stared at my mother's card. "I thank you. I will call them both. Now then." He tucked the cards into his shirt pocket. "What can I do for you today?"

"Ugh. I hate this, I really do. But, you know how Pearl was working on flower arrangements for a big, mysterious event next month?"

"Yes. The white callas with the impossible red tips."

"Well, they were for Shelby Wooley and—"

"What about Shelby Wooley?" Pearl demanded from the entrance of her store. She wore the mauve wool coat she always wore unless it was over ninety degrees outside, with her purse on her shoulder.

"Oh, uh, he passed away last week. On Friday"

"I know." She unbuttoned her coat as she walked toward me.

"You do?" My eyes stung and watered.

Her looked left, then right, then seemed to look behind me. I almost turned to see if someone had snuck in from a mysterious door somewhere without me knowing. "I saw it on the news," she added.

"Right, well. You know how you've been working on perfecting a red dye to tint the ends of some callas?" I rubbed my eyes.

"Yes. I have been suffering great anxiety over that."

"Right, um, I think I heard you mention that before. Well, they were for Mr. Wooley. For an event for him."

Pearl took off her coat and draped it over her arm so slowly the Grand Canyon had enough time to deepen another inch. Her eyes remained locked on mine. For some reason, I felt afraid. I cleared my throat.

"So, uh, yeah, I came here, in part, to cancel the uh, that order for the special event next month."

Pearl lifted her chin.

"I know you've put in a lot of time and expense already experimenting for it," I said, rummaging through my purse for a tissue. Damn that store. "I'll make sure you get pa—"

"I want no money for any of that." Her knuckles were white, the skin stretched tight against them as she clutched her purse strap.

"Oh, that's nice." I glanced at Madder while I blew my nose. He was right. She was in a weird way. Pearl had mastered passive aggression years ago. She spoke to everyone like a doting, yet suffering for you, prematurely aged, spinster auntie faking happiness for your sake and the least you could do in return is pay her promptly. "So, anyway," I wiped my nose. "His daughter asked me to handle his funeral. We're hoping to hold it this Saturday. I'm sure I'll have several clients wanting me to take care of sending flowers on their behalf—"

"Of course we'll be happy to provide," Pearl said. She rounded the consultation counter and stood opposite me.

"That's great." I raked at my eyes.

"I suppose you still want me to do white callas with red tips." Her head dropped to one side as if her neck could barely take the weight of it.

"Well," I sniffed, "if it's not too much trouble."

"Don't you worry about me, toots." She gave me a phony smile. "It's just too bad I never perfected the color."

"What about paint chips?" Madder piped in.

"What do you mean?" I blew my nose again.

"Do you think you could find the right shade of red on one of those strips of color you get in paint stores?"

"Oh! That's a good idea." I searched for another tissue in my purse. "Would that be helpful for you Pearl? If I found the perfect red that way? Could you match it?"

"It would be so much easier than guessing what color he was

seeing in his mind's eye," she half murmured as she turned away from me.

Madder and I watched her walk to the back office.

"Yeah, I think I see your point about her soul," I said to Madder, though it come out as, *I tink I see yer pont 'bout 'er soul.* "I'll pick up a paint strip."

Chapter 17: Ready Or Not

I left the toxic air of the florist's shop and gratefully stepped out onto the Center City sidewalk where I did my best to take a deep breath of the exhaust-filled atmosphere through my nose. As I walked toward the high rise that held the law offices of Bernard and Bernard, I vowed that one of these days I would figure out whatever it was in that shop that bothered me. Certainly it wasn't any of the standard, normal flowers we get in the Philadelphia area. I'd never experienced allergies until I started getting flowers from Pearl's shop. Unfortunately, many of my clients insisted I used only her as she was the best florist in town. I was going to have to deal with it as best I could, or figure out which flower was the problem so I could avoid it.

A block away I entered a tall, glass-and-metal high rise where I took the elevator to one of the upper floors. Within minutes I was in the open reception area of the law firm where attorney Johnnie Bernard was a partner with his father, Mervin Bernard, who coincidentally had dated my mother when they were in high school.

By the time I stepped out of the elevator car, my itchy eyes were no longer bothering me. The drippy nose had ceased, only to be replaced by stuffed sinus cavities. It happened every time I left that damned store, in that order: itchy eyes, runny nose, clogged sinuses.

Mervin's secretary, Stella, greeted me with her polite client smile until she realized I was toting a lunch bag. Then I got one of her hugs.

"Honey, aren't you a sight for sore eyes." She led me to the break room. "My doctor broke the HIPPA code and told my daughter I need to lose some weight. Now that busybody stops by my house every day and raids my kitchen. Don't tell anyone." She lowered her voice even though we were the only two within earshot. "I've had to resort to stashing an emergency supply of Reese's Cups in a tampon box in the bathroom. Now what did you bring to me?"

Stella is a giant in all senses of the word: height, width, and personality. I'd met her daughter on a few occasions and had always been surprised by how small, even delicately built she was. I couldn't picture her wrestling a box of Tastykakes out of her mother's hands.

"A little chocolate-peanut butter something," I said.

I melted the butter in the microwave then mixed it in with the milk, oil and the dry ingredients in a large coffee mug. I plopped a spoonful of peanut butter and a few chocolate chips into the center then let Stella take a peek. She grabbed the bag of chocolate chips and dumped in a few more. After a furtive glance around the room, she rolled up the bag and stuck it in her ample cleavage.

"I hope you don't forget about that." I shut the door to the microwave.

"Do you honestly think I'd ever forget about chocolate chips?"

I punched in one minute on the microwave. "You never know. It's possible you could get distracted by an exercise bike or something." I grinned at her.

"Now don't you go acting like my daughter. You young people don't know what it's like to be menopausal and craving sweets."

"You should talk to my mom. Here." I dug out another business card and handed it to her. "She's got all sorts of herbal remedies for menopause and for curing sweet cravings."

"Hmmm," she studied the card. "Maybe I'll give her a call."

"Do that, but uh, if you're having hot flashes, don't you think those chips will melt?"

"Good thinking." She removed the chips from between her breasts and stuck them in the pocket of her slacks. "Thank you. Now what's up with you? You sick? You sound all stuffy."

The microwave dinged. I pulled out her mug cake. "I was just in

Custom Floral. They have a flower in there I must be allergic to because every time I go in there—"

"Your eyes burn and your nose runs." She held out her hand to me.

"Right." I didn't give her the mug cake.

"Happens to just about everyone who goes in there. It's not a flower, honey. It's Pearl Slack's perfume. Now, why are you teasing me?"

"Her perfume? Huh. Never thought of that." I clutched the mug cake to my chest. "No cake 'till you tell me why Mervin insisted on talking to me in person. Am I going to regret coming here? Is this about my mother?"

"No." She chuckled. "He got the charges for lewd and lascivious behavior dropped against your parents. You gotta get new curtains up in their home soon, honey."

"I'm working on it." I relinquished the mug cake. "So what's he want with me then?"

"He needs to talk to you about Wooley's will."

"What about it?"

"It's a pretty crazy will. I think Mr. Bernard should handle telling you about it." With eyes closed, she took a long, deep whiff of the mug cake and smiled. "You know, Pearl should try to smell like this. Maybe more people would like her then."

A few minutes later I was sitting in Mervin's office. While stereotypical in design and color scheme—rich mahogany wood, dark green walls, Oriental carpet on the floor—it was still very comfortable and somehow relaxing. He often had spa music playing in the background. This morning it was no different.

"How are you, Peri?" he asked as he shuffled through some papers.

"I'm doing okay, I guess."

"I smell chocolate. Did you feed Stella?" he looked at me over the tops of his reading glasses.

"I did." I grinned.

"Do you know a good sign man? I need one that says *no feeding the secretary*." He laughed. "Maybe you could talk to your mom and get some recipes that are healthier for her."

"I just gave her Ma's business card."

"Good. She needs help." He pulled a paper from a file. "Here it is. Are you ready?"

"No. Absolutely not."

"You don't even know what I'm about to say."

"I do know that, unless I'm on a roller coaster that's about to start, I'm never ready to hear what people need to say after asking that question. Particularly when those people are attorneys who insist on seeing you in person."

"You're as wise as you mother." He nodded. "Well, ready or not, here it comes: Mr. Wooley left you in charge of his estate."

"What . . . what does that mean?"

"That means he wanted you to handle the dispersal and disposal of his worldly goods. I was quoting him, there. That's not a legal expression or anything."

"It's almost a Catholic one. St. Francis spoke of disposing one's worldly goods. My gram talked about it when she told me she was leaving me her home. But what do *you* mean, oh St. Bernard?"

He smirked. "This will explain." He leaned over the desk to hand me the paper. "In a nutshell, as you know Shelby Wooley was a very wealthy man."

"Yes." I only glanced at the paper as I knew he'd explain.

"As executor, I will take care of the banks and government in regard to his estate, however, once that's done, it is all to be entrusted to you. At that point, as explained in that paper there, if Jacqueline doesn't want to live in his home, you will need to sell it and add the assets to the trust mentioned. You will then be responsible for managing the trust and setting up an allowance for Jacqueline to live off of. Then he would like you to create a foundation with the rest of his assets to support a worthy cause."

"Which worthy cause?"

Mr. Bernard smiled. "He left that up to you to decide. He said he trusted your judgment better than anyone else's."

I wasn't sure how to respond. On the one hand, this seemed like something I should have expected I would have to do for a client one day. On the other, I didn't feel qualified to start a foundation.

"Um," I started, not completely willing to ask my question

because I was afraid of his answer. "Huh. Does Jacqueline know this?"

"Yes."

"Could that be what she meant when she told me I was now responsible for her?"

"Could be."

"I'm not, really. Right?"

"Well, she is an adult of sound . . . that is, she is a legal adult. Regardless, the money is never to be given to her in one lump sum. You will always have control over her trust. So you would be the person to say how much she needs, to assure she pays her bills, help her make large purchases, etc."

"Oh God."

"I'm sure Shelby's financial planner, Edward Monihan would be glad to handle it directly. His contact information is on that page I just gave you."

Again, I glanced at the paper. "Okay." I sighed. "Any guidelines on what he'd consider a worthy cause?"

"No. that's up to you."

"I see." I shuffled through the pages. "Do I have a few days to process what all this means?"

"You do. Though I have to warn you: Jacqueline will be free to roam the city streets within a few hours."

I stood. "Oh, wait. I almost forgot. Jacqueline asked me to handle the funeral arrangements."

"Of course." He shuffled through the files some more. "I should have realized that. Here are the instructions."

He handed me a few more pieces of paper. Just glancing through, I saw he wanted the service at the Cathedral Basilica of Saints Peter and Paul and that he wanted to be dressed in a black evening gown. "Hoo boy," I said aloud.

"I think that's what I said when I made it." Mervin stood. I stood, too. We left his office together. He walked me out to the reception area. "How's your mother doing, by the way," he said when we were all alone in the hall.

"She's doing well. She always does, right?" I smiled at him, knowing what was coming next.

"Yes, she does." He took a deep breath. "I think I still love her."

"I know." I hugged him. "Look on the positive side. You're better fed this way."

In the parking lot, I sat in my truck scrolling through the e-mails on my phone that had come in while I was speaking with Pearl and Mervin. There was nothing that couldn't wait. I checked the phone log and noticed Todd had called twice, leaving no messages. Curious, I called him back.

"You rang?" I asked.

"Yeah. I been texting Ez all morning and he's not answering. He okay?"

I was almost impressed. Had Todd been worrying about his son? "I'm sure he's fine. He's in school. If he's caught texting someone during school hours, they take away the phone."

"Is that legal?"

"I'm pretty sure."

"Man, that sucks. Glad I'm not a teen anymore."

"Funny, I thought you never quit being one."

"Well, you never were one. Bet I have more fun."

"Whatever. I'll tell him to call you when he gets home." I punched off the phone and looked at the time. It's Your Mission MMA had an open studio for another forty minutes. I could go and punch Todd, that is, a bag, for about a half hour.

Gabe had a different idea. He set me up in a cage with the first man I'd met at the studio, the one who had called me a chick, his brother, Michael. They both wore loose gym shorts and black shirts with *It's Your Mission MMA* on the front and feathered wings stretching down the back. As Michael strapped protective padding around his midriff, I got the meaning.

"So how many brothers are there?" I asked Gabe while he tightened boxing gloves over my hands.

"Three." He grinned.

"Let me guess, the other is named Raphael?"

"Actually, the dog's name is Raphael. My other brother is Uriel." He winked.

I flicked my eyes to the dog at his feet. "So I'm about to fight with an archangel?"

"Better than a devil in disguise, don't you think?"

He spun me around and guided me in my foot placement. Within a few minutes I was throwing left and right jabs at Todd's face, I mean, Michael's padded hands. I had just mastered adding in an uppercut when Gabe yelled at us to stop.

"Your phone won't stop ringing," he said as he handed me my purse.

"Could you get it for me?" The fighting gloves made it impossible for me to unzip my purse. I continued struggling with them while he read off the phone log. I had received eight calls from Ezra's school. Before he could hit *return call*, another came in. He hit speaker.

"Hello?" I shouted. My heart rate, which was already up from the exercise, had reached a mountain peak. Since they'd called so many times, I knew it could only mean one thing: something bad had happened to Ezra.

Chapter 18: What Else

"Ma?" Ezra said. "Where are you?"

"I'm . . . It doesn't matter. Are you okay?"

"My pump battery is dead and the spare ones I have in the nurse's office are all corroded. Can you bring me some more? The stupid alarm keeps going off in class. It's embarrassing."

I was shaking so hard, I fell to my knees.

"Yeah. I'll get them to you right away." Gabe clicked off the call for me. He and Michael simultaneously undid my gloves while I explained to them my son was diabetic and wore an insulin pump and it ran on triple-A batteries and that I was a horrible mom for not thinking to check on the spare batteries at school and that I was even a worse mom, because how could I be away from my phone for so long knowing he could need me and . . .

"Hey," Gabe grabbed me by the shoulders and forced me to look in his eyes. "Is he in pain right now?"

"No."

"Is he in danger of dying before you get to him?"

"No."

"What's the worst thing that happened to him before he contacted you?"

My breath eased as I thought about it. "He was embarrassed in class."

"Good. That means he experienced something everyone does at some point: social embarrassment. Now he has one less thing to fear because he knows it's survivable. Right?"

"I guess so." I sighed and dropped to the floor again. This time to put my shoes back on.

"What's wrong?" he asked, kneeling in front of me.

"It's a mom thing. Now I'm scared he'll feel like he can't rely on me anymore."

He rubbed my back. "Then he'll grow up a little more and realize he needs to rely on himself."

"You're not a parent, are you?" I asked.

"No. I'm just a big believer in self-reliance."

"You sound like my father."

I stopped by a drugstore for new batteries then dropped them off at the school before heading home. I don't know if it was mental exhaustion, emotional exhaustion, or what, but after I took a quick shower, I couldn't keep my eyes open. I lay down on my bed, thinking I'd nap for just a few minutes. I wound up crashing for the entire afternoon. My cell phone woke me shortly before three o'clock.

I didn't recognize the number on the screen. Because it was a local one, I answered.

"This is Vivian Catelli. I'm Alex Foster's personal assistant."

"Yes?" I remained in my bed, propped on one elbow.

"I believe a woman who goes by the name of Honey Potts is your mother."

"Oh God."

"I'm not quite sure I understand the details of what happened in Mr. Foster's office today. He had agreed to meet with your mother because he had hired her services in the past." The woman paused.

She seemed as if she was unwilling to say anymore.

"I see, and now you're calling me because . . ." I prompted.

"Apparently, your mother is under the assumption that Mr. Foster had something to do with Shelby Wooley's passing. I'm not sure how you came into the conversation . . . well we had to have building security remove your mother. I was going to call the police, but Mr. Foster insisted I notify you to have you speak with her about not returning here again."

"Sure, I can do that."

"I'm not certain what exactly she said or did."

"It doesn't really matter. Thank you for not calling the police." I clicked off, rolled onto my back and dialed my mom. The call went to voice mail.

Seemed like a good time to make some coffee and finally get started on the laundry.

I filled Melissa in on my meeting with Mervin Bernard and my mother's recent visit to Alex Foster, just for laughs. "What did you find on Carolyn?" I asked her.

"I followed up with every single person I could who is related to her past, and that's everyone she's mentioned. None of them are in the area."

"Hmmm. So what do you think we should do next?" Before she could answer, the doorbell rang. "Stay here," I ordered and ran to the front of the house.

I opened the door. Gabe was standing on my stoop. And so was Raphael.

"Hi," I said through the screen door. "This is a surprise."

"You left this." He held up the cardigan I'd taken off to beat up Todd/Michael.

"Thank you." I stepped outside to take the cardigan. "That was really nice of you. How did you know where I lived?"

"The forms you filled out at the studio."

"Aha! You should be a detective."

He laughed. "Your son all right?"

"Yeah. He's fine. He's actually coming up the walk, now."

Gabe turned around. The dog did, too. Both stepped aside as Ezra came up the steps.

"Hey Ma," he said, nodding *hello* at Gabe. "Dad just called. He's going to New York tomorrow and wants—"

"You cannot go to New York tomorrow. You have school."

His jaw went slack. He stopped walking. "He just wants to take me to dinner tonight. Said he hasn't had a decent cheese steak since he's been in town. He wants to go down to Tony Luke's. Is that too far?"

"No. I'm sorry." I looked up into his eyes. He's just a few inches taller than I am, which because it always reminds me he'll be of age to leave home soon, always scares me to notice. "Seriously. I am. Your father is just too full of surprises sometimes. After sweeping you off to AC yesterday, and the promise of Japan . . . I just don't know what to expect from him lately."

"I get it." Ezra glanced at Gabe again before entering the house.

"That's your son?" Gabe asked.

"Yeah." I paused, waiting for the acknowledgement to show up on his face.

He grinned. "How old is he?"

"Fifteen. I was a young mom." I crossed my arms, dangling the cardigan in one fist.

"So was my mom," he nodded. "That happens sometimes. Look, uh . . ."

I stood there as nothing came out of his mouth.

He cleared his throat and scratched the back of his neck. The dog leaned into his leg. "Uh, I was wondering. Maybe we could get a bite to eat sometime?"

"Oh." The question surprised me, after all he'd spent most of his time with me when I was at my craziest.

"I mean, it's okay if you can't or whatever." He took a step back. The dog moved with him. "Please. Don't feel awkward at the gym. I get it. I'm sorry—"

"No, I mean, yes, I'd like to go out with you some time. I'm the one who's sorry." I reached out and put my hand on his arm. The dog stepped between us. I pulled back. "I was just surprised. That's all. I mean, I haven't exactly exhibited any signs of being a stable person around you."

"Ha!" He tilted his head back and laughed. "You're so real. That's what I like about you. And, um, since it looks like your son isn't going to be home for dinner, you want go somewhere tonight?"

"Yeah, you know that sounds nice."

Of course, Melissa had been peeping out the front window, listening to the exchange between Gabe and me the whole time.

"Holy cow!" she pounced on me as soon as I shut the main door.

"Who is he? Where were you that you left your clothes lying around for him to pick up? And . . . well, that's it, actually."

"Yeah, Ma. That doesn't sound like you." Ezra said from the doorway to the dining room. "What does she mean leaving your clothes—"

"Mel doesn't mean anything," I snapped. "I had gone to that MMA place I told you about and worked out. That guy is the owner and that's where I was when you called today. I ran out of there so quickly to get batteries to you that I forgot my sweater." I flicked the cardigan out for him to see.

"Okay, okay!" He spread his hands in front of him. "I just thought maybe my mom was finally having some fun. That's all." He turned to go back to the kitchen.

"Finally having some fun?" I stormed after him. "What does that mean?"

"That means," he said as he opened the freezer to pull out the carton of ice cream, "that I thought you were finally doing something besides work. You work all the time. When was the last time you went out on a date anyway?"

"The last time . . ." I stopped. The last time had been well over a year ago and it was with Johnnie Bernard. That's when we learned my mom and his dad had been on the hot and heavy side back in their day. The idea creeped us both out a little, so we happily stayed friends. "Does that really matter?" I asked. "Is your pump working right?"

"Yeah," he grinned, letting me change the subject. "It's fine. Thanks for the batteries."

"Think about that. What would you have done in Japan?"

He paused, holding the scooper above the carton. Mel swooped in like a hawk over a pond; she snatched the ice cream from him on her way to the cupboard to get a bowl. Ezra shot her a dirty look before answering me. "I can't respond to that question without sounding like I'm being sarcastic or disrespectful," he eventually said.

"What do you mean?"

"I mean, I'm pretty sure they sell batteries in Japan."

"But . . ." He was right, of course. What I wanted to say was *but I won't be there to make sure you get them.* That's when I realized maybe Todd wasn't the only problem parent. Maybe my being an overprotective, hovering, possibly controlling mother meant I was a problem parent, too. Gabe was right when he had gently pointed out that it was good if Ezra learned not to rely on me.

I sat at the table with my head in my hands.

"Ma," Ezra sat next to me. "You okay?"

I nodded as best I could while still holding my head. "I'm okay. I'm getting old. I guess I'm uptight. And I might just be a control freak. Aside from that, yeah, I'm okay."

"Well, look on the bright side," he said.

I looked at him from under my hands, apparently before he was ready for me. He bugged his eyes out at Mel.

"At least you're still managing to get guys to ask you out," she offered.

"Yeah. There's that," Ezra said. "I guess."

My head slammed against the table.

"**W**hat else do I have but time, now, dear Peri?" Jacqueline asked. She'd arrived simultaneously with the beep going off to tell me a fresh pot of coffee was ready. Now she sat at my kitchen table, semi-reclined so that her head could rest on the back of a chair. "When they released me, it was on the condition that I stay in town. I have lost my father and now—" she let out a long wailing sigh. "I have lost my freedom."

"You wouldn't be leaving town, anyway, Jacqueline," I said. "Your father's funeral is this weekend."

"Yes, yes, there's that." She rolled her head on the seat back to look at Mel. "Otherwise, I have nothing to look forward to. Nothing to live for now. I have lost everything."

"Um, right." I pulled my notepad from a kitchen drawer and poured a cup of coffee before joining them at the table. "Well, maybe you just need something to do. Why don't you help me plan your father's funeral? Maybe it will help bring you closure with his death."

"Why would it do that? Why would I want to have closure?"

"Jacqueline, trust me on this. I know from personal experience. Whether or not you want it to, life goes on."

"So that's what I have ahead of me now? Your life?" She sat

upright. "A life filled with petty errands and funeral planning? Ah!" She leaned her head into her crossed arms on the table and burst into sobs and wails.

Mel and I exchanged looks under lowered lids. She smirked. I cheered her with my coffee cup.

"And now what?" Jacqueline eventually asked. She removed a white cloth handkerchief from her clutch purse to dab at her eyes. Neither her eyeliner nor her mascara smeared a bit during her sobbing episode.

"Well," I opened the notepad. "According to the will, your father wants to have his funeral at the Cathedral Basilica of Saints Peter and Paul."

"We can't do it there," Jacqueline said. "May I have a cup of coffee?" she asked.

"Sure," Mel said. "The cups are in that cupboard there." She pointed.

"Oh, of course." Jacqueline stood, smoothed out her tight black pencil skirt and floated to the cabinets.

"Why can't we have the funeral at the cathedral?" I asked.

"Daddy was an atheist, remember? They won't let him in." She took out a cup. Held it up to the light, perhaps ensuring it was opaque before setting it on the counter. She went through the same motions with the coffeepot before pouring.

"Regardless, that's what he stated in his will. Perhaps we just keep mum with the priest about his true beliefs." I suggested.

"We just can't. The lighting is terrible there." She found the sugar dispenser next to the coffee and poured in what appeared to be a half cup. "I'm disappointed in you, Peri. You should know better. The press will be in attendance. They'll need better lighting."

"It's not really a matter of my preference, Jacqueline, nor yours. Nor what the press needs." I shook my head. "That's what your father wanted. So we'll do it there. I figure we'll get the monks—"

"Oh yes, the monks!" Jacqueline's eyes lit up. She sipped with her pinkie finger perfectly arced.

"We'll need to call everyone who was on the party invite list."

"Hmm. I suppose I could tackle that." She frowned at Melissa. "Will you coach me? Maybe give me a script to work from."

"I'd be happy to," Mel smiled at her.

"Mel doesn't work—"

"Oh, it's fine, Peri. I'm here to help you, remember?" Mel's smile had a hint of wickedness when she aimed it at me. "I'd *love* to help Jackie."

I sipped of my coffee. "Very good. I'll handle the monks, the church, and the rest of the funeral details. You two will handle calling everyone. The only thing left will be to arrange for a reception somewhere afterward."

"Somewhere with good lighting," Mel added.

I glared at her.

"Yes, yes." Jacqueline's head bobbed over her coffee. "Why don't we have it at the art museum?"

That was actually a good idea, as it would be something Mr. Wooley would have wanted. We could do it in one of the larger eating halls. I made the necessary calls from the kitchen table. Once I had the time schedule set up, I excused myself from the two of them to prepare for my date with Gabe, while they phoned Mr. Wooley's invite list.

Chapter 19: Tasted Like Steak

I'd decided to take the flat iron to my hair to make it perfectly straight. I had just sectioned it off to start on the back of my head when Carolyn called my cell. I put her on speaker.

"Something horrible happened," Carolyn said when I answered.

"What? Did you hear from that person again?"

"No! But I think Gerard might have." Her voice dropped to a panicked whisper. "I have to go and tend to him right now. I will call you later. Please. You must help me get to the bottom of this."

I sat quietly mulling over the call, wondering just what the hell the woman expected of me. I couldn't wonder too long, though, because Brittany Johannsen called.

"Did you secure a site yet?" she asked.

"I did. I signed the contract yesterday. I—"

"Why didn't you e-mail a copy to me?"

"I was planning to do it tomorrow—"

"You have to keep me up to date on everything, you know. I heard only good things about you. Why aren't you treating me like the rest of your clients?"

She was right, of course. I should have been on top of things for her. I should have confirmed the date of the party with her yesterday. I should have scanned and e-mailed her a copy of the contract. I should have ordered sample invitations. I should have started scheming out decorations to show her ideas. I should have been in control.

I sighed at myself in the mirror.

"Did you just sigh?" she yelled. "Call it off. Call the whole thing off. I will find someone else to do this party. You'll never work for me again." Her end of the line clicked.

I think I sighed at myself again in the mirror. That was the first time in my entire career, in the only career I'd ever had, that a client was disappointed in me. It was the only time I'd failed one of them.

I stared at myself for a few minutes longer, not quite able to comprehend how and why that happened.

Then I noticed the roots of my hair looked very dark at the top of my forehead. Leaning closer to the mirror, I unclamped my hair and fingered through it, pulling it taut against my skull.

"Oh, hell." My natural blond was starting to go.

Gabe rang the front doorbell at the same time Todd pounded on the back door. I met my archangel while Mel let the devil in.

"Hi," I said to Gabe as I opened the door for him to come in. "I just need to tie up a few loose ends."

He settled on the sofa while I ran to the kitchen. Jacqueline was still there. An open bottle of wine was on the table between her and Mel's chair.

"Looks like a party," Todd said, clapping his hands. "Should Ez and I stay in?"

"No." I opened the basement door and called for Ezra. "No. You shouldn't." I turned to him.

"Listen, no one can get an exact carb count on those cheese steaks."

"I don't even know what that means, babe," Todd grinned at Jacqueline.

"It means she's worried I can't handle eating without her," Ezra said when he came into the kitchen. "Honestly, Ma. I've had, like, a million cheesesteaks. Lighten up." He kissed me on my burning cheek.

I wasn't sure if he was being disrespectful or not. I was sure I wanted to assume he was and that I wanted to blame it on Todd. I was also sure I didn't want to get into a pissing match that would postpone my date with Gabe and possibly have everyone in the kitchen tell me I was uptight. So I let it go.

"I was just looking out for you," I said to him.

"I know." He tied his sneaker. "And I appreciate it, really. But Ma, I can handle a cheesesteak."

I opened the backdoor and practically had to shove Todd out.

"He's a cutie," Jacqueline said. "Who is he?"

"My son's father."

"Oh, is that boy your son?"

"Yes."

"Were you like twelve or something when you had him?"

"Sixteen."

"Oh," she said again and frowned at me. "So is he single?"

I almost wanted to ask if she meant Ezra, just to be mean, but Gabe was waiting. "In fact, he is. Want me to introduce you to him?"

"When I'm done mourning my father, maybe."

"**Y**ou look great," Gabe said when I returned to the living room. Not knowing where we were going, I had chosen black, straight-legged jeans with a black, tunic-length form-fitting sweater with a wide, scooping boat neck. He wore jeans and a black pullover. Seeing how dark the top of the dinner table would now appear, I opened the hall closet to get a scarf for a little color accent.

"Thanks. So where are we heading?" I chose a hand-knit scarf colored like a peacock's tail in purples and blues. After realizing the tail end of it, as was all the other scarves, had been dangling low enough that they had been resting on the potentially radioactive box of china, I changed my mind. We'd just have to look like bank robbers while we ate.

"There's a great little Brazilian place not too far from here."

"Picanha?"

"Yeah. You like it?"

"Love it!"

"Feel free to bring a doggie bag," Mel said. "Hi!" She held her hand out to Gabe. "I'm Melissa, Peri's cousin."

"Nice to meet you." They shook.

"She's serious, you know," I said, opening the front door. "She doesn't cook and relies on me for meals when she's not eating out. By agreeing to this date tonight, I agreed to let her starve." I fluttered my eyes as I smiled at her. "Though she could always call Ed's First Pub and order a pizza to go."

"Yeah. I suppose I could. Or maybe I could take your car—"

"If I wasn't in mourning, we could go out, Mel," Jacqueline entered the room. With one hand on her heart and leaning back a little, she took sweeping strides toward Gabe. Since my living room is on the small side, it was really only about two and a half sweeping strides that ended with her ungracefully stepping over the coffee table. She placed her hand in front of Gabe's face.

His eyes darted to me while he gently shook her fingertips. I tilted my head toward the open door. "We can go now."

"Great. Uh, nice to meet you, too," he said, sidestepping his way out of the house. "Are they both your cousins?"

"No. Just Mel, the other is the daughter of . . . ha! She's a long story." We ambled down the steps to the walk. He led me to the street and stopped beside a little red car.

"I have a confession," I said.

"I'm not sure if I'm qualified to hear it." He raised his eyebrows. "But I'd be happy to figure out some form of penance especially for you."

"Ha! Well, my client decided not to use my services for that party. It's off." I sighed. "I'm sorry."

"Actually, I'm relieved." He opened a car door. "Now it's all pleasure and no business between us."

"So no penance?"

"Hop in." He nodded toward the car. "I'll let you slide for now."

But I still had a price to pay. His dog was in the backseat. "Oh . . . Hello . . ." I struggled to smile at Gabe while I lowered myself into the passenger seat.

He jogged around to the driver's side and got in.

"So I see Raphael likes Brazilian food, too, huh?" I turned my head to make eye contact with the dog.

"He likes any kind of meat," Gabe laughed. "Joao, the chef, always makes sure to give him a nice chunk of steak."

I got the feeling Raphael's eyes were saying he thought I'd taste like steak. "So, like, uh, you're quite the dog person."

"You're not?"

"I've never had a pet."

"That's a shame. They're good for you. Helps you stay relaxed." He glanced in the rearview window. "Right Raphie?"

The dog must have used telepathy to answer him, no doubt neglecting to mention he thought I probably tasted like steak.

We parked street side around a corner from the restaurant. I got out and waited on the sidewalk while Gabe and the dog exited the other side of the car. My neck muscles ached. Probably from the strain of the fake smile I had insisted on aiming toward the dog.

Gabe stopped in front of me, his hands in his pockets. "You know it's true that they smell fear," he said.

"What? Who?" My breath felt hot in my nostrils.

"Dogs." He grinned. "I'm joking." He reached out and touched my arm. "I'm sorry. I didn't realize you are afraid of dogs."

"I'm not afraid."

"Oh, well I'm sorry you're uncomfortable around them."

I blinked long and slow as I struggled to find the words. "Dogs have never really liked me," I tried.

"I see. Well, I promise you it'll be different with Raphie. He's a good dog. He's my. . ." Gabe's smile looked as forced as mine now. He scratched the back of his neck. The dog leaned into him. "He's my therapy dog."

"What do you mean?"

"I suffer from . . . " He pulled on his earlobe then rubbed Raphael's head. "He helps with my Post Traumatic Stress Disorder."

My eyes shot up to his. "He does what?"

"He's been trained to work with PTSD sufferers. He's able to sense when I'm stressing. It's like he can smell my body chemicals and stuff. He keeps me from having panic attacks and from being anxious." He stared hard into me. I knew he was waiting for a reaction from me, like maybe my face would show pity or disgust. I'd seen enough of those faces to understand how difficult it was for him to tell me what he just did.

"I never knew dogs could do that," I said. "Dogs and cats have always had the opposite effect on me."

"You're afraid of cats, too?"

"I was attacked by one named Kisses."

"An attack cat named Kisses?"

"Yes. I have scars on my leg to prove it."

"Well I have scars on my head from when I was attacked in Iraq. We'll have to compare battle wounds sometime."

"No need. Yours sound worse than mine. You win that one."

"Maybe, though your life sounds more interesting than mine."

"You have no idea." I held out my hand for him to take. "Let me tell you about my mom. She would absolutely adore you."

It's funny that I started our date talking about my mom because it ended with me wanting to kill her. Gabe and I were settled in at a table. The waiter had just poured us each a glass of wine. Unfortunately, we couldn't toast to a pleasant evening because Johnnie Bernard called my cell.

"I'm sorry for calling in the evening, Peri," he said. "My dad's bailing your mom out of jail right now."

"Was she naked again?" I said not even thinking about the inferences Gabe could make from the statement.

Johnnie laughed. "No. She is fully clothed this time. She was at a man's house insisting on talking to him about Shelby Wooley. She refused to leave so the guy called the cops."

"Was it was the home of an Alex Foster? His assistant said they had building security remove her earlier."

"No. I think it was Jules or Julian Westman. Something like that. I'm calling you because you know how Dad gets around her. I didn't think it would be wise if he took her home. He and Mom are in a good place these days. If he spends too much time around your mom . . ."

"I got it. I'll call my dad."

"I just did and got his voice mail."

I groaned. "Okay. I'll go get her." I clicked off. I looked at Gabe, looked at my wine, and even looked at Raphael. I might have sighed, heavily. "I'm so sorry, Gabe. This is going to sound crazy. I hope you'll think this is one of those interesting things about my life. Um, I'm kind of in the middle of a murder investigation. I didn't kill anyone. But my mom is determined to figure out who did. Tonight she somehow got herself in trouble with it all and now I need to go to the police station to pick her up. Her attorney posted bail."

He laughed. "Yeah, I do think that's interesting." He waved his hand for the waiter. "I'll take you to get her. But I think it's only fair that you fill me in on all the details on the way."

Chapter 20: Pound Out Some Stress

I told Gabe everything about Mr. Wooley's murder, even about the seaweed delight Detective Beatty and I shared with my parents. He thought it was the funniest thing he'd ever heard. I thought it was too bad he needed the dog nearby. He was the first male I'd been interested in who was interested in me despite my parents, which could have been a very good thing. I almost found it suspect. How stable could he be?

Thankfully my mother was, indeed, fully dressed at the police station. She wore mint-green silk palazzo pants and a matching camisole over which she had a long, turquoise duster fringed with strands of tiny crystal beads. Her dreadlocks hung loose, almost extending to the back of her knees.

"Oh, you brought a friend!" She sidled up to Gabe and took his hand. "I love it when Peri introduces me to her friends."

"Yeah, uh, Ma, this is Gabe. Gabe, this is my mother, Honey Potts."

"Nice to meet you Mrs. Potts."

"No, no. It's Honey. Everyone calls me Honey."

"Right, well let's head out of here and get you home so Gabe and I can–" I almost said *have dinner.* Luckily I realized, just in time, how hard she'd make it for us *not* to have dinner with her. So I said something almost as bad. "So we can finish our date."

"A date! *You're* on a date? That's so wonderful!" She clapped her hands. "She never goes on dates," she said to Gabe.

"Yeah, well, let's get a move on." I shoved her down the hallway.

We made it out of the building and were about halfway to Gabe's car in the parking lot when my wannabe-detective mom made a discovery.

"Aaaack!" She stopped and grabbed my arm. "He has a dog! A DOG!" To make sure I got the point, she shook my arm, hard, and pointed to Raphael. "A dog!"

"Yes, Ma. You're right. He has a dog." I cleared my throat and waved my hand toward Gabe's partner. "This is Raphael."

She dropped to her knees so she was eye to eye with the animal. "Hello, Raphael." They stared at each other until suddenly she popped back up.

"He's quite the gentle soul. No wonder you're not freaking out poopsie." And just like that, she started walking again.

"Poopsie?" Gabe whispered to me.

"I think she likes it better than *Peri*."

He clicked his car unlocked and opened the door. Raphael jumped into the backseat. Mom insisted on sitting back there with him. I felt no need to encourage her to do otherwise.

I gave Gabe the address to plug into the GPS then we were off. We drove in silence for a few minutes until I just couldn't contain myself any longer.

I turned in my seat to look at my mother. She and Raphael stared back at me.

"So I got a call today from Alex Foster's personal assistant."

"Can I just tell you something?" she asked. "That man has lost both his sense of humor and his sense of justice."

"I'm not sure if I want all the details. But what made you think you'd get a different reception from Julian Westman?"

"He's a different man."

I sighed. "What are you saying to them to make them call the police?"

She giggled. "It was great fun, you know. I went in with guns blazing. Well, if I had a gun it would have been blazing. Instead, I just walked into his home and started asking him questions." She reached between the front seats to touch my arm. "You should have seen me! I was like this powerful Amazon woman leering over him as he ate his dinner, which, by the way, was not anything he should be bragging about. By the looks of his skin, the last thing that man should have been eating was that slab of meat on his plate."

"Yes, Ma, but think about it. Ever see one of your beloved TV detectives strutting into people's houses like that?"

"I don't need to think about it. You have no idea how many times I've shouted at the TV telling them to give it a try." She leaned back in her seat. "They should make it a legal thing to do."

"Well now that you know it's not legal, please don't bother anyone else." I faced forward in the car.

"What do you mean? Someone has to clear your name."

"My name isn't in need of clearing. In fact, the police arrested someone else today."

"They found the killer?"

"No. But I think it means they're not looking at me anymore. They haven't tried to arrest me."

"It could just be a matter of time."

"I'm innocent, Ma. There's nothing they could find to point to me."

"Unless you're being set up."

"Did anyone ever tell you, you have an overactive imagination?"

"Did anyone ever tell you, you should be more grateful?"

"What the hell?" I turned to face her again.

"I'm doing my best to help you, to protect you, to take care of you. The least you can do is say *thank you* instead of *please don't get involved.*"

"Excuse me?" I must have lunged toward her a little because I felt the seatbelt dig into me all of a sudden. "Ma, your parenting style could never be called involved."

"That's not true."

"It is! Look, I love you, however—"

"I have always been there for you."

"You know what I think, Gabe?" I leaned against the door to look at him and keep her out of my sight. "I think I have a secret sister. One that had an involved parent and now my mother has the two of us confused."

"Peri Mercury Potts!" Mom scolded. "I have always been there for you. I just never directed you. That's the difference. You, apparently wanted a parent to tell you what to do, how to live your life, and who to be."

"Don't you think that's what a parent is supposed to do? Direct their kids?"

"No! Children need role models. Like every animal in the kingdom, the young ones observe the older ones and if the parents behave like proper animals, the puppies learn proper animal behavior."

"I had a kid when I was sixteen!"

"And?"

"And you think that was proper?"

"It was not maladaptive behavior. And nothing bad came from it."

"You have arrived at your destination," said the voice inside the GPS.

Gabe pulled to the side of the road. He got out of the car as did Raphael and my mom. The dog looked like he wanted to go with her.

"Okie dokie, poopsie," she said, bending inside the driver's side of the car. "So your father and I were forced to put sheets up over the front windows. At first I hated it. Then I moved that Chinese screen in front of it to block my view and *voila!* I had an epiphany. Paper parasols!"

"What?"

"Can you find someone to cut the handles off a bunch paper parasols? You know, the Chinese umbrellas?"

"I guess so."

"Good. I don't want your father near a power tool again. I'm still not certain that beam in the bathroom will last the year."

"What beam? Oh, never mind. I'll send a contractor to you, too."

"Good. Well, I'm going to china town tomorrow and buying a whole slew of paper parasols. If I drop them off with you, can you get someone to lop off their handles?"

"Sure."

"Good. I'm going to have to borrow your glue gun, too."

"I think you still have it."

"Then that makes it easier!" She blew me a kiss. "Love you!"

"Love you, too, Ma."

Gabe and the dog returned to the car.

"You okay?" he asked.

"Yep."

"You sure?"

"Yep."

"Did you and your mom just have a fight and make up already?"

"Yep. That's the way we do it."

He nodded. "Like I said, *interesting.*"

I couldn't convince him to take me to a bakery for dinner, so we wound up at a hole-in-the-wall pizza joint in south Philly where he promised they had fabulous cannolis. He was right. Afterward, he took me home, kissed me on the cheek and promised to call me soon.

I'd heard that line before so I figured he'd had enough of me and my family's weirdness. I never expected to see him again, unless I went to the gym to pound out some stress.

Ezra's blood sugar number was unusually high the next morning.

"Did you check for ketones?" I asked him.

"I forgot."

"What are ketones?" Mel asked.

"Ketones are things that show up in your pee, if your body isn't using the sugar in your blood right. Anytime his number is over 240, he's supposed to check for ketones." I frowned at my son. "And you want to go to Japan?"

"Ma. It's just one high reading. Look." He showed me his insulin pump. "I'm taking care of it right now."

"Promise me you'll go to the nurse and get a ketone strip to check your pee the next time you have to go, okay?"

"Do you know how embarrassing it is to pee on a stick in school?"

"Do you know how important this is?"

"Do you know how—" he threw a hand the air, exasperated. "I'll check at lunchtime, okay?"

"Okay."

He ran out the front door then slowed to a saunter on the

sidewalk where he met with Theo. I watched him the whole way. It took every bit of restraint I ever had not to yell to Theo to look after him. Instead, I channeled that energy into folding the linens Mel had used on the sofa.

"He was going to ask me if I knew how uptight I am," I said to her.

"Either that or if you knew what a control freak you are."

"I'm getting really sick of hearing people use those terms to describe me!" I slammed the hall closet door shut.

"Hey! Did you just put my blankets in the radioactive closet?"

"Oh my God, sorry!" I took them back out and handed them to her. Before she could do anything with them, I took them away from her to find another place. "We've gotta get that stuff out of this house."

I stowed the linens on a chair in the dining room, tucking them under the table as I gazed at the dresses on top of it. Even though the event wasn't until the following month, I should have already placed the dresses in a consignment shop with the order to put them up for sale on a specified date in the future. I rubbed my eyes.

"I lost my first client yesterday," I said to Mel. "I don't know what's happening to me. I've never been fired. These dresses have been here since Friday. Why haven't I taken them to the shop yet? Why is that china still in the house? Did I tell you I'm supposed to find a foundation for Mr. Wooley's estate? I haven't even thought about that. What's happening to me? I'm always on top of things."

"It sounds like I came along at the right time. You need help. And don't worry about that client. As soon as we solve this thing for Carolyn, you can tell everyone you're adding P.I. work to your list of services and you'll get more jobs, I'm betting."

"On the one hand, that sounds really cool. On the other, it sounds like I'm turning into my mother."

"I just poured the last of the coffee into a cup, so I think that means I'm turning into you."

I sighed. "Does that mean you'll eventually turn into Honey, too?" Her laughter followed me into the kitchen. "She should be coming by this morning. She has some fabulous idea about using paper umbrellas for her front window covering."

"How is that possible?"

"I'm not sure. At least she's not parading naked for everyone happening by outside to see."

"She has a better body than either one of us, you know. I'd show it off too, if I were her."

"It's still illegal regardless of how good the bod."

"Maybe you should get her input on the Carolyn thing." Mel seated herself at the table with that last cup of coffee. "Since she's into the whole detective thing right now, too."

"After getting arrested for barging into people's houses, do you really think she has some answers for this?

"You have any other ideas?"

Chapter 21: Taking A Hiatus

I called Ma from the house phone to see when she'd be by so I could make sure I was home. She heard me running the water to fill the coffeepot and asked me what I was making. In a moment of sheer stupidity, or possibly due to a lack of enough caffeine to make my brain work right, I told her. Sure enough, she took that as a sign she should come over immediately and bring something "better" for us to drink.

"Just remember, Ma," I said when she bounded in the back door, "Ed doesn't know Mel's here. So don't let on if you see him."

"Nothing to worry about, poopsie," she said as she put a teakettle on. "I don't have a problem lying when necessary.

"Do I want to know what that means?" I opened the brown paper bag she'd brought with her and sniffed at the green and brown plant matter inside. "Is this from your compost pile?"

"Does it really matter how I answer that? You won't believe me regardless of what I say now." She kissed me on the cheek and pulled three cups out of the cupboard. "Mel, honey, I have to say I'm glad you're taking this hiatus from your marriage. Every woman needs to do that now and again."

"She's not taking a hiatus from her marriage and what do you mean: 'every woman?'" I asked, inhaling a longer sniff. I could detect cinnamon, licorice and something else, something familiar.

"Do you take hiatuses from Dad?"

"Certainly!" She waved her hand in front of her face. "Otherwise, I'd do more than just have the occasional lunch with Mervin Bernard, you know." She winked at Mel.

"Ugh. Did you bring the parasols?" I shook the bag and took another, longer whiff of the contents.

"Oh, dear. I forgot." She took the bag from me and doled out heaping spoonfuls into the cups. "I'll bring them by later."

"Well, it's good you're here, anyway," Mel said. She pulled a chunk of something out of the cup to inspect it. "We could use your help solving another mystery."

Ma clapped her hands, once. "Wonderful!" The teapot shrieked. "What can I do? Did Peri find another dead body?"

At that moment I thought perhaps I needed more help than she could give me. Unfortunately, she was already in the kitchen. Mel gave her a rundown of everything that had happened regarding Carolyn Hoskinson to date while Ma poured the hot water into three cups and served us at the table.

I finally recognized the third smell.

"Um, mom." I put my hands over their cups. "Is there pot in this?"

"It's hemp tea, yes, but it won't make you high. Hemp's not water soluble. Besides, it's mixed with a bunch of other herbs."

"What is wrong with you?" I pulled the cups to my side of the table. "You brought marijuana into my home? I have a fifteen-year-old living here!"

"It's probably not his first exposure," she said and pulled her cup out of my grip. "Besides, it won't make you high unless it's steeped in milk. You were exhibiting signs of excessive yin and coffee wouldn't help you. This will help you!" She picked her cup up and cheered me with it. "Cannabis will stimulate your yang, for the short term anyway."

"I have no idea what you're talking about." I heard the doorbell ring and stood. "No one move while I see who's here."

I don't know why I was surprised to see Detectives Beatty and Jameson standing on the other side of the front door. Who else would show up when my mother had just made tea with pot?

"What brings you guys around?" I asked through the screen door.

"Something came up," Jameson said. "We need to ask you a couple more questions. Do you mind if we come in for a few minutes?"

I did. But my mother didn't.

"Col! How wonderful!" she yelled from behind me. "Peri, invite the man in. Ooo. It's *men.*" She smiled coyly at Jameson. "Hello. I just made some tea would either of you like some?"

Beatty's eyes questioned mine. With the back of my head facing my mother, I nodded "yes" while mouthing "no" to him.

"Thanks, Mrs. Potts. Maybe some other time."

"Suit yourself," she said as I let them in. "And please, remember to call me Honey."

We settled in the living room. My mom took the armchair and pointed to the couch for the men to sit. I remained standing.

"Now, is this about the Wooley case?" Mom asked.

"In part. We just—" Jameson started.

"Has the coroner been able to establish the approximate time of death yet?"

"He died at approximately eight o'clock in the evening. Now then—"

"Oh, that's good. Now you know for sure my Peri didn't do it. She was working. Now, tell me, did you ever ask that daughter why she called nine-one-one and said someone killed her father?"

"How did you know that?" Beatty asked her.

"Yay!" Ma leaned back in the chair and pumped her fists in the air like a cheerleader would pompoms. "See that? I didn't! Pure speculation on my part. So, did you ask her? What did she say?"

After staring at my mom for a few seconds, Detective Beatty looked at me. "Do you suppose we could talk privately somewhere?"

"That will do you no good, young man." Ma reached over and slapped his thigh. "She'll just tell me everything after you're gone."

"I don't think that's the issue, Ma." I rubbed my eyes. "I think they need to speak without being interrupted."

"Why didn't you say so?" She sat up straight and sucked in her lips.

"Right, um," Detective Beatty pulled his notepad from his pocket. "We need to ask you a few questions about your visit to the condos at Washington Square yesterday. An older man was pinned against a wall and—" He wrinkled he brow. "What is it?"

"I wasn't there yesterday."

"Yes, you were."

"No, I wasn't."

"A license plate reader read your tag number as you entered the parking lot at one-forty-three in the afternoon," Jameson offered.

"It's wrong. I was napping then."

"She's suffering excessive yin," my mother said, as if explaining.

We all looked at her, briefly, and simultaneously decided to ignore the comment.

"Well, while you were sleeping," Jameson said, "your Ford Explorer was in the lot behind that building yesterday. Where was your son?"

"At school."

"Does Todd have a key?" Ma asked.

"Think harder than that, Ma." I headed to the kitchen, but I didn't have to go that far. Mel was in the dining room eavesdropping.

"Did you borrow my car yesterday?" I asked. She nodded. I took her by the hand and led her out to the living room. "My cousin was the driver. You remember meeting Mel, right?"

"Right. You have a tendency to disappear on your husband," Beatty said.

"Oh Collie, please don't tell Ed she's here. She's on a hiatus."

"Excuse me?"

"Ma, Detective Beatty doesn't even know Ed. Anyway," I shoved Mel to the center of the room, "were you at Washington Square yesterday?"

Mel nodded, again.

I almost asked why. Then I realized we'd probably have to explain to the detectives what had been going on with Carolyn and that might create even more problems.

"One of my biggest clients lives in that building," I offered.

"I see," he said. "Well, a resident of that building, a prominent judge, was accosted in the parking lot by a young man, possibly a teenager."

"Hhhhhnn!" I shrieked. I could feel my eyes popping. "Is he okay?"

Beatty looked confused. Jameson frowned.

"I believe so," Beatty said. "He was just roughed up. Slammed against his car by a young, white male. A security guard heard shouting and came running. The attacker got away on foot, by running out of the parking lot." He narrowed his eyes at Melissa. "Can you tell me if you saw anyone suspicious in the parking lot?"

Mel twisted her mouth to one side, as if she were thinking about his question. It was clear to me she was acting. I glanced at my mom. Her eyes were shining and she was grinning, which made me realize it was clear to her, too, that Mel was putting on a show. I was too scared to look at either Beatty or Jameson, in case I'd see it was clear to them as well.

"I'm sorry, I just didn't see a thing," Mel eventually said. "I wasn't even supposed to be there. I pulled into the lot and parked for only a few minutes. As soon as I went into the building, I spoke to the concierge and realized I was in the wrong place entirely."

"And you didn't notice anyone running through the lot shortly after your arrival?" Jameson asked.

"Nope." She shook her head.

"Thank you." He stood.

"Wait a minute!" I said. "Is that why you arrested Jacqueline?"

"I'm not making the connection." Beatty tucked his phone into his pocket.

"Sorry, you have to be in my head sometimes to keep up." I moved aside so the men could escape the sofa. "I was thinking about what my mother said earlier. Did Jacqueline call in and say her father was murdered?"

"Ask your mother if I'm at liberty to tell you." Beatty winked at Ma and turned to Melissa. "If you happen to remember anything else, please let us know. This gentleman is active in the art community, as was Shelby Wooley. We want to make sure his attack was completely unrelated to Wooley's death."

"I'll call you if anything stands out to me," Mel said.

"Great. And Peri, one more thing," Beatty said, "we can't seem to find contact information for Noreen Parkerson, his housecleaner."

"Who?" Ma asked.

"No one, Ma," I said as I ushered him to the door. "He was just asking if I could locate a housecleaner for Mr. Wooley's place." I shoved him outside. Jameson followed us. "Let me walk you to your car," I said loud enough for my mom to hear.

I stopped at the bottom of the steps. "Sorry about that. I got Noreen the job for Mr. Wooley after . . . well, she used to be my mother's housecleaner and they kind of clashed. It wouldn't be a good idea to bring up Noreen in front of my mother."

Beatty laughed. "One day I'll pop by your cousin's pub and you can tell me the whole story. Right now we need contact information for her."

"I didn't bring my phone out with me. Will you e-mail me a reminder to send you her cell number?"

"Sure." He shook his head. "What'd I tell you, Jameson? These women are funny."

They headed toward their car and I returned to my house where I immediately pounced on Mel.

"What the hell is going on?" I demanded.

Chapter 22: Side Topics

"**L**et's go finish our tea before it gets cold," Ma suggested. She led each by the hand to the kitchen.

"I swear to God, Mel. My head feels like it's about to explode. Why did you go there?" I accepted my cup from my mother and sipped. The tea was lukewarm and tasted the way it smelled. "You sure I won't get high from this?"

"You won't. But if you ask me, that's part of your problem," Ma said. "You seem very uptight these days, like maybe you should get a little high or something."

"Stop!" I gripped her am. "Do *not* talk like that when Ezra's in the house."

"Oh, pork chop bubbles, first of all, he's not here. Second, if he was, I'm sure he'd agree with me. Anyway, Mel," she sat at the table, "what were you keeping secret from the detective?"

"I went to Carolyn's building to see how easy it would be to get in and get access to the residents. That concierge is a jerk, by the way. I couldn't get past him."

"Well he's supposed to be that way," I said.

"Here's the thing," Mel leaned over her cup. "You know that kid who was here the morning Carolyn first told you about the notes?"

"Yeah."

"Well, when you made me go back upstairs that morning, I went to your bedroom at the front of the house and looked out the window to see if I could tell who was here. I saw that kid who lost his phone."

"So?"

"So I think *that's* who was running out of the parking lot."

"Really?"

"Yeah. Don't you think that's coincidental?"

"I certainly do," Ma chimed in. "At least I think I do. Who is this kid?"

I filled her in on the lost phone. "Oh my God!" I said as things came together in my head. "I found his phone right outside the freight door to Carolyn's building. On Friday!"

"And the second note said he'd seen her, except that she hadn't gone anywhere but here, when he was here," Mel added.

"Right."

The three of us sat silently, sipping our tea.

"Now what do we do?" Mel asked.

I looked at my mother. At first she seemed flustered, then she must have realized she wanted to be a private detective. "Well, I guess we should call his mother and ask why he's been haunting your client," she offered.

"I don't think that will do, Ma," I stood. "I think we have to be absolutely certain that it was him before we confront him. Now, think about it—what would motivate him to threaten Carolyn?" I rinsed my cup in the sink.

"Do you have his mom's phone number?" Mel asked.

I wrote down the number that showed up in my call log from when I spoke to her.

"I'll research her online to see if anything comes up in connection with Carolyn or her husband. Maybe he's been arrested before and had to appear before that judge? Who knows?"

"How can you do that?" Ma asked.

"Shame on you," I teased her. "What kind of detective would you make?"

"One that needs Mel, it seems."

We took her to the dining room. Mel educated my mom on the powers of People Finder and Intellius. I sorted through my e-mails, made a list of all the clients who wanted to send flowers to Mr.

Wooley's funeral and printed the rest of my to-do list for the day.

Unfortunately, I didn't get started on any of it.

"Promise me you won't freak out, Ma," Ezra said on the other end of the phone.

"You have ketones, right?" I blew air out of my pursed lips in what was probably a thinly veiled attempt to keep from freaking out.

"Yeah. The nurse let me use the principal's private bathroom," he said, as if I cared where he peed on a freaking stick. "So what do I do? I can't remember exactly."

"I'm going to come get you. While you wait for me, drink a bottle of water and however many units of insulin your pump says to dose, multiply it by one and a half."

"I'll drink the water and dose. Please don't come get me for an hour. I really want to get to physics class. Team assignments for our project are posting today. I want to make sure I'm not on some team with a loser."

Against my better judgment, simply because I was sick and tired of him thinking I'm uptight, I agreed to wait.

I paced in circles around the dining room table until Mel got tired of me bumping her chair.

"How the hell am I supposed to type if you keep doing that?" she asked.

"Let's run down to my house and pick up those parasols, poopsie," Ma said.

"What parasols?" Mel asked.

The doorbell rang.

"Maybe I'll make more tea, instead," Ma said.

Jacqueline was at the front door. She held a white box with a Potitos Italian American Bakery label affixed to it. I decided Jacqueline could become a good friend after all.

"Oh Peri, I have no meaning left in my life," she said as she paused inside my living room. I shut the door behind her. She remained standing still, the pastry box balanced on upturned palm, chin pointing above my head. I realized she was expecting someone to take the long, black cape she was wearing off her shoulders.

"It was kind of you to bring cookies," I said removing the box from her hand.

"Actually, I brought a dozen Sfogliatelle." She removed her cape herself and flung it onto the sofa. "They were a favorite of Father's," she said as she followed me to the kitchen. "You should be sure to have them at the funeral reception."

"I will." Though I never understood the appeal of them. Why ruin good pastry dough by stuffing it with something like cheese, fruit and nuts? The filling almost made them healthy.

In the kitchen, I introduced her to my mother.

"I greatly admired your father." Ma pulled out a chair for her. "Such a terrible loss for us all, most especially for you. We're about to have some tea, would you like some?"

"That would be lovely." Jacqueline pulled off her elbow-length black gloves.

I placed the Sfogliatelle on a platter and took out enough plates for us all, though I really doubted my mother would eat any of them. At the table, I noticed Jacqueline's face was paler than usual. Her eyes, usually heavily made up to appear almost as large as an anime character, were pale to the point of almost blending into her face. They were bloodshot, too.

"Are you all right?" I asked her, setting the platter and plates on the table.

"No Peri." She shook her head. "No, I'm not." Tears dribbled out of her eyes, down her cheeks. "I haven't been anything other than all right my whole life. At least, I think so. I was a baby when my mother left and Father always made sure nothing bad happened to me again after that. I thought the worst thing that could ever happen was not landing a role. A role I could prepare for. I wasn't able to prepare for this. Honestly, I don't know what to do about it." She dabbed at her eyes. "Look at this!" She showed each of us, one by one, the shiny tip of her finger. "Those are real tears. From real sadness. What am I supposed to do with this?"

She wiped her finger on the napkin my mother handed her.

"I'm sorry, Jacqueline." I put my hand on hers. "I truly am."

"The police won't leave me alone." She sipped her tea. "This is divine. Where did you get it?"

"I brought it to her. I'll make some up for you, too, dear." Ma patted Jacqueline's arm. "Why won't the police leave you alone?"

"They think I killed my father." Jacqueline seemed unaffected by the statement. In fact, she said it the way she would say something like, *They need directions to the local doughnut shop.*

"Why did you say he was murdered when you called the police?" Mel asked, winking at my mom. I was dying to know the same information, although I was going to ease into it a little.

Jacqueline cast her eyes to the table as she carefully set the cup down. She bit her lip then slid her eyes over and up to me.

"You know that china I gave you?" she asked.

"Yes."

"Well, I'd been experimenting with ways to poison Father."

"What?" Mel and I said in unison.

"You should have had her call me, Peri. Next time you have a client who needs to poison someone, have them call me."

"You . . . I . . . Oh my God! Ma! Please. I can't take any more of these, these side-topic confessions today."

"What on Earth do you mean?"

"You lie. You take hiatuses from Dad. You know how to poison people." I squeezed my temples. "Just stop saying things like that for a little while. It's too much for me to handle right now." I sighed. "Jacqueline, why did you kill your father?"

"I DIDN'T KILL HIM!" She jumped up, knocking over her chair. "Why do people keep saying that?" She clenched her hands in front of her mouth. "Peri! You're supposed to be taking care of me for the rest of my life! You can't accuse me of murder whenever you want!"

"I'm not supposed to be taking care of you. I'm only responsible . . . Ugh! It doesn't matter. That's another side topic." I dumped my tea in the sink and hit the coffeepot's *on* button. "Let's get back to square one. Jacqueline, why were you *poisoning* your father?" I picked up her chair.

Jacqueline pulled herself together and returned to her chair.

"Do you know what it's like knowing your father was going to become your mother?"

"You know, Archie and I experimented with that once," Ma said.

"Who is Archie?" Jacqueline asked, somehow making herself heard over me shrieking. "Jesus! Ma!"

"Archie is my husband. We started our parenting adventure by deliberately reversing our roles so Peri wouldn't grow up with the stereotypes of what a woman is supposed to be like, or a man. We wanted her to decide that for herself. It was very amusing. Except, we kept forgetting to follow through. Eventually, we got confused as to who was supposed to do what, so we decided to just let Peri teach us how to be parents."

"That explains so much," Mel said, cheering me with her teacup. I nodded in return. If I had ever believed tears were useful, I may have allowed myself to cry.

"Well, Ma, that's not quite what Jacqueline means." I sniffed. The coffee aroma calmed me. "What she's talking about is that Mr. Wooley was planning on becoming, medically and completely, Miss Wooley."

"I see." Ma sipped her tea. She poked a Sfogliatelle as if she worried it might attack. "Arch and I never tried that, though I can see how Mr. Wooley would be so inclined. The man had a gift for color coordination."

"So anyway, Jacqueline . . ." I encouraged.

"So anyway, I thought I'd make him a little sick. Just a little. Just enough so his doctor might postpone the change."

"Aha," Mel said.

"How were you poisoning him, dear?" Ma asked.

"Well, I tried to use rhubarb leaves. That happened in a movie I auditioned for. Who knew that in real life rhubarb leaves are bitter? He couldn't eat enough of the pie I'd made him for it to have an effect."

I returned to my chair with my precious cup of caffeinated ambrosia in hand.

"Then I tried to convince him to eat lightly steamed lima beans."

"Lima beans are poisonous?" Mel asked.

"You betcha," Mother said. "That's why you have to cook them for hours with the lid off."

"She's right," Jacqueline nodded. I think she nodded anyway. While I was staring at my mom, I saw an up-and-down movement out of the corner of my eye that I assumed to be Jacqueline's head, nodding. "They have a high level of cyanide in them that gets cooked out."

"I'm surprised you could even find them raw," Ma said.

"I had to have them imported from Peru."

"That makes sense," Ma said. "I may want to get your contact there."

"No. No she doesn't," I interrupted. "Go on, Jacqueline."

"Well, I accidentally cooked out all the cyanide. So I had to go back to the drawing board. Actually, back to the Internet. That's when I stumbled upon the red china."

"Aha! It's radioactive."

"Yes. I thought I'd let it soak into some cheese every day until it damaged his kidneys enough that the doctor would tell him he wasn't healthy enough to undergo the hormonal part of the change."

"And you were giving him that recently?"

"Yes."

"How did he die?" Ma asked. "Do we know the cause of death?"

"The police said poisoning. Not radioactive poisoning," Jacqueline said. "That's as much as they would tell me."

"Interesting," Ma said. She picked at the flaky crust of the Sfogliatelle, letting the crumbs fall to the plate. "Well, did Peri tell you I'm dead set on getting to the bottom of this case?"

"No." Jacqueline shook her head.

"I am. Ha!" She tilted her head back in laughter. "I said *dead set* without even meaning to. Whew! I'm so funny." She ripped open the Sfogliatelle. "So don't you worry none, little Miss Jacquelini, I'm on the case. Honey Potts will save the day!"

"Honey Potts?" Jacqueline asked me.

I could only nod.

We ate quietly for a few minutes. Mel and I tackled our Sfogliatelle. Jacqueline nibbled at hers. Ma explored the one on her plate like a surgeon examining an alien body.

Before anyone could come up with anything else to say, the phone rang.

"Mrs. Milano?" the school nurse said on the other end. "I hate having to tell you this. We just called an ambulance for Ezra. He was vomiting and acting very confused."

Chapter 23: Evidence of Tears

Ma said I passed out again. I'm sure she was right because I remember things being black and then looking up at the scared faces of her, Mel and Jacqueline. After they helped me up, Mel drove us all to the hospital. We found Ezra in the ICU where Mom had to claim Mel and Jacqueline were my sisters to get them in. I led the race down the hall until we found the room where a team of specialists were inserting a dozen or so tubes into my son's body.

Sometime later, an endocrinologist handed me Ezra's insulin pump.

"It appears to have malfunctioned," the doctor said. "The school nurse explained to the EMTs that he'd been dosing accordingly, nevertheless his glucose was 728 when he arrived."

"Is he going to be okay?" I asked. My mother's arm was around my shoulder in a déjà vu-like moment from the first time he was in the hospital. Back when it took three days for them to promise me he'd be *okay*.

"There's no brain swelling and while his potassium is low, it's not low enough to impair heart activity. As you may know, we cannot reverse it quickly. We have to slowly dose him with insulin and slowly replace the electrolytes. He won't be leaving here today."

"He survived much worse," I said to him, or maybe I was just reminding myself.

I handed my mother my phone. "Call whoever you think needs to know. I need to busy myself," I said before I went to work rearranging all the supplies in Ezra's hospital room.

I could feel everyone's eyes on me as I worked. Wisely they stayed out of my way. That is, until I went to the room next door.

"Come on, Peri," Mel took my hand to lead me back to Ezra. "Look, if you need to do something, then—"

"I need to do something."

"I need to go shopping," Jacqueline said. "Want to go shopping with me? I need more black clothes. Could I bring back flowers for him? Or since he's a boy, should I get something else?"

"Actually, I need to get flowers." I pulled my billfold out of my purse. "Mel, somewhere in the dining room is my to-do list for today. Will you look at it and see what you can take care of? There's also a list of people who want to send flowers to Mr. Wooley. Use this card." I handed her my business credit card. "You should find contact information for Pearl Slack at Custom Floral Designs. Use her. She already knows the funeral details."

"That Pearl is a whack job," Ma said. "Why not use someone else?"

"She's good."

"She's nuts. And I know all about nutty people."

Mel laughed as she hugged me. "She sure does," she whispered into my ear. "I'll take care of it all. Don't worry," she added in a louder voice. She kissed my mom good-bye and left the room, taking Jacqueline with her.

Ma pulled me down next to her on the uncomfortable couch in Ezra's room. "I called your father, Todd and Mick. Anyone else need to know?"

"No, that's all." I fell against her. "God, I want a cookie."

"Why didn't you say so?" She jumped up and replaced her body with a cushion from the rocking chair. Her bony frame was actually softer. "I'll go get you one."

"No, Ma, really. I—"

"I'll get something that comes in a manufactured package. It's trying times, I'm aware." She disappeared.

I pulled myself together enough to call the pump manufacturer to tell them what happened. They promised me they'd send Ezra a new pump overnight. According to them, everything would be just fine.

I worked hard to believe them.

Todd was the first to arrive. He walked in the room hunched over as if he were afraid I was waiting with a bow and arrow aimed toward his chest.

"Did I do this?" he asked, standing beside Ezra's bed.

"I wish you had," I said. I did my best to fluff up the cushion from the rocking chair.

"Why do I deserve that?"

"You don't. But, if it were your fault, then I could yell, rant and make sure it never happens again." I flipped the couch cushions. The wooden platform they used to create the sofa was filthy.

In the bathroom connected to Ezra's room, I wetted some paper towels in the sink. I returned to the sofa to wipe it down.

"How did it happen?" Todd remained standing by Ezra, staring at his unconscious body.

"His insulin pump malfunctioned."

He didn't respond. I continued to clean the sofa until I had to tell myself it wouldn't get any cleaner. I threw the paper towels away, replaced the cushions. Eyeing up the blinds, I decided they could use a good dusting. Unfortunately, I had no duster. No vacuum, either. And the paper towels were linty–they would make the fabric blinds worse.

I stood there, fingering the cord. My breath came in shorter and shorter. My throat clogged and soon enough, I emulated Jacqueline as I dabbed at my eyes. Tears meant I wasn't in control.

Things went black.

When the light returned, I could hear my mother's voice.

"No, no, no! She does this all the time. It'll just freak her out to get a doctor to look after her."

My eyes came into focus. I discovered I was lying on the sofa in Ezra's hospital room. Mom and Todd were staring at me.

"I fainted again, right?"

She nodded.

"You're awake now, though. That's what matters. Lookie here!" Ma waved a small package in front of my face. In lieu of a cookie, she found a granola bar, a whole grain, organic, granola bar. I didn't even have to bother trying to look at the ingredients. I knew white table sugar wouldn't be listed.

I forced myself into an upright position, smiling at her. She meant well.

Todd sat beside me. He put his arm around my shoulder. "Look. I can only handle one emergency at a time," he said. "Please don't do that again."

I shrugged out of his embrace. "Sorry to be such a burden." I sat in the rocking chair beside Ezra. Without thinking, I opened the granola bar.

"I didn't say you were a burden," Todd said. "God. Nothing I ever do is right with you, ever notice?"

"Ever notice you only do the wrong thing?" I asked, chewing. It wasn't even close to a cookie.

"Ever notice that you are both always right and both always wrong?" Ma took my former place next to Todd on the sofa. "It's a simple matter of perspective. The two of you need to understand you will never find common ground until you realize that. Isn't that right, Archie?"

My father entered the room with Mick at his side.

"I'm sure you are, my dear." They kissed hello in a way that made us all avert our eyes.

"Here you go, kid," Mick said, extending a bag of Milanos to me.

"You're a godsend, you know that?" I dumped the granola bar into the trash. My mother didn't notice. She was still embracing Dad.

Mick nodded hello to Todd. Todd stared at him in return.

I explained what had happened to Ezra. Then we set up camp the way dysfunctional families do when a member is on his back with a bunch of tubes connected to his veins. Todd kept quietly to his corner of the sofa. Mick took my place in the rocking chair. Once properly fortified with cookies, I began organizing the supplies into what I was sure was a more orderly and efficient arrangement. My parents chatted as if it was just an ordinary day.

"So we're going with adding 'the best batch we've ever had' to the label," I heard her say to my dad as I returned with the cleaning supplies that I had found in a maintenance closet.

"Brilliant! Simply brilliant!" my father said.

"Do I want to know?" I asked.

"I'm making my own honey," Ma said. "Seems only a natural outcropping of my talents."

She and my father looked at each other and burst out laughing. I think I sighed. Todd grinned, with his head down, as if he didn't want anyone to see. His grin made me feel guilty.

I cleaned the bathroom again. But I still felt guilty when I was done.

"Um, Todd," I said when I came back into Ezra's room. "I'm hungry. Do you want to go with me down to the cafeteria? Maybe we can scare up some food for everyone?"

Whatever you call an expression that's a mixture of confusion, curiosity and a hint of horror is what you'd use to describe Todd's face. "Uh, sure. I guess. If you really want me to," he said after he pulled himself together to look like a normal human being.

We headed to the elevator bank where there were too many people around us for me to attempt an apology. Besides, Gabe chose that moment to call me. I replied with a text message that probably freaked him out. *My kid's in hospital. Will call when I can.*

Naturally, all the people hanging out around the elevator got in it with us. We were packed tight, at what appeared to be maximum capacity. Yet Todd and I somehow managed not to touch each other, despite the fact we were side by side.

Once we hit the main floor, everyone scattered. Now was my chance. I just didn't have my nerve. Finally, as we crossed through an open mezzanine area, the high ceilings and expansive space somehow made room for my emotions.

I stopped walking and turned to him.

"Look," I said as I waited for him to meet my eyes. "I know I can be on the uptight side. I know some people think I'm controlling. It's not because I think everyone is doing everything wrong."

He held my eyes for a second longer, then flicked them away. "Got it," he said. We continued walking. The urge to slap him returned, which I suppose meant things were back to normal.

In the cafeteria, I piled up two plastic containers with field greens and mixed vegetables.

"That for your parents?" Todd asked.

"Yeah. What'd you find?"

"There's a guy doing mini pizzas made to order, but the crust is whole grain."

"Yuck."

"You got that right. The only other decent option is the Mexican station. It doesn't look like real Mexican food, though. It looks more like something your mom would call Mexican."

"Should I call my cousin? Maybe he could bring us some real pizzas?"

"That'd be cool." He pulled four bottles of water from the refrigerated case.

"We need five," I said.

Todd chewed on his lip before tucking two bottles under his arm. He reached in the case and pulled another out.

"Why's he here, anyway?" he asked.

"Mick loves Ezra. And me." I waited for a heartbeat. "He loves you, too."

"Yeah. That's the rumor anyway." Todd turned away from me. In the reflection of the cooler doors, I watched him jostle the water bottles so he could wipe his eyes.

"Maybe Ed could sneak in a of couple beers," I said when he turned back around.

He smirked. "I was thinking that but I figured you'd yell at me if I suggested it."

"I am human, you know." I led him to the cashier.

"I know. I mean, you're doing a great job with our kid. He's really cool." He shoved my purse out of the way and handed the cashier a credit card. "He's the real reason I'm coming back. I could easily stay in Japan. I'm living good there. I just feel like I'm missing out on too much of Ezra."

Ez was awake, sort of, when we returned to the room. His eyes were open and glassy. But he was still too out of it to ask what was going on, or why he was in a hospital.

When the doctor checked on him, he said his electrolytes were back to normal, which is what we needed to happen. They could up the insulin dosing now without problems. We were assured he'd be back to normal soon and he'd come home the next day. Mick left immediately. He kissed my mom on the cheek, hugged my dad and me, nodded at Todd.

My parents ate their salads. Ma, of course, removed the lighter-colored leaves first, since, according to her, they were a waste of energy to chew them. Within the hour, Mel and Ed brought pizza and beer. My mother sniffed the air like a hound dog. She took hold of my father's hand.

"Come on, Archie. Let's give the young people their space." As she hugged me, she whispered in my ear: "Will you please have Ed call me to discuss the nitrates in pepperoni?"

"No." I shook my head. "I can't take on another project right now."

She pinched my cheeks. "I'm so proud of you poopsie! You can say *no!* Do you realize how few women have the strength to do that?" She kissed the end of my nose before dragging Dad away from the pizza box.

"Thanks, Ed." I hugged him. "Oh God! I think I was supposed to tend bar tonight. Jenna had something going on, right? I'm so sorry! I forgot."

"I called him for you," Mel said. "I saw it on your to-do list, so I called. I came clean about everything with me, too."

"Good. Are you mad at me?" I asked him.

"Oh yeah. But I'll be a good guy and take it out on you later." He punched me in the arm. Todd caught me as I nearly fell over. Ed didn't even notice. "I covered for you for a while until I got Katie from Pub Four to come in. It was fun being behind the bar again. But man, Derek's a mess."

"I know. I'm trying to figure out what to do to help him." I pulled a slice of pie out of the box, plated it and handed it to Todd. I doled out another piece for Melissa, who already had a slice on a plate.

"I am an adult you know," she lifted her plate in a *cheers* gesture.

I sighed. "I didn't mean it that way. I was just trying to be helpful. Jeesh." I kept the slice. "Anyway, Ed, do you think Noel is sleeping with his sister-in-law?"

"Absolutely," Ed handed me a bottle of beer.

"See?" Mel said. "You guys have all the fun out front. I never get to know this kind of stuff. I'm stuck in the back, by myself with only the walls keeping me company."

"So come back!" Ed said. "You can tend bar if you want to. Do whatever you want."

"I don't want to tend bar. Seriously Ed, as of right now, I have no desire to ever set foot in one of your pubs again."

"What about coming back to me?"

"I'm still deciding."

"Okay, so I'll figure out what to do with Derek *and* Mel," I said to Ed, touching his arm with my free hand. "Please, don't go nuts on her right now. My kid's almost awake. Can we all just pretend to be normal, happy people for his sake for this one night?"

So we did. Ed, Mel, Todd and me. We ate, drank, and made a little bit of meaningless small talk. Eventually, Ed went back to his pubs. Mel went back to my place promising to bring me a fresh change of clothes, a toothbrush and a comb the next morning. Todd and I slept in Ezra's room: me on the uncomfortable couch, him in the rocking chair with his feet resting on Ez's bed.

Chapter 24: A Rosier Aura

They discharged Ezra first thing the next morning. Todd drove us home, packed tightly in his sporty rental car. I made Ezra an all-American breakfast of scrambled eggs with pepper jack cheese, buttered toast and orange juice.

"I forgot what a pain in the ass these shots are." Ezra sat in a chair in the kitchen with his arm propped on the table.

"Pain in the ass, really? Is that any way to talk?" I asked as I wiped his arm with alcohol.

"I'm the one getting a shot so I can eat my breakfast," he said. "I think I know the best words to describe the situation."

"You're such a joy to have around when you're grumpy, you know that?" I jabbed him and squeezed the syringe to empty it into his precious body. After I pulled the needle out, I wrapped my arms around him. "I mean it. Even when you're grumpy, you're a joy to have around."

"Thanks, Ma. Can I eat now? I'm starving. You know I'm not nice when I'm hungry."

"Like mother like son," Mel said as she poured me a cup of coffee.

"So, like, am I going to have to give him shots when we're in Japan?" Todd asked, face white.

"It's no big deal, Dad," Ezra said. "I used to give them to myself all the time before I had the pump. Ma's just being a control freak. I could do it if she'd let me."

"I'm not being a control freak," I said. Strange how that word, *Japan* made my neck cramp and twist my head to the side. "We're both out of practice. I just think you should do it a few times on an orange, like when you were first diagnosed, as a refresher. I don't want you to hurt yourself by accident."

"You didn't practice on an orange as a refresher," he said, sprinkling salt over his food. "Does that mean it's okay for you to hurt me by accident?"

"Ezra, really. The attitude is not winning you brownie points." I shot an evil glare at Todd. He didn't notice because he was pouring himself some juice. Mel did, though. She grabbed my arm, as if sensing I was about to tackle him. She should have known better. I did, after all, have a fresh cup of my favorite brew in my hand. I wouldn't dare risk spilling any.

"I'm not trying to be disrespectful, Ma," Ezra said. He hung his head. "Just sometimes you act like I'm incapable of being alive."

"That's not what I mean to do," I sat next to him at the table. "I just want you to have the best life possible. So yeah, I'd rather accidentally hurt you with a bad jab than let you feel disappointed in yourself by doing it."

He met my eyes. "I know," he said. "I'm sorry, Ma. I just . . . it just sucks being diabetic."

Mel took the seat across from Ez. "This shouldn't last long, right?" she asked. "Didn't the rep say they're sending a new pump overnight to us?"

"Yeah," I sipped my coffee. "It should be here sometime today."

Todd took the last chair.

"Cool!" Ezra shoveled a forkful of scrambled eggs into his mouth. "So see, Dad? It'll be easy in Japan. We'll just have to change the inset every three days. No biggie."

I couldn't stop staring at my son as he ate his breakfast.

No biggie. It was no biggie to change the inset every three days. It was no biggie to order supplies far enough in advance to make sure you have the necessary stuff to change the inset every three days. It was no biggie to have alcohol wipes on hand for the change day. It was no biggie to remember to change the inset before you have a meal so you can test to make sure it's working before ketones set in. It was no biggie to always have spare triple-A batteries on hand for the pump. It was no biggie to have glucose tabs or jelly beans everywhere possible, in the case of a sudden drop in blood sugar. It was no biggie to have plenty of test strips for the meter. It was no biggie to make sure the meter was always charged and ready to use. It was no biggie to have fresh lancets available so that he wasn't pricking his fingers with a dull blade. It was no biggie figuring out how many carbohydrates were in each meal. It was no biggie doing the math to know just how many glucose tabs he should eat to raise his blood sugar when it dropped. Nothing was a freaking biggie!

"You all right?" I heard Todd's voice say. Something was touching my shoulder.

"Get her head below her heart," came Mel's command. Someone listened to her because a hand grabbed me by the hair and shoved my head between my knees, hitting my forehead on the table in the process.

But, I stayed conscious.

"I don't think you should drive anywhere today," Mel said a few minutes later when I was able to stand. She followed me as I left the scene of the crime that would have been committed if had I stayed in that kitchen any longer with Todd. We went out to the front porch. "What's on your agenda for today?"

"I have no idea." I rubbed my face with my hands. "My God! When did everything get so out of control? I always know what's on my agenda."

"That's why you need me," Mel chirped. "I was thinking about it yesterday while I staked out Carolyn's building."

"You did what?"

"I hung out at her building again while you were at the hospital."

"Why?"

"I'll get to that in a minute," she sipped her coffee. "I was thinking. I know why you're so uptight all the time. You have too much to do. I should become your partner. We can take on a bigger workload, including private detective work, so we'll both be paid. Also, I researched the detective business. You can make good money tracking down deadbeat dads and spying on cheating spouses. So really, the extra workload won't be much. You'll end up working less."

"I'm not following you."

"You'll have more spare time to go box or do whatever that workout is where you punch things with that good-looking guy from Monday. Who knows? Maybe you'll finally get laid again."

"Hey!"

"Anyway, you'll be less stressed."

"But –"

"But you'll have to realize you're not God and relinquish some of the control you think you need to have over the world."

I didn't respond with another *but* because Detective Beatty was walking up my front walk.

"Good morning," he said as he stepped onto the stoop.

"Good morning," I responded. Mel cheered him with her cup. I waited for him to ask why she was stalking Carolyn's building.

"Any idea where we might find Jacqueline Wooley right now?" he asked.

"Oh no." I covered my eyes. "Are you about to tell me she skipped bail?"

"Not if you can tell me where she is."

"She said yesterday that she was going shopping for black clothes and to get some flowers. I haven't seen her since."

"Why are you looking for her?" Mel asked. "Did something happen?

"We have a few more questions for her. She's not answering her cell phone. Nor did she ever come home last night. Before we put out an APB on her, I thought I'd check with you, Peri. Your home seems to be the place everyone goes when they disappear." He smiled a full-on toothy smile at Mel.

"I gave her your mom's contact info," Mel said to me.

"Why?"

"She wanted more of that tea."

I stood. "Let's give my mom a call, then."

Inside, we headed to the dining room where my cell was charging.

"Are you getting married?" Beatty asked. He fingered the gowns still piled on the table.

"What? No!" I put my cell on *speaker* and clicked on my mom's name.

"Thought these might be bridesmaid gowns."

"No. They're for a project for a client," Mel said for me.

"Good morning, poopsie!" Ma's voice boomed through the speaker. "How goes everything with my dashing grandson?"

"He's doing great, Ma. We're home now. Listen," I held the phone aloft so everyone could hear clearly. "The police need to ask Jacqueline Wooly some questions. You haven't seen her lately have you?"

"Actually, I see her right now. We're enjoying the view from the roof garden, nibbling granola together. You should join us. I made some fermented garlic and aloe juice smoothies, too."

"I am soooo very busy today. I have a lot to make up for, after not working yesterday. Though I'm sending Detective Beatty down your way, so keep Jacqueline there, please."

"Actually, I think my partner, Micah Jameson, would be closer." His face took on a green sheen.

"Nonsense! Collie baby! You get your tushy down to my house right this instant. I insist! Otherwise I'll have to hunt you down at the precinct!"

"I'll, um, I'll be there soon." He pulled at his collar. I clicked off from my mom.

"She will hunt you down, you know," I said. "When she finds you, she'll force whatever goodie she made especially for you down your throat. Trust me, she's stronger than she looks."

"Wanna take some Pepto Bismol with you?" Mel asked him. "I always do whenever I visit Honey on her turf."

"I'll just stop by a pharmacy on the way down." He nodded. "And Peri, you haven't e-mailed me that housecleaner's number."

"I'm so sorry." I scrolled through the contacts in my phone. "I'm doing it now."

He waited for his phone to refresh. "Great. Thanks uh . . ." We made eye contact. "Wish me luck."

"Godspeed Collin Beatty," I said.

"Are you getting him a housecleaner?" Mel asked after he saw himself out.

"No. Remember me telling you only a handful of people knew Wooley was in town?"

"Yeah."

"Well, don't tell this to my mom. After she had a spat with her housecleaner, I felt guilty, so I got her a job cleaning Mr. Wooley's house. She's another person who knew he was in town."

"Who is she?"

"A woman named Noreen Parkerson. I don't know much about her, really. I'm not even sure where Ma found her."

"What kind of spat did they have?"

"Noreen has a unique look."

"So does your mom."

"On the opposite end of the spectrum."

"I don't get it."

I scrolled through the e-mails on my phone that I'd been ignoring since the school nurse called. "Ma felt that Noreen wasn't embracing her inner beauty. She tried to convince her to get a makeover. Noreen was offended but tolerated it for a while. However, you know Ma. When she's on a mission to help someone, she's on a mission, right?"

"Right. Kind of like you." Mel sat in a dining chair.

"I'm not sure if I resent or resemble that. Anyhow, things kept escalating until Noreen couldn't take it anymore. She exploded, verbally, on my mother. Who, according to Dad, took it quite calmly. When Noreen finished, my mother told her her problem was that she was 'unlayable' and that if she'd fix herself up enough so that someone would want to have sex with her, she'd be a happier person and have a rosier aura."

"Unlayable?"

"Yep." I sat at my desk to download the e-mails to my computer in order to remove them from the server, hence from my phone. It made me anxious to see so many e-mails on my phone. On my computer, I could handle them better for some reason. "Okay. Enough about Noreen and my mom. Let's talk about you." I spun my chair to face her. "Why were you at Carolyn's condo?"

"Nope. Not till you answer my question. Are we partners?" She reached out a hand for me to shake.

I think that sigh was more of an exasperated huff. "Who'd you call yesterday for the flowers?"

"Oh, I just used some online place."

"Ugh! No! You can't do that!" I flopped back in my chair. "Okay.

Here's the deal. Yeah, I think I could use some help. So let's do a trial run for the next month or so. If, and I do mean IF, you become my partner, you can't do things like use some online company for flowers. You have to use the best of the best. Pearl Slack with Custom Floral is the best of the best of the best florists."

"I have to say that your mom was right. She's a whack job. I called her first. It was like I was tormenting her while she was doing this ginormous favor for me. She kept going on and on about how no one appreciates what she does. That she could never satisfy Wooley with the right colors anyway so why try?"

"You just have to know how to butter her up," I said as I printed my to-do list. "Come on. I promised her I'd get a sample of the right red. And we have a boatload of things to do today. Let's go."

I opened my grandmother's sideboard. Tucked inside, along with her antique serving platters and good silver, was a small metal box where I store keys to my clients' homes. I looked at the to-do list one more time before pulling several keys out. Once I got them onto a supersized safety pin, I returned the box to its regular place.

I went into the kitchen and opened the basement door. "Yo Ez! Todd! Mel and I need to run out. You good?"

"Yeah."

I tried, I really tried to hold back, but I was a woman possessed by the demons who frighten only the moms of diabetics. "Ezra, you know you can't just—"

"Eat anything without a shot. Got it, Ma!"

Chapter 25: Proper Response

In my SUV I handed Mel my to-do list.

"What's this?" she asked.

"That's what we have to do outside the house today. The list for phone calls and computer research is still at home."

"Why did you print it out?"

I backed out of my driveway into the alley and stopped to look at her. "So I don't forget anything. Also, if something comes up regarding any of that, I have a handy piece of paper to take notes on."

"Why not use an app on your phone?"

"Because phones get stolen, lost, and broken." I raised my eyebrows at her. "Any other questions?"

"Who's Penny?" She pointed to the first item on my list.

"She's an interior designer." I explained Madder's idea for paint strips. "Penny will have full Pantone charts so we can match the color to Mr. Wooley's favorite red in his house instead of looking through paint strips, going to his place to compare and then possibly having to go back to the paint place for more strips. I wish I had thought of doing this before. You'd be surprised how many shades of red there are."

"No, I wouldn't. After all, remember how many shades of coral lipstick there are?"

Within minutes, I pulled behind an old warehouse that had been turned into a design center where Bon Monde designs had their office. We entered the main doors of the building and headed through a long, wide corridor with various design-related businesses flanking both sides. Near the end, we reached Bon Monde. I stopped walking instead of going in.

"What's wrong?" Mel asked.

"Look." I pointed across the way to a closed shop. A sign on the front glass read: *RIP Sy. Heaven is more beautiful with you there.* "That's so sad. I've used him for a couple of my clients who had specifically requested him. He could do an ultra-modern, minimalist style like no one else. I can't believe I didn't hear about his passing. I would have sent flowers or something. He was a really nice guy."

We went inside Bon Monde. Penny was on the floor surrounded by an assortment of pink and purple fabric swatches.

"Peri!" She scrambled up. "Oh no! I must have forgotten! Did we have an appointment?"

"No. I'm the one who should apologize. I should have called to warn you I was coming." I touched Mel's arm. "This is my cousin, Melissa. She's helping me on a project. We were hoping we could borrow a Pantone chart from you to match a red color."

"Are you talking paint or fabric?" Penny asked as she headed to a messy office area.

"Paint." I smiled at the disarray. I may have been attempting to camouflage my clenching jaw. Every artistic person I know blames the state of their desks on the fact that they are creative. I've never been able to see the connection. Seemed to me, if they were all that creative, they'd think up a unique system to keep it all organized. My fingers itched to take over her desk and set it right.

"This should do the trick then," she magically pulled out a fan-dex of color samples from a pile of ribbons and trims.

"Great! How soon do you need it back?"

"I have a couple more floating around here somewhere. Take your time with it." She walked us toward the door.

"Oh, hey!" I stopped. "What happened to Sylvester Weissman? I just saw that sign."

"He died a couple of months ago." Penny's eyes opened wide. "You didn't hear?"

"No! I feel terrible. I would have gone to the memorial or something. What happened? Was he sick?"

"No one knows." She bent toward me. "Leeann, his wife, thinks someone killed him."

"What?" Mel asked. "What's going on in this town? I thought only people on the street got killed around here."

Penny stared wild-eyed at Mel for a full second before continuing. "Yeah, it was really weird. He was fine. He came in that morning as usual. Went home for lunch. Came back and within an hour or so he got really sick. His assistant called nine-one-one. They took him to the hospital and he died."

"Why does the wife think he was killed?" Mel asked. She fingered a group of tassels hanging off a hook by the door.

"He died of a cardiac arrest, whatever that means. Leeann thinks it was impossible for him to have had heart problems. He'd just had a checkup. Everything was fine. She's so sure something triggered the heart thing that she insisted an autopsy be done, even though Sy was Jewish."

"Did they find anything suspicious?" Mel asked.

"Well, Leeann thinks so. It turned out that he had traces of some kind of toxin that may have caused the arrest thing. There was nothing definitive. Now she's ready to sue the police force for not looking into it being a homicide."

"Wow. She must really be hurting," I said.

"Yeah. She's super unstable these days. I don't think she'll ever reopen their shop. It's a shame, really."

Out in the truck, I scribbled a note on the to-do list.

"Send a card to Leeann Weissman," Mel read aloud. "You know, I left a message on the Weissman's voice mail a couple days ago when I was calling the people on Wooley's invite list."

"Yes! They *were* invited to the party. Oh no! I feel horrible. I wouldn't have had you call them had I known. I'm sure the last thing Leeann wants to do right now is go to another funeral."

"I think there's something you're missing right now."

"What do you mean?"

"How did that Weissman guy know Wooley?"

"I'm not sure."

"Don't you think it's coincidental?"

"What's coincidental?"

"That guy is killed by some kind of poisoning. Your Wooley guy was killed by some kind of poisoning. They knew each other. Think there could be a connection?"

I stared at her while I processed what she'd said. "You know, Mel. I think you're better at this than my mom. Yeah. That does seem coincidental."

"Well, that's all I got." She flipped the visor down to open the mirror. "How do we figure out if it's more than coincidence?"

"I think we would need to find out how Mr. Wooley and Sy Weissman knew each other. How they're connected." I started the truck then waited for her to apply a fresh layer of lipstick before putting it in gear. "Maybe I should call Leeann and apologize for being inconsiderate instead of sending a card. Will you change my to-do list?"

"I'm writing, 'visit Leeann Weissman' to *our* to-do list." Mel dropped her lipstick back into her purse and pulled out a pen. "I think we should do it in person, maybe she'll be more willing to open up about the passing of her husband."

"Oh, I don't know if that's right. What if she's still grieving?"

"Penny said she's disappointed with the police. Maybe she'd like to hire a private detective." She nudged me with the pen.

"I don't remember agreeing to that yet."

"Just think about it, will ya?"

With Mel by my side, I clicked off some of the more mundane tasks on my list in record time, as I guess I should have expected. We stopped by a client's house to put away her monthly supply of nonperishable groceries, which she receives from Amazon.com on the twenty-eighth of each month. We purchased a set of crystal doves for another client to give away as a corporate gift. Finally, we let an irrigation company have access to a third client's basement so they could open up the sprinkler system for the warmer months ahead.

"Just how many keys to how many houses in the Philadelphia area do you have?" Mel asked as we followed the irrigation company's truck down the lane.

"I think about seventy or seventy-five."

She whistled. "You know how dangerous you could be?"

"I do and if you start thinking like that, you won't be my partner. Got it?"

"Got it."

"What's next?"

"Um, window film at twelve thirty. What's that mean?"

"Oh, that's for Carolyn. We'll be there for a little while, so we'll pick up something for lunch. That means we have time to go to Mr. Wooley's place and compare reds."

"Can we get in?"

"Of course. I have keys, remember?"

"No, I mean, shouldn't it be a crime scene or something? Can you just traipse through his place?"

I called Beatty. He was still at my mother's.

"You just can't get enough of her can you?" I teased.

"I'm about to call for backup to help me get out of here." I could barely hear Beatty's voice through the speaker of my phone. He must have been whispering. "She keeps forcing me back in the chair. She said I have dampness in my spleen. What does that mean?"

"That sounds like a term from when she studied acupuncture."

"Yeah," Mel added. "She used to say I had too much wind in my gall bladder. I think she used an herb on me."

"Please don't take any herbs from my mother," I said. "Listen. I have to get into Mr. Wooley's house. Do I need a police escort or something?"

"Technically, not anymore, but I think I need to assist you today. Don't go in without me. I'll meet you there in minutes."

He beat us to Mr. Wooley's townhouse. As did my mother and Jacqueline. They all stood waiting for me on the front stoop.

"Peri Mercury Potts Milano!" My mother yelled at me and stamped her foot as I walked toward her.

"Uh-oh poopsie," Mel whispered. "She sounds pissed.

"Yes, Ma?" I unlocked the front door, pausing to give her my best showroom smile. Really I was hesitating. I wasn't sure if I was ready to relive the scene of finding him.

"Why didn't you tell me you were coming here? How am I supposed to solve this mystery if you keep withholding information?"

"Actually, I'm the one who's supposed to be solving this

mystery," Beatty said. "And I, too, would like to know why you need to be here."

"I'm matching Mr. Wooley's favorite shade of red to one of these." I showed them the Pantone fan-dex I'd tucked under my arm. "That way I can tell the florist what color to dye the tips of the callas for all the flower orders for his funeral."

"That's so very thoughtful of you, Peri," Jacqueline said. She wore a skintight leopard print dress with a thin red belt, matching shoes, short black gloves and the veiled pill-box hat she'd worn the day before. All she was missing to be a pinup girl was a long, thin cigarette. I supposed she felt the world was aware of her mourning via the hat and gloves. "You always understood how important it was to Daddy for people to pay attention to detail."

"Right." I opened the door. Inside, I gagged. "Ugh. What is that smell? Ew! Is it from his . . ." I couldn't finish the thought.

"No." Beatty sniffed. "Smells like bad fruit."

I turned to Mel. "We need to make a note to get this place cleaned soon."

"You're selling this place for me, right, Peri?" Jacqueline asked from the doorway.

"If that's what you want."."

"It is what I want."

"Okay, I'll talk to Mervin Bernard about who should list it."

"Thank you."

"And at some point we need to discuss what kind of foundation your father would want set up in his honor."

Jacqueline said nothing. She remained in the doorway, staring at me with both fists pressed against her mouth.

"Are you all right?" I asked her.

"No. No I am not." She clamped a gloved hand to her heart and closed her eyes, "I can't stand the thought of being in here. I think I'll just stay outside and weep on the front stoop." She turned around and stepped outside without waiting for a response, which was probably best for her.

"Who the hell says 'weep' in normal conversation?" Mel asked.

"Jacqueline," my mother and I said in concert. Then Ma added: "Will you be seeing Merve in person, poopsie? I can go with you if you'd like."

"That won't be necessary, Ma. I'll just call him."

It didn't take me long to match the painted red nails of the ball-and-claw dining-room table to Pantone Red 032 C.

"That's almost disappointing," Ma said.

"What?" I asked, fanning through the rest of the deck to be sure.

"There are so many shades of red with exotic names and he chose just 'red.'"

"Looks that way." I glanced up at her. She was tapping her chin. "Also looks like the wheels are turning in your head. Do you want something painted red?"

"No. I'm thinking it was pure genius to paint the toenails on the furniture."

I winked at Mel. "What color do you want?"

"Lime green." She paused, pursing her lips. "Yes. That would be fabulous. While I was out buying the parasols yesterday morning, I picked up a few green ones. Oh, that reminds me, dear poopsie, I still need to get them to you. You have someone who can cut the handles, right?"

"Yes, I have a guy." I went to Mr. Wooley's kitchen to find the offending fruit. My mother followed me.

"I'll also need him to attach them to each other somehow. I tried experimenting with the glue gun yesterday. It's quite messy you know. What I really want is a screen type of thing made from just the tops of the parasols. So if he could somehow attach them to each other for me to make one big screen then put it on casters, *that* would be ideal. I'll be able to wheel it out of the way when I want to look out the window." She opened Mr. Wooley's cabinets.

"I think my guy can do it. He's pretty handy." I used a paper towel to pick up a black and oozing banana from the counter. "What are you doing?" I asked her.

"I'm always curious about what other people have in their cabinets. I'm surprised he had so many prepackaged items. I thought he had better taste than that."

"A lot of pre-packaged stuff tastes pretty good."

"It's horrible for your health."

"Hey Mel," I hollered into the front of the house.

"She's out front with Jacqueline," Beatty replied. "Do you need her?"

"No, I'll just send myself an e-mail." I tried to hand him the banana so I could get my phone from my pocket. He took out his cell.

"What do you want to remember?"

"To pack up all his food to give to a food shelter."

"I have some homemade kale, ginger and soy protein bars," Ma said. "Do you want to give them some of those, too?"

"I think they only take prepackaged stuff because it lasts longer on the shelves."

"That's a shame." She walked away from the cabinets. I shut them behind her. "My stuff would be so much healthier for the people."

I threw away the offending banana along with the remaining bunch that was still on the holder and some moldy oranges. I took them outside to the trashcan behind Mr. Wooley's townhouse. Inside, I re-shut the doors to the pantry and cabinets that Ma had apparently re-opened before ushering everyone out the front door.

Ma pinched Beatty's rear as we walked toward the street. He hightailed it to his car, which is probably the proper response to such a nonverbal *good-bye*.

"So Per," Mel said as we all walked toward the street. "Jac just told me her dad knew Sy Weissman from the Horticultural Society."

"Oh I know Sy Weissman from the Horticultural Society," my mother said.

Chapter 26: Shaggy Hair

"You knew him," I corrected Ma and stopped by my Explorer. "You *knew* Sy Weissman."

"What do you mean?" Ma asked.

"He passed away a couple months ago. His wife thinks someone poisoned him," Mel said.

"What? You are supposed to tell me everything, Peri Mer—"

"We just found that out," I interrupted.

"Ah! And you didn't want to say anything in front of the detective! I get it!" Mom hugged me. "You are a shrewd one. Now, what else d'ya got?" She rubbed her hands together as if warming them up to receive a cash reward.

"Nothing. And just for the record, you're jumping to conclusions. We have no reason to believe Sy's death and Mr. Wooley's are even related."

Mom's shoulders drooped. Her hands flopped.

"We're going to visit his widow," Mel said. I gave her the evil eye.

"I'll go with you!" Mom announced.

"No. Uh, you can't." Since the evil eye wasn't working, I bugged my eyes out at Mel in what I thought was the universal sign for *say something else!*

"That's right," she said, bugging her eyes back at me because apparently I was the one who was to come up with the right idea.

"You have an appointment, don't you?" Jacqueline asked, somehow saving us without bugging her eyes at anyone. She adjusted her hat using the clean window of my Ford as a mirror.

"How could I forget?" Ma smiled. "Your friend Madder is coming over today."

We left my mother and Jacqueline, who were apparently now bosom buddies to go their way as we went ours. We picked up lunch on our way to Carolyn's Washington Square high rise.

"So where did you find that kid's phone?" Mel asked as we got out of my truck.

I explained how the delivery men thought I dropped the phone when I had to force the door open. "Maybe he lives here," I added.

"Maybe." We went in the main entrance and bid hello to Stephen the concierge who pointed out the window film installers sitting in the lobby. I escorted everyone to the elevator then let them in Carolyn's unit. She wasn't home.

Beatty called while Mel and I ate.

"No one is answering that cell number you gave me for the housekeeper," he said. "Do you have another contact number?"

I scrolled through my phone while he waited. "That's the only one I have," I said.

"Did she clean for Wooley on any particular day of the week?"

"No, not when he was in town. When he was out of town, I'd let her in twice a month just to keep the dust and toilet ring under control. She liked to do it on Tuesday mornings because she said it was near another customer. When he was in town, he'd request her whenever he felt the place needed it."

"Any idea when she was in last?"

"I could look in my records at home to be sure. I'm thinking it was probably Monday last week."

"And spell her name for me."

I did.

"Know what kind of car she drove?"

"No."

"Know who any of her other clients are?"

"No. I don't know who referred her to my mom, either. She only worked for her for a couple of months before they parted ways."

"Would you be able to ask your mom who referred her?"

"Ick." I sighed. "Do I really have to?"

He laughed. "Yes, you really have to."

I clicked off and realized I was alone in the kitchen.

Mel was in the master bedroom, the master bathroom actually, nosing through the medicine cabinet.

"What the hell are you doing?" I dragged her back to the kitchen. "You can't just go nosing around like that."

"Sorry. I got bored. And medicine chests can say a lot about people." She sat on a bar stool at the high counter.

"Really?" I put my hands on my hips. "Tell me, what did you learn about Carolyn and Gerard?"

"They take very good care of their teeth." She turned her nose in the air and laughed. "So how long has that concierge guy been working here, do you know?" she asked.

"I think since the building was built," I said. "At least longer than I've been doing this gig. Why?"

"Would he know if anyone had a teenager named Ricky?"

"Definitely."

So of course when the installers were done, we took them back down in the elevator and let them leave while we stopped to chat with Stephen.

He was certain no one in the building had a teen son named Ricky.

Which was weird, because as we left, I spied Ricky sitting in the lobby area on a sofa, as if waiting for someone.

"You know, I think I left my planner in Carolyn's place," I said to Mel, as we passed Stephen's desk, heading back toward the elevators.

"What pla—" she started. Perhaps my death grip on her elbow prevented her from continuing her sentence.

I nearly dragged her down the hall. We passed the elevator doors, continued beyond the bank of resident mailboxes on the wall, only stopping when we made it to the fake palm trees flanking the freight entrance.

"What are you doing?" Mel asked.

"Ricky is sitting on a sofa in the waiting area."

"What? I didn't see him!"

"Obviously. Now what do we do?"

We stared at each other in silence. I began doubting our private detective skills. Fortunately, Carolyn accidentally saved us. I spied her entering the hallway. A few seconds later, Ricky showed up walking behind her.

Mel and I made a mad dash to the elevator bank. We arrived simultaneously with Carolyn, being sure to block the boy from her.

"Hey there," I said. "We just saw the window film guys out." I pointed my thumb to the freight entrance, as if hinting I had them exit that way. "Everything is just fine. Maybe even on all fronts."

I smiled broadly at her.

Mel nodded and smiled in similar fashion.

Carolyn's eyebrows went up, clearly confused. Eventually she smiled, too. Not broadly, but in a way that suggested she was questioning my sobriety. "Thank you, Peri." She hugged me as the elevator dinged. I let her get on the elevator while Mel not-so-smoothly prevented Ricky from doing the same. The doors shut.

He shoved Mel aside and punched the up button.

"It's no use, Ricky," I said, looping my arm in his. "You can't get to her apartment without a special key."

He pulled away.

"What d'you mean?" He shook his head hard enough that his shaggy hair briefly exposed his ears. While I got a glimpse for only half a second, it was long enough. I'd only ever met one other person with ears like that.

"Let's go chat in the lobby," I suggested. "Then maybe I'll introduce you, in the right way, to your mother."

"Who? What?" Mel asked.

"How did you know?" Ricky asked.

"For years, your mother has considered having plastic surgery to alter the shape of her ears. But she's deathly afraid of anesthesia so she's been hiding them with her hair. Kind of like you."

The skin on his jaw grew taut. His face reddened. I thought he trembled. "That bitch gave me up. She threw me away so she could live this rich, high-class life. Don't call her my mother."

"She wasn't really given a choice at the time, Ricky. She certainly didn't do it so that she could live well off. Why don't we have her tell you about it?" I called Carolyn on my cell to see when she was expecting Gerard. He wasn't due back until late that evening, so I asked if we could bring a visitor up.

She greeted us as we exited the elevator car and led us toward the living room.

"You look familiar," she said to Ricky.

"He should," I said.

"You're in the student art program at the museum, right?" she asked him.

He nodded.

"Are you his mother?" she asked Mel.

"So sorry, Carolyn," I interrupted. "She's my cousin. I had to enlist her special expertise in this matter. I'll explain later."

"Oh, I see, I guess." She waved her hand to the replacement sofa. "Please, have a seat," she said as she sat opposite us on a chair. "What can I do for you?"

Ricky stared at the floor. I studied the side of his face as he clenched his jaw, squinted his eyes. I couldn't tell if he was about to attack her or cry. It was so obvious that he was using all his might to hold in whatever the emotion was, though, that it put me on edge. I stood in my newly learned fighting stance, just in case I needed to jump on him. One of the few things my sparring exercise with Mikey taught me was that if I stood with my weight on my toes, I could bounce up and pop someone with a right uppercut without them seeing it coming.

Mel stood too, flatfooted on the other side of the boy, eyeing me up in total confusion.

Ricky broke into tears. I relaxed my stance.

"Ricky's the one who's been leaving the notes," I explained to Carolyn. Her eyes grew wide as she blinked at us. "He's your son."

She gasped. Her hand went to her throat, then covered her mouth as her tears welled. I moved aside for her to sit next to him. She did, wrapping her arms around him.

"I'm so sorry," she said, sobbing against him. "I'm so very sorry."

Mel and I snuck out of the room. We got in the elevator silently, as soon as the doors shut, Mel let out a holler.

"Woo hoo!" she hugged me. "Now *that's* what I call detective reasoning."

"Deductive reasoning," I corrected.

"Whatever. How the hell did you know that?"

"Like I said, the shape of the ears. When he shook his head, I saw how pointed they were and that the lobes were attached to his face. They're like elf ears. Carolyn's are identical. Really, I was guessing. I just happened to guess right."

"Wait 'til you tell your mother. She's going to be sooo jealous," Mel said as we exited the elevator. "Now what do we have to do?"

"We take the Pantone thing in to Pearl and show her the right red. Then I think that's it for the to-do list."

"Good. We'll have time to go pay our respects to Leeann Weissman."

We drove the short distance to Custom Floral. Madder was behind the counter when we went in.

"I heard you had an appointment with my mother," I teased him.

"I just got back," he beamed at me.

"And?"

"I think she understands me." He winked as he turned toward Melissa. "Who do you have here?"

I introduced him to Mel.

"First your mother, now a cousin," Madder shook Mel's hand. "I feel like I'm becoming part of the family. It's nice to meet you, Mrs. Potts."

"Potts?" Pearl hollered from the back. "Which Mrs. Potts?" she asked as she came into the room.

My eyes burned immediately.

"Oh, this is my cousin, Melissa Potts." I dug through my purse for a tissue. "Mel, this is Pearl Slack. She's the owner and floral designer extraordinaire."

"We spoke on the phone the other day," Mel said.

"Yes, yes. But I didn't realize you were a Potts."

"Only by marriage."

"And she married into a lovely family," Madder said, nodding his head. "I got to meet Peri's mother, Honey Potts, this morning."

Pearl's head snapped in my direction. She narrowed her eyes at me. "*The* Honey Potts?" she asked. "She's *your* mother?"

I sniffed. "Yes, please don't hold that against me."

"Humph." She slowly spun around to Madder. "And why did you meet with that woman this morning?"

"I went to her for nutritional help."

"I hear about you visiting her again, I will fire you." Pearl stormed into the back room.

"I'm so sorry Madder," I said and blew my nose. "I really am. I had no idea."

"That's okay, Peri." He grinned and lowered his voice. "Your mom offered me a job. I was going to put in my notice today, anyway."

"A job?" I whispered back, though I think my whisper might have been louder than his. "Doing what?"

"Is everything all right, out here?" Pearl reemerged into the shop.

"Oh, yes." I felt my spine straighten. "I found the right shade of red for the tips of Mr. Wooley's flowers." I pulled out the fan-dex to show her. "You can keep it for a couple of days if that helps."

"If you had thought of this months ago, Madder, it would have saved us all time and aggravation. When I think of all the hours I put in for all those flowers." Pearl shook her head. "I do whatever I can to serve my clients." She smiled at me. I think she sneered at Mel.

"Okay, well," I said as I started walking backward. "That's all we need to take care of here for now. I'm sure I'll be in touch with more flower orders soon."

Chapter 27: Half the Battle

"Is she always that weird?" Mel asked as we walked back to where we'd parked.

"She's always been passive aggressive and, well, miserable would be the word, I guess. She used to be . . ." I clicked the locks as I struggled to define Pearl Slack. "I don't know. She used to always make me, everyone, feel like she was burdened by whatever you were asking for, but since you were a helpless animal, she'd take pity on you and do it anyway. Now it's as if she's just burdened."

"Good. Then I won't take it personally." Mel opened the passenger door. "Think we could make a couple more stops? I'd like to get my purse and phone from the pub. Then maybe we could swing by my house so I don't have to borrow any more of your clothes. Or are you going to do some laundry today?"

I waited until we were both in the SUV before I answered.

"We can stop by your place for clothes and you can feel free to help with the laundry anytime you want." I batted my eyes as I smiled at her.

"Got the message, boss." She batted her eyes and smiled back at me. "I can call you that, right? I mean, you're gonna take me on as a partner, right? We did good on Carolyn's case."

"I did good."

"It was me stalking her condo that got us suspicious about

Ricky."

I started the engine, sighing.

"Hey!" She grabbed my arm. "Do you know what you just did? You sighed. You know why you sigh?"

She didn't wait for me to answer.

"You sigh because you're turning into Pearl."

A bolt of lightning shot through me. Just for that tiny flash, I pictured myself like Pearl: older, alone, miserable, overworked, tired, sighing all the time.

"Really, if you think complimenting me is the way to get what you want, you're not doing a good job." I pulled out of the parking lot. "So what's next?"

"We go see Leeann Weissman."

"Okay. We'll go home to look up her address. But I'm still not sure I feel comfortable just showing up on her doorstep."

"Can't we just log in to PeopleFinder from your phone to see where she lives?" she asked.

"We probably could. I also want to check on Ezra."

"Ez is fine. He'd call you otherwise."

"He could be unconscious."

"In which case Todd would call you."

"I just want to check on my son!" I slammed my palm on the steering wheel. "What's so wrong with that?"

"Nothing, really. It's just that sometimes what you call 'checking on,' others might see as—"

"Are you about to tell me I'm a busy body?"

"I think that's a nicer term than I was about to use."

I fumed quietly while I worked my way through traffic.

"You okay, Peri?" Mel asked after a few minutes.

"Why wouldn't I be?" I turned onto Roosevelt Boulevard, heading north. "I mean, within the past couple of days, I've discovered I'm a control freak, I'm stressed, uptight, and apparently I'm a busy body. It's funny. I always thought I just took care of people. But no. I guess I was just annoying the hell out of them. Now that I know that, I guess I'm okay. I mean, right? Knowing what the problem is is half the battle or something. Isn't that what people say?" I took a cleansing breath and held it as long as I could before exhaling. "Look at that. I'm already making progress. I almost freaking sighed." My nails dug into the steering wheel.

"So you're not okay. Look, I wasn't trying to be mean. I was trying to help you."

"By insulting me?"

"It wasn't an insult!"

"Because abuse is a sign of affection, right?"

"I wasn't . . . Ugh! You're impossible sometimes. You know that?"

We drove in silence for several more minutes until my cell dinged with a text message.

"Will you get that out of my purse for me?" I asked. "Though I'm sure it's a wrong number because I am the one calling everyone else, right? I'm in everyone's faces all the time apparently."

"Really, *Pearl*, you are just a joy to be around." Mel found my phone and read the screen. "You got a message from It's Your Mission MMA."

"Oh, that's Gabe. I forgot to call him back yesterday."

"He wants to know if you and your son are all right," she said. "And he added 'no pressure' at the end."

"I don't know why I agreed to go out with him," I said as I tried to nose in front of a taxicab.

"What do you mean? He's hot. He seems nice."

"I don't have time."

"You would if we were partners."

"He has a dog."

"So? It's not like the dog will be going on dates with you."

"Actually, it is."

I guess my detective skills were still pretty primitive because somehow I didn't notice Mel's mischievous grin until I pulled in behind my row house.

"Oh God," I said as she ducked out of the Ford. "What did you do?"

"Nothing. Only if I were you, I'd make sure my hair and face looked the best I could make them by, oh, say sevenish." She ran up the back steps.

"What?" I stormed after her and discovered a tornado had already been in my kitchen. "What the HELL IS GOING ON?" I screamed.

Ezra and Todd pounded up the steps from the basement before I had a chance to catalogue the mess.

"Oh, hey there, Ma." Ezra gave me his most charming grin. "You usually call to see if I need something when you're on your way home. Otherwise, this place would be spotless. Right Dad?" He dragged Todd to the sink.

The tips of my ears burned. "Funny. I would have, but *someone* made me feel like I was a busy body and butting into everyone's life all the time." I glared at Melissa. She placed her hands together and tilted her head against them as she smiled at me like a cherub. I pressed my fingertips against my temples. Maybe I was trying to keep my head from exploding.

"Ma, really, it looks worse than it is," Ezra said. He cleared the bowls of food from the table. "We got this. Go chill or something."

"Chill?" I gripped Todd's arm. "Did he get that from you? Did you tell him that's what you thought I needed? To chill?"

He pulled his arm away. "Actually, we didn't talk about you all day. He'd been explaining diabetes to me and we played video games. I think you're the one teaching him to talk to you that way." He turned his back to me to put an unopened bottle of *his* soda in my refrigerator.

"Yoo hoo!" Ma yelled from the front door. "Who's home?"

Mel shoved me to the front of the house. Either to see my mom or to save Todd.

"Lookie here poopsie!" She dragged a box of paper parasols across the floor. "As promised."

"Great, Ma. Let's put them in the dining room and I'll get my guy on it."

"What's the matter?" She tilted my chin to look at my face.

"Todd and Ezra made a mess in the kitchen," Mel answered for me.

"Well then, you should have them clean it up." She pinched my cheek.

"They are now." I sighed.

"Nice!" Ma strolled back toward the kitchen.

I dragged the box of parasols into the dining room.

"It's getting tight in here," Mel said.

"Yeah. It's kind of my holding pen. Sometimes it's full, sometimes empty." I collapsed into my desk chair. "Mel, would you make some coffee? I'm afraid if I go in there something violent might happen."

"I got your back." She left.

I turned to my computer to download my e-mail. There were several more requests from clients to order flowers for Mr. Wooley, a note from the funeral home that they needed clothing for his body and there was a message from Beatty.

Get the food out of Wooley's townhouse.

Don't forget to ask your mom about the cleaner. Still can't find her.

It's always fun when you're around.

I was sure he really meant it's always fun when my mother was around.

I dialed Noreen Parkerson, thinking it'd be safer to ask her than to ask my mother. Her voice mail picked up.

"Hi there, Noreen," I said into the recording. "I'm sure you've heard the news about Mr. Wooley." I paused, wondering if she really had. How would I know? "Um, anyway, I'll be cleaning out his food to send to a shelter tomorrow morning. It'd be great if you could get in there tomorrow afternoon or maybe Friday to clean the place. Please call me back and let me know when would be a convenient time."

With my to-do list updated and my e-mails answered, I spun in my chair, doing my best to ignore any and all sounds coming from the kitchen.

The front doorbell rang. I bolted to answer it.

Jacqueline was now an official frequent visitor.

"Jacqueline, you're just in time for coffee, I think," I said as I led her to the rear of the home.

"Oh, I'd rather have some of your mother's tea if you have any."

"I'm not sure . . ." I stopped to gather strength before I entered the kitchen. It was spotless. Todd and Ezra had disappeared. Mel and Ma sat at the table. "Let's look."

Once we four women were gathered around the table, two drinking coffee, the other two waiting for the water to heat for their tea, Mel and I updated Ma on the Carolyn case.

"Wonderful!" She clapped her hands.

"Yes. That would make for an excellent made-for-TV movie. How old is the mother?" Jacqueline asked.

"You're not old enough yet," I said.

"Oh, well maybe in a few more years, then," she said. The teapot screamed.

Ma filled two cups with hot water.

"So we have one mystery solved. Only one more to go," Mel said. "Who killed Mr. Wooley?"

"No clue, yet," I answered. "But, if someone kills my mother, we'll know it's Pearl Slack for taking her employee away from her."

"Maurice is an absolute delight!" Ma set the cups of tea down for her and Jacqueline.

"Maurice?"

"Maurice Adler is his full name. That's where Madder comes from."

"Oh," I said. "I'm almost disappointed. I had assumed he had an anger management problem."

"Madder is still a sexy nickname." Jacqueline pulled on her earlobe. "I took quite a fancy to him myself."

"Nice." I winked at Mel. "Anyway, what did you hire him for?"

"He's helping with everything. My herb and natural product business is too much for me to handle by myself these days. I barely have time to still consult with patients. He loves his flowers, but he's more interested in the actual plants and how they can be used medicinally."

"Uh, Ma, did Madder tell you where he learned flower arranging?"

"Yes. In prison."

"For drug trafficking."

"Yes, he told me all about it." She sipped her tea.

"And he's had major problems with addictions. Do you think it's safe for him to be around all your herbs? Like the one in your tea?"

"Oh poopsie, don't you worry none about that. He'll get counseling from your father, too. While he's working with me, he'll learn good uses of our gifts from nature and their medicinal value. That can be quite empowering."

"I'm not sure you're getting my point."

"Oh, I am. *You* are not getting a significant fact of life." She put her cup down. "Everything is potentially harmful. However, the reverse is not true. *Not* everything is potentially healthy. And, until you give up your sugar habit, I don't think you're in any place to look down upon any substance Madder may have abused in the past."

"I cannot get arrested for eating cookies."

"If it were a perfect world, you would." Ma chinked her teacup to my coffee cup before drinking. I may have sighed before I sipped my coffee.

"Anyway, Pearl's harmless. She's all bitterness and bile; no action." Ma set her cup down. "I tried to help her. I really did."

"Help her what?" Mel asked.

"Be happy."

"Who's Pearl?" Jacqueline asked.

"She's that florist we were calling the other day," Mel answered.

"Oh, she is miserable." Jacqueline nodded.

"How do you know her?" I asked Ma.

"We met years ago at an herbology class." Ma waved her hand. "It was one of those stereotypical cases of the average student being jealous of the star pupil. I was the star pupil, of course."

"Of course." Mel kicked my leg under the table.

"I did my best to befriend her. I'd just finished my Reichi training and had even offered to do an energy clearing for her."

"Ooo! That sounds wonderful!" Jacqueline piped in. "Can you do one for me? After the funeral, of course."

"Absolutely, my dear. I'd be delighted." Ma patted her hand. "Anyway, Pearl refused. She wanted nothing to do with me. So I let it go. I didn't see her for years after that. Not until the flower show of twenty-eleven."

"That's when you met Mr. Wooley, right?" I touched Mel's arm. "And Sy Weissman."

"Right. What wonderful men. They both understood where I was coming from artistically. Many of the florists, including Pearl, did not. They were too entrenched in what they thought a flower show should be." She leaned back, shaking her head slowly. "In the end, they won."

"Do you remember anyone else from back then?" Mel asked. "Anyone on the side with you, Wooley, and Weissman?"

Ma twirled a dreadlock as she thought about it. "Most people tried to stay out of the fray. I'm sure there were a couple others. I just can't recall their names right now."

Chapter 28: Forewarned

After Ma and Jacqueline left, I tried calling Leeann Weissman. Her phone went to voice mail. I hung up instead of leaving a message because I wasn't sure exactly what to say to her.

Mel said she had some ideas for research so she hit the computer. I called Pearl Slack to place more orders for flowers for clients who wanted to send some to Mr. Wooley's funeral. I also placed an order for a dozen red roses for another client's mother.

I looked over the list of clients who had sent Mr. Wooley flowers. It seemed odd to me that so many people wanted to send something for him when very few were close enough to him to know what was really going on in his life. Although he was relatively famous. His face was in the social pages of the paper back when everyone read papers. Now it was often on the Web. At least it was until he went on his "world tour."

Regardless, he was well known. Very well known. People would recognize him on the street when he was dressed as a man.

Could it be he was fooling himself thinking that no one knew who he was when he strutted about as Ms. Shelly?

He had a few places where he habitually went as a man or a woman. He liked to have coffee at La Colombe near Rittenhouse Square and he frequented The Franklin for a little gin in the evenings. Could he have been at one of those places and been recognized last week? Certainly someone would remember seeing a man in drag at least. If so, would they have noticed if maybe, just maybe, someone had followed him outside?

I sat at the dining-room table to handwrite a list of Mr. Wooley's favorite haunts. I figured Mel and I could make our rounds and ask the people working in those places if they'd seen him recently.

Feeling like a proper detective with good ideas, I made a pot of coffee.

While it brewed, Ezra's new insulin pump arrived. He tore up the stairs faster than an underage drinker runs out the backdoor when the police show up. He ripped open the packaging insisting on setting it up himself, which meant I needed to do something with my hands.

Shortbread seemed to be the perfect thing. It needed only a few ingredients: flour, cornstarch, sugar and butter. And it required much squishing and hand mixing until it formed a nice, crumbly ball. Somehow I managed not to smash it against Todd's head when he asked Ezra why he didn't just drink the insulin.

I pressed the shortbread into a round, spring-form pan, imprinting the tines of a fork around the edges. I poked the top in several places then very lightly I carved *NEP* in the center, for Nora Eloise Potts, before popping it in the oven.

Ezra finished programming his new pump and inserted an inset into his stomach. Todd's face found a new color spectrum as it took on a shade of green that Pantone had yet to discover.

"How often do you have to do that?" Todd asked.

"Every three days," Ezra said. He turned the oven light on to look through the front glass. "How soon 'til that's done?"

I checked the timer. "Just a little over a half hour."

"Cool." He kissed me on the cheek. "C'mon, Dad, let's get back to GTA," he said before disappearing down the stairs.

Todd hesitated. "Are you worried about him going to Japan?" he asked.

"I'd worry less if I knew you were worrying, too."

"Man!" He rocked back on his heels and ran his hands through his hair. "I never understood how intense things could be with him. I mean, he's a champ the way he handles it and all but . . ."

"But yeah. A lot could go wrong." I folded my arms and leaned my backside against the counter. "And you haven't even seen him have to deal with a low yet."

"I can't take the offer away now, though, can I?" he asked.

"It wouldn't be nice. He'd be upset. He'd probably blame it on me, thinking I talked you out of it."

"What should I do?"

"Educate yourself as much as you can. I'll make sure you're stocked up on supplies. Then you gotta help him stay on top of it all."

He visibly swallowed as he held my gaze.

I felt my jaw drop, not in a surprised-with-delight-kind-of way but in a you're-a-complete-jerk-kind-of-way.

"Or you can just skip out on him and leave it up to me to figure out a way to make it right with him. I've had lots of practice with that." I spun around and turned the faucet on at the sink to wash the dishes.

A little while later, I scrunched my hair into curls and waves with a diffuser attachment on my hair dryer. I figured the added height and texture would hide my darkening roots better. I was looking forward to getting out of the house. Todd was still there hanging with Ezra. While I knew his presence was good for Ez, it was giving me so much angst, I was almost tempted to steep Ma's tea in milk.

I followed up with Carolyn as I did my makeup.

"How did things work out with Ricky?" I asked her as I oh-so-carefully lined my upper right eyelid, pulling out and up to make a wing-like effect.

"They couldn't be any better," she said. "He's having dinner with Gerard and me tonight. He's a delightful boy."

"Did he say how he found you?" I truly was curious. As a potential private detective, I needed to know how people did these kinds of things.

"Well, he always knew he was adopted. His adoptive mother had told him only *some young woman in the Poconos gave you to us.* He loves art. I guess he gets that from me. Anyway, he started taking courses at the museum. One day, he saw my ears somehow and looked me up. My name there is listed as Carolyn Clark Hoskinson. He went on the Internet and found some kind of public record for when a Carol Lynn Clark in Meadowbrook, Pennsylvania gave birth to a boy on his birthday and didn't list his father. Isn't he a smart boy?"

"Yes, he is." Though I had People Finder, which was just as good. My cell buzzed with a text. I ignored it.

"So he confronted his adoptive mother with the information. She said it sounded like his birth mother. And that's that."

"Are you sure? The note sounded so angry. Does he want anything from you?"

"He just wants to know me and why I gave him up. I told him everything. He forgave me. Now we both want to try having some kind of relationship. Oh Peri, I feel like you've just given me the gift of life. I feel so complete now."

"I'm so glad I could be of help," I said. "Though I have to be completely honest with you. I had to confide in my cousin."

"About me? Why?"

"I needed her help. You can trust her not to expose any of your past. We're becoming business partners and extending my services to include private detective work."

"I see." She paused. "Actually, I think it makes perfect sense for you to do that."

I remained silent, sending up a prayer that she wouldn't add something about it being a *natural outcropping of my many talents*, like my mother would say.

"I do. You're so good at researching and problem solving," she said, answering my prayer. "I shall post a check for twenty-five thousand in the mail to you today. Though what you've done for me is priceless. Thank you, Peri! And thank your cousin."

"I will." I clicked off. The message that had come in was from Noreen: *Friday. 10:00.*

Todd and Ezra were in the living room and I was still upstairs when Gabe arrived. Todd must have let him in because he was at the bottom of the stairs getting ready to call up for me when I started bounding down the steps.

He remained silent, his eyes fixated on my chest.

I was showing a bit of cleavage in my purple, cowl-neck silky top.

Judging by Todd's reaction, I may have over compensated a little in my desperation to appear anything other than stressed, uptight, and un-chill.

"Can I get by?" I asked.

Silently Todd stepped out of the way.

"Hi, Gabe," I smiled at him and took a breath. "And hey there, Raphael." I bent at the knees, stiffly, to pat the dog's head. "I don't think I introduced you to my son the last time you met. Ezra, this is Gabe. Gabe, Ezra." I did my best Vanna White impression. Todd made a noise behind me. "And, that's Todd." I pointed with my thumb. "Ezra's dad."

I opened the radioactive closet and shut the door without grabbing a jacket. I'd rather be cold. "So there are leftovers in the fridge," I offered my son.

"We finished them at lunch today," Ezra said. "Dad's taking me out for sushi."

"Sushi?" I asked Todd. "He's never eaten sushi." I sucked on my lips, lipstick be damned.

"Yeah, well, I figured I'd introduce him to it since he'll be eating a lot of it in the summer."

I inhaled sharply and held my breath.

"You'll be happy to know I got this app on my phone," Todd continued. "It helps us with the carb counts."

I exhaled, forcing a smile. "Great. Good job." I realized I was clenching my fists and relaxed my hands. "Okay, so I guess I just need my purse. I'll be right back," I said to Gabe.

Mel was still at the computer in the dining room. "Want me to bring you leftovers?" I asked.

She swirled around in the chair. "Wowsa!" She grinned. "You look amazing! Todd's bringing stuff back for me. But, yeah, leftovers would be good. I'm not sure I like sushi."

"Sure." I tried to look behind her at the computer monitor. "Whatcha doin'?"

"Research." Her grin broadened.

"I see. Promise me you won't go anywhere without me tonight."

"I'll do my best to stay home."

"That's not the same thing."

"I don't want you to get mad at me for two reasons—for my

promise and for not staying home."

I sighed.

"You're going to hyperventilate one of these days from doing that too much." She swung back around to face the computer. "Go. Go have fun."

"I will. If you have a chance, find someplace to get rid of all that china in the closet. It's creeping me out. I'm going to have to buy new coats. I don't think I can wear any of the ones hanging in there anymore."

"I'm already watching a Geiger counter auction on ebay."

Outside, I discovered I didn't need my jacket after all. It was warmer than usual for a late April evening, which was a pity because I had no reason to encourage an arm around me.

"It's so nice, do you just want to walk somewhere?" I asked anyway. "Or did you have a plan?"

"No plan. Where can we walk to from here?"

"My cousin, Ed's pub is nearby. It's called Ed's First Pub."

"Ed's your cousin?"

"Yes. You met his wife the other day, Melissa. How do you know him?"

"I live a couple of blocks away from Ed's Fourth Pub. Great pizzas."

"Indeed. So are you good with a pie from Ed's First?"

He was. So was Raphael, it seemed. I caught Gabe up on the lack of progress we'd made regarding Mr. Wooley's murder and explained what had happened to Ezra.

"Sounds like a tough life for the kid," he said as he opened the door to Ed's First Pub.

"It can be." I said over the *Yo, Peri!* yells. "The pump makes it easier to manage the disease."

We sat at a table for two. Raphael laid by Gabe's feet.

"Looks like you're on good terms with your son's dad," Gabe said glancing over the menu.

"I don't know if you'd call it that. He lives in Japan and visits Ezra maybe once a year." I tossed my menu aside. I wasn't even sure why I picked it up since I knew it by heart. "He's saying he wants to move back here next summer to be a bigger part of Ez's life."

"That's a good thing."

"Maybe. He's not very reliable and . . ." I sighed. "You know what?" I reached across the table and tilted his menu away from him. "I'd rather not talk about that. It'll just put me in a bad mood and I want to have a nice time tonight."

"Deal." He threw his menu down. "Are we sharing a pie or do you want something else?"

"Let's share." I scooted my chair so my back was to the bar. The other tenders didn't keep it as neat and clean as I did. Given all the stressors in my life lately, I knew I'd find it mighty difficult not to go back there and set it right.

"Hey Per! Can you get me a beer?" Lou yelled. He was sitting a new woman, which probably meant his Special Eddy hadn't worked on Saturday night.

"No, but Jenna can," I hollered back.

Gabe laughed. "What was that about?"

"I bartend here sometimes."

He nodded. "I thought you were a . . . a lifestyle something."

"Lifestyle Manager. I am. I do this to supplement my income whenever someone calls in sick here."

"Yeah, being a single mom can be tough, I know."

"It sure can. However, my cousin Mel is going to become my business partner. We're planning to add some services. Hopefully I won't have to tend here much longer." I rolled my fingers on the table wondering just what in the hell Jenna and Katie were doing that was making them dawdle instead of pouring everyone drinks. Lou wasn't the only one with a dry mouth. We were still waiting for someone to approach us.

"What kinds of things do you do?" he asked. "Besides the party planning."

Something pressed against my leg. I reached down and touched fur. "Aaa!" I jumped out of my chair. "What does it want from me?"

Gabe's eyes were wide and serious. "I don't know. What happened?"

"That dog . . . Raphael was on my leg. He was leaning against me."

Gabe smiled. "He must have sensed you were tense. He was trying to calm you."

"Why would he do that?"

"That's what he's trained to do."

I felt myself swallow.

"He was trained to work with me. He doesn't usually pick up on vibes from other people. He must like you. Otherwise he wouldn't have bothered."

"Why would he like me?"

"Doesn't everybody?" He smirked as Jenna finally set a couple of coasters down on the table.

"Sorry it took so long to get over here, Peri," she said. "Katie and I were trying to talk Derek into going home before he gets hammered."

I glanced over at Derek before returning to my chair. "I'll take care of him," I said.

We ordered our drinks and pizza. I saw Noel leave the men's room.

"I'm sorry," I said to Gabe. "I should have realized what it would be like here before I suggested it. I promise, I'll do my best to have no more interruptions after this one."

"What do you mean?"

I held my hand up to him then grabbed Noel's as he walked by on the way to his table.

"Hey Noel, can you take Derek home?"

"Aw, Per, why do you always ask me?"

"Because you live across the street from him."

"Just about everybody in this bar lives close to him. Including you. You have to pass his house. Why don't you take him home?"

"Look, Noel, he's not the only one who needs help here, am I right?" I pulled him down to sit in the seat next to me. "Don't think everyone hasn't noticed. Your wife always leaves here with her sister because she doesn't want to be out as late as you. You always leave about five minutes later. When I have you take Derek home, you're in danger of Lorraine seeing you drop him off and you not coming home because you're probably going to meet up with—"

"Fine. I'll take him home." He stood.

"And Lorraine, too. Why don't you go over there and say, 'Hey, honey, let's call it an early night'? Then try to have a good time with your wife, huh?"

He worked his jaw. "Everyone has noticed?" he asked.

"Except for Lorraine."

He turned around and slapped Derek on the back. The drunk fell over.

"Come on, man," Noel said, picking him up. "Let me pay my tab and I'll take you home."

Noel walked toward his table.

Gabe winked at me. "You're a sly one."

"See that? You'll never get one over on me."

"I consider myself forewarned."

Chapter 29: All Alone

Somehow my date with Gabe ended without us having to leave early to get my mother out of jail. I took it as a good sign. He (and Raphael) walked me home. He was quieter on the trip home and pulled back when we reached my stoop.

"You okay?" I turned to ask.

"Yeah." He smiled in the porch light, though his eyes reflected something that wasn't so happy.

"You sure?" I sat on my steps.

"I'm good, uh," he scratched the back of his neck. I recognized the move and glanced down. Raphael was leaning into him. Gabe was definitely nervous, or anxious, or some other –ous that was not smile-worthy.

"Uh . . ."I took his other hand.

"You take care of everyone, don't you?"

"That's what people say."

"Look, um . . . is that why you went out with me?"

"What do you mean?"

"Did you think I needed someone to take care of me?"

"I didn't even think of that."

"Then why did you go out with me?"

I sighed as I dropped my head to the side. "You mean besides the fact that you're hot, you're nice and you seem to have a good sense of humor?"

"Okay, okay." He tugged on my hand. "I just wanted to make sure I wasn't another project for you." He pulled me up and lightly kissed my lips.

The next day, Mel waited until Ezra left for school and for me to start drinking my second cup of coffee before she broke the news.

"So I didn't go anywhere last night," she said sitting across from me.

"Mel's a very good girl," I said in a baby voice before I realized that was probably a preamble to something I didn't want to hear. I changed my tune. "What did Mel do?"

"I had a long, a very long, chat with Leeann Weissman."

"On the phone?"

She nodded. "I think we're BFFs now."

"Oh my God!" I covered my mouth with my hand then burst out laughing. "You're insane, you know that?"

"Maybe. But I'm having so much fun." She laughed. "It's so good to hear you laugh again, Peri. Did you get laid last night?"

"What? No! It was our second date!" I sipped my coffee. "Anyway, did you learn anything helpful?"

"Maybe. I learned her husband had a poison in his system called grayanotoxin when he died."

"From what?"

"She doesn't know."

"Did you research it?"

"Not yet. Here's some good news: she officially hired us to be the private detectives to find out who gave it to him."

"Seriously?"

"Seriously."

I set my cup in its saucer and leaned toward Mel. "Explain."

"I found your standard contract on your computer, changed it up a little and used your hourly rate for non-retainer clients. Actually, I doubled your hourly rate for non-retainer clients. I e-mailed it to her and she e-mailed it back, with an e-signature, this morning."

I leaned back in my chair. I could feel my mouth hang slack.

"Impressed, aren't you?" she grinned, nodding.

"I think we should have become partners years ago."

After our celebratory cup of coffee, we went over the to-do list for the day. She was going to research grayanotoxins while I went to Mr. Wooley's townhouse to pack away all the nonperishable foods and throw out everything else. Afterward, we'd hit La Colombe to see if he'd been there recently, then maybe go out to The Franklin at night.

As I drove out to his place, I realized the best part of having Mel as a partner is that she loved to research stuff on the computer. I, on the other hand, loved to be physically doing things. We were a good pair that way. And twice my regular hourly rate for detective work?

I wiggled with joy in my seat while I waited for a red light. That pricing move was sheer genius.

I stopped by a storage company to purchase boxes, and then stopped again at a Wawa convenience store to get a large cup of coffee. Soon enough I was standing outside of Mr. Wooley's back door thinking I'd rather be eating dinner with my mother than entering that townhouse, especially from that door, all alone in the morning. Just like last Friday.

I was completely spooked. More than spooked, I was downright scared. I wasn't sure of what. I just had this feeling in my stomach that something bad was going to happen to me in there.

I put the key in the lock anyway.

"Really, Peri," I said to myself. "What worse could happen than what already did?"

Even though I could turn the key, I couldn't make myself open the door. I wanted back up, moral support. Not my mother, though. She'd be too distracting. Mel needed to work on the research. However, Jacqueline might be perfect.

I stayed outside while I called her.

"Good morning," I said as cheerfully as I could. "I'm over at your dad's townhouse. I'm about to pack all his nonperishable food to give it away to a food shelter."

"That's very nice, Peri. Good thinking."

"I was wondering if you'd like to help me."

"Oh, no. That sounds like something you should do."

"I will. I, I didn't mean it like that." Completely distracted from my case of the heebie-jeebies, I opened the back door and entered

Mr. Wooley's kitchen. "What I meant was, maybe now would be the perfect time for you to pick out exactly what you'd like to keep. I'm sure you don't want to sell everything with the house, right? There must be something of sentimental value here for you."

"Hmmm . . . I suppose you're right. I hadn't thought of that. Yes." I heard a click, as if call-waiting was interrupting our call. She paused. "Stay tuned. I'll call you back in a flash." She hung up.

I sighed and slipped my phone into my back pocket. Inside his home I opened the pantry closet and eyed up what was there. Then peaked in the cabinets.

I went out to my SUV to get the boxes. Back in the kitchen it was deathly quiet while I worked. Though periodically I thought I heard a creek, or a crack, or some other unexplainable sound. The hair on the back of my neck wouldn't stay down. And despite being warm from the rush of work, I had goose bumps.

Jacqueline took her time calling back. I had finished all the cabinets and had started on the pantry when her call came through.

"I so appreciate your thoughtfulness, Peri," she said. "And yes, there are a few things I want."

"Great. You want to swing by now, while I'm here to pack them up?" The sound of a car going down the alley startled me. I looked through the back window too late to catch a glimpse.

"Heavens, no," she said. "I really can never go in that building ever again."

"I understand." I sighed. "So what do you want?"

"The silver tea set. Father and I used to enjoy our loose leaf tea together. That would be the only thing of his I truly want."

"Just the tea set?"

"Yes. Though it's a large set. The coffeepot, a hot water kettle and burner, a chocolate pot and a giant silver tray are all in the hutch in the dining room. The teapot, sugar bowl and tongs, creamer, and honey pot are all in the glass-front cupboard in the kitchen."

I turned around and saw the gleaming silver. "I see it, now," I said. "I'll bring it home with me today."

"Very good. I'll head over there later to meet you."

I put my phone back in my pocket. Not much was left in the pantry. I stood with the door opened and stared inside. Again, I thought I heard something. Then all was quiet.

In the pantry there were only root vegetables stored in clear, plastic bins. A musty odor came from the potatoes. The onions were rank. My eyes stung. I reached toward that bin. Before I could actually grab a hold of it, someone pushed me against the shelves and slammed the door behind me.

Chapter 30: An Awful Lot of Sense

"AAAAAAAA!" I pushed my back against the pantry door. It opened a half inch then slammed back again. I felt the doorknob turn and jerk against my hand. Someone must have jammed something under it, locking me in. "Hey!" I pounded my fist on the door behind me.

As I should have expected, whoever had shoved me in had no interest in letting me out.

I didn't have much room. The pantry wasn't of the walk-in variety. It housed shelves and little else. Not even a light. There was about a foot of space between the shelves and the door. I filled that space. I couldn't even turn around.

I did have room to move sideways a little, which allowed me to remove my cell phone from my back pocket. I dialed Detective Beatty's number.

"Someone just locked me in the pantry at Mr. Wooley's townhouse," I said when he picked up.

"Who?"

"If I knew, I would have said their name!" I yelled. "Get me out of here!"

"We'll send someone right away."

Next, I dialed my house. Mel answered.

"Someone locked me in the pantry at Mr. Wooley's townhouse,"

I said to her.

"Really? Who?"

"You're kidding me!" I shouted. "How the hell would I know?"

"Sorry. That was stupid," she said. "You want me to come get you?"

"I just called the police. I think they're coming. I . . . I don't know. I just wanted some company." I could feel tears in my eyes. "I think I'm scared! And I can't be! There's no room in here for me to pass out. There's no room to fall down. The blood won't return to my head! I won't—"

"Stop!" she yelled. "There's no need to be scared."

"What? Then what do I need to be?" I may have been shrieking.

"Think about it," she said, calmly. "If someone wanted to hurt you, they would have. They wouldn't have shoved you in a closet."

That made an awful lot of sense at just the right time.

"Whew!" I relaxed against the door. "You're right. They just wanted me out of the way . . . why?"

"Beats me."

"Ugh. I'm not sure we're cut out for this detective business."

"We're just getting started," she countered. "So tell me, what kind of plants are around Wooley's townhome?"

"I don't know, why?"

"Grayanotoxins come from plants. Specifically plants from the Ericaceae family, though I don't know if I'm saying that right."

"I have no idea. That sounds like a question for my mother."

"Yeah, I was thinking that, too. I called her and got her voice mail."

"Peri?" yelled Beatty's voice.

"I gotta go. Police are here." I clicked off. "In here! In the pantry!"

I stayed while the police dusted for fingerprints. I gave my statement to some detective who wasn't Beatty, though the latter was there within hearing distance.

"Do you think this is connected to Mr. Wooley's death?" I asked him as I watched the buzz of activity around us.

"I have no proof. However, it seems more than coincidental." He walked through the kitchen. "Are you done in here?"

"For now, I guess so. I just gotta put these boxes in the truck and get his silver. His daughter, Jacqueline wants the silver."

He took my hand and pressed my thumb directly into the front of the microwave. "Dust this," he said. They did and got my print.

"That way we know which prints are yours. There's really not much else to go by unless you can tell if something is missing."

"I don't think so. I mean, I wouldn't know if something was taken out of the drawers. Should I call Jacqueline?"

"That'd be a good idea."

I called her cell. She was at my house. I had to lie and tell her the police were insisting she come. Mel agreed to come with her for moral support.

Only Beatty and a uniformed officer remained to take her statement. There were, after all, other crimes going on in the City of Brotherly Love. While we waited, he asked the inevitable question.

"Did you ask your mother who referred Noreen Parkerson to her?"

"Actually, I left a voice mail for Noreen, herself. She'll be here tomorrow at ten o'clock to clean. I'll have to let her in so I'll get more contact information from her then."

He made a note in his phone.

"I'll do my best to come by to talk to her myself."

Jacqueline had very little to say. She spent all of three and a half seconds inside the kitchen with her eyes cast downward the whole time, which I supposed meant she was telling the truth when she said she couldn't tell if anything was missing.

The uniformed officer left. Mel and Beatty helped me load the boxes of food into my Ford while Jacqueline paced the alley with the back of one hand pressed against her forehead. When we were finished, I called to tell her I was going to lock up.

"Could I trouble you to get that silver now?" she asked. "I honestly never want to come to this place again."

"Sure." I pulled one more empty box from the Explorer. Inside the townhouse, I gathered the items in the dining-room hutch first, then the stuff in the kitchen. Outside, I showed it to her before closing the box.

"Where's the honey pot?" she asked.

I went back inside but couldn't find a silver honey pot.

"Are you sure?" she asked when I returned the second time. "It wasn't a match to this. This is all Tiffany. The honey pot was Gorham. The bottom was crystal, the top silver. Oh, it's not really a honey pot. I think many people would say it's a jam jar. Go look for a jam jar."

I shook my head. "Whatever you call it, there's nothing else silver in there."

"Well, where is it?" she asked. I looked at Beatty.

"What did it look like?" he asked.

"It is probably as tall as my hand." She held up her palm. "The bottom is clear crystal with lily flowers etched into it. The lid is silver with the same floral pattern going around the edge with a little knob on top."

Beatty helped me drag Jacqueline back into the kitchen to find it.

It wasn't there.

"Do you suppose that's why I was shoved into the pantry?" I asked. "Someone stole it?"

"Maybe." Beatty shrugged. "It could be someone saw you opening the back door and thought a back-alley robbery would be easy. After he locked you in the pantry, maybe he panicked, grabbed one item and ran. Though I don't know why he wouldn't have taken the largest piece of silver he could carry."

"I'll make sure the standard alerts go out to local pawn shops," Beatty said. "If anything else happens, make sure you call me right away."

Mel and Jacqueline followed me to the food shelter. After unloading the donated foods, we all went to my house.

"God, I need coffee," I said as I entered the front door of my row home. I was now too spooked to go in the back.

"I think you'll be pleased," Mel said.

In the kitchen was a clean carafe with grinds and water at the ready. All I had to do was hit the *on* button.

"We should have become partners years ago." I hugged her. "And Jacqueline, I'm with you. I never want to go back to that townhouse again. At least not alone."

"How do I get my honey pot back?" Jacqueline asked.

"I don't know, Jac." Mel put her hand on her shoulder. "I mean unless it's somehow related to your dad's, um, you know, we may not ever find it."

She sat in a chair, resting her chin on her hand, pouting.

"Anyway," I started. "Jacqueline, I need to set up a foundation for your father. Any ideas about what he'd like?"

"Well, he liked art and dressing up." She leaned back to pull her gloves off, plucking one finger at a time. "Can you do a foundation for that?"

"I'm not sure how that would benefit anyone?"

"Is there a foundation for transgender people who don't have the funds to do the job?" Mel asked.

I leaned against the counter as I waited on the coffee. "I don't understand you," I said to Mel. "Sometimes you surprise me with the most brilliant suggestions and other times you, well, you don't."

"I don't understand which time this is." Mel sat at the table.

"A brilliant one." I laughed and pulled my ringing cell phone from my pocket. My Dad was calling.

"Hi, Dad."

"Peri, my sweet, please sit down and put your head between your knees," he said.

"Oh God." I handed the phone to Mel and did what he suggested.

Her voice came to me through a tunnel that connected me to a different universe.

"Uh uh. . . Really? . . . When? . . . What?. . . OH GOD! . . . Where?"

The next thing I know, we're standing in the hospital looking at my sedated mother in a hospital bed.

"Ma doesn't do hospitals," I said to Dad. "What the hell is going on?"

"Here's the doctor now, sweetheart." Dad turned me around. "If you feel the need to clean her room later, I've already found the janitorial closet with the supplies. I'll point you in the right direction."

Dr. Singh politely explained my mother's condition.

"She was found by her employee and brought in to the hospital," he said.

"What employee?"

"Maurice," Dad chipped in.

"Madder?"

"Yes. He came to the house just in time."

"As I was saying," Dr. Singh continued, "when he brought her in, she was presenting symptoms of a heart attack."

"My mother has the healthiest body of any person on the planet. She doesn't have heart attacks."

"She was experiencing atrial-ventricular block—"

"In layman's terms that means?"

"It means her heart had slowed down. The beats were too far apart for it to do its job."

I didn't say anything because I still wasn't sure what he meant. My mother's heart could never slow down. Her heart could never stop. At least not now. Not out of the blue like that. I needed my mom's heart to continue beating.

"Upon further examination," Dr. Singh said, "we believe she is suffering from some form of toxicity."

"Oh." Mel was at my side, clutching my arm.

"How does that make atrial slow heart whatever?" I asked.

"Certain toxins cause an inability to inactivate neural sodium channels, which—"

"You know what? Never mind." I shook my head. "What happens now?"

"Well, as you can see we had to sedate her. She was in quite the agitated state. The first thing to do, of course, was to get the heart pacing corrected. We are also giving her activated charcoal through the tube in her nose there." He pointed to her beautiful, tube-covered face. "It will absorb any toxins that haven't made it into her bloodstream yet. If we could find the source of the toxin, then we may be able to supply an antidote."

"It was probably grayanotoxin," Mel offered. "Does that help?"

"Yes." He frowned at her and lifted his hand as if only partially convinced he should nod. "If you can supply the source, that would be ideal."

Mel dragged me over to Dad.

"We need to go to your house."

"That's fine. It sounds like you know what you're doing." He kissed me on the cheek before returning to his chair by my mother's bed.

"Are you worried, Dad?" I asked him.

"Why would I be? As you said, your mom's probably the healthiest person there is. This is just a blip for her." He smiled at me. "Besides, you need to do something to channel your worrying. So go, my dear. Go do something. If she wakes up, I'll tell her where you went."

Chapter 31: A Delightful Thing

Mel drove Jacqueline and me in my SUV. I called Todd on the way to my parent's place and explained the situation to him.

"Will you hang with Ez, maybe take him to the hospital if he wants to see my mom?" I asked him.

"Sure. I'll wait for him at your place now."

"Good. There's a key under the back mat."

"No there isn't," Mel said. "I used it when I moved in last Saturday. I don't think I put it back."

"You'll have to wait for him outside." I hung up. "I kind of like that better," I said to the other women with a small laugh. "Actually, while I hate to admit it, I guess his visit is good timing."

"So maybe he's not pure evil?" Mel asked.

"I have no idea what he is." I dialed Beatty's number to tell him to meet us at my parents' place.

We parked street side in front of my parents' house. I used my key to open the front door. Inside, I immediately caught Mel as she tripped over the foo dogs that were still in the middle of the foyer.

"Now what do we do?" she asked.

"Ever notice how you only have part of the ideas?" I asked.

"Yes. It's because you're supposed to have the other half."

"I have an idea," Jacqueline piped in. "We should look in the kitchen. That's where people usually are when they are preparing or eating food to get poisoned, right?" She led the way as if she owned the place.

Once in the kitchen, she gave a shriek. "The honey pot!"

We all ran to the counter where a crystal and silver honey pot sat next to a ceramic teapot.

"What's it doing here?" Mel asked.

We stood as if we were a silent trio paying homage to a beautiful jam jar until the gong went off alerting us someone was at the front door.

"I'll get it," I said knowing it was probably Beatty. I was right.

"Wooley's honey pot is here." I took him to the kitchen.

"I'm not making the connection," Beatty said. "How did the honey pot get in your mother's kitchen?"

"We don't know that part," I said. "All we know is that my mom's in the hospital right now with poisoning. We think the honey might be toxic honey."

"How is that possible?" he asked.

"Mel," I called. "You're up."

She used her cell phone for back up. "If honey is made from bees that used plants from the Ericaceae family," she said, "then the nectar and the honey they produce from it will contain grayanotoxin." Which was news to me, I had assumed the poison had been put in the honey.

"What family of plants?"

"E-R-I-C-A-C-E-A-E. I don't know how to pronounce it." She put her phone in his face. "It includes rhododendrons and andromedas, plants that are all over Philadelphia according to the Horticultural Society."

"Does anyone know where your mother was earlier today, when you were locked in the pantry at Wooley's former residence?"

I shook my head, suddenly nauseous at what he was implying. My ears rang.

"I need to . . . go sit down." I ran to the living room.

Mel followed immediately. Jacqueline came a few seconds later.

"He's calling for a crime-scene team."

"What does that mean?" Mel asked.

"We'll dust for fingerprints and check for other evidence to see who else has been in this kitchen," Beatty said as he entered the room. He squatted in front of me. "Are you alright?"

"I don't know."

"She's in good hands." Mel sat next to me.

He stood. "I'll wait for the team. Don't touch anything."

Outside, he stood in front of the curtainless window, as if he wanted to keep an eye on us.

"It sounded to me," I said, "like he thinks my mom locked me in the pantry today. Is that how he sounded to you guys?"

"Yeah," Mel said. "Do you think it's possible?"

Jac sat on my other side.

"I don't think Honey's the kind of person to do that," she said. "Frankly, I find it very suspect that my father's honey pot with potentially toxic honey in it would be in your mother's house. If you ask me, someone is framing your mother for my father's murder."

Which was a delightful thing for me to consider at that moment.

"Say, shouldn't that sexy detective be sending out the honey to see if it *is* toxic?" Jacqueline stood. "I'm going to talk to him about it. Right after I powder my nose." She sashayed out the room.

"Is that what you're thinking?" I whispered to Mel as the powder room door shut behind Jacqueline.

"It puts your mother in a more innocent light than what I was thinking."

"Yeah. Me, too." I pulled out my phone. "I mean, I can't imagine my mom killing anybody. It's just that ... ."

"Sometimes she doesn't seem all that sane. Yeah, I get it. And," Mel went on, "I can see her not wanting any harm to come to you, so she'd shove you in the closet instead of telling you she needed to get the honey pot from Mr. Wooley's townhouse to hide how she killed him."

As Jacqueline had suggested, once Beatty's team came by to check for fingerprints and whatever, they took the honey to be analyzed.

I called Dad to check on Ma. Nothing was different. She was still sedated. She was expected to sleep there all night. There was nothing we could do so Dad said we should just go home.

I didn't want Ezra to worry, so I followed his suggestion.

Gabe called as we headed in that direction.

"Been thinking about you all day," he said. "Is your son's father still in town? Can you go out again tonight?"

"I probably could. I'm not sure if I'd be good company, though."

"What's wrong?"

I explained my mother's situation.

"I really just want to bake some cookies," I said. "I like to bake when I'm stressed or worried."

He laughed. "Can I bring some milk over?"

"A dessert wine would be better."

"I'll see you after dinner."

That was disappointing. I had hoped to have the cookies and wine *for* dinner.

I baked. Mel researched. Jacqueline disappeared, presumably to her condo. Ezra and Todd played video games in the basement.

Around six thirty, the boys came upstairs.

"What's for dinner, Ma?"

"Cookies." I pulled a sheet of oatmeal-raisin-chocolate-chip cookies from the oven.

"Seriously?" Todd took a bite of a chocolate-peanut-butter drop.

"Is Grandmom going to die?" Ezra asked, eyeing up the variety of cookies taking up all the counter space in my tiny kitchen.

"No!" I slammed the oven door shut and put the tray on a rack on the counter.

"You're obviously worried about her." He tugged on my arm until I finally turned around. "I can handle it. Tell me."

"I don't know what's going to happen to her. And there's nothing I can do about it but bake."

He hugged me.

"Dad," he said. "Ma bakes when she's stressed. Maybe we can do some kind of take-out—"

"Chinese would be great!" yelled Mel from the dining room.

"Maybe we could get some Chinese take-out," Ezra finished.

"We'll be right back," Todd said as Ez dragged him out of the kitchen.

"He's a really good kid," Mel came in. "And speaking of Chinese, I found a guy near Fabric Row who will be delighted to unload us of the red plates."

"How is that connected to Chinese anything?"

"It's china, right? The plates?"

I could only make my mouth open in response. No words came out.

"Which ones are the best?" she asked, picking through the cookies.

"The coconut macaroons."

She piled several on a plate while eyeing up the white-chocolate-macadamia-nut cookies.

"Those are for Gabe and me."

"Ah yes, to go with the dessert wine." She opened the fridge to get the milk. "Any word from your dad?"

"Nope."

"That's probably good. It means nothing bad is going on with her."

"I like that theory."

"You're still worried she might have killed Wooley, though."

"I am. I just can't figure out why she would do it." I sighed as I slid into a chair. "What are you doing?"

She took the opposite chair with her macaroons and milk.

"I just finished looking up everyone who was associated with that flower show the year your mom was on the advisory panel."

I stole one of her cookies. "And?"

"And, the only people to have died since then are Wooley and Weissman."

I coughed, nearly choking on my cookie. "You get right to the point, huh?"

"So I'm all out of ideas about how to make a connection to those men. They both know your mom. They both did that flower show."

"Maybe their deaths aren't connected at all," I said. "Maybe we got a little ahead of ourselves on that one."

"That would just suck because I have no idea how to figure out what happened to Weissman."

"We'd have to ask my mom." I sighed as the doorbell rang. "Hopefully, she'll make it through this heart-poisoning thing so we can ask her about it during visiting hours at the jail." I reached over and stole another cookie. "I have another idea. Tomorrow let's go visit a couple of Mr. Wooley's favorite places. He lived in drag for this past year, supposedly in secret. I'm wondering if people who saw him on a regular basis might have recognized him. Maybe they'd say he was in last Thursday and left with a particular so-and-so."

"Sounds like you're grasping at straws."

I stood to answer the front door. "I have nothing else to grasp right now."

Gabe and Raphael came in. I brought them to the kitchen.

"Wow!" Gabe said. "You were pretty busy."

Mel found the corkscrew and handed it to him. "Yeah. You have perfect timing. The last batch just cooled."

Gabe opened the wine as she pulled out three glasses, not two. Before I could say anything to her about her poor math skills, my cell phone ring.

"This can't be good," I said showing Mel the Philly PD name on my screen.

"Think they picked up Jacqueline again?" she asked. "Maybe it's her way of flirting with Detective Beatty."

Instead, it was Madder.

"Peri! I'm so glad you answered," he said. "I need your help."

"What's up, Madder? Why are you calling from the police department?"

"I was arrested."

"What?"

"Yeah. They think I poisoned your mom."

"What?" I said again because really, there's only so much a woman can take in one day before she loses her vocabulary.

"Yeah, my fingerprints were all over a honey jar that poisoned her. I didn't do it, Peri, honest. Can you help me? I have no money for bail."

"Don't you have an attorney or something?"

"No." His voice dropped to a whisper. "You know what my record's like. I'm surprised they're even offering bail. I got no one right now. I'm calling you because I really thought your mom was gonna be my new beginning. I took her to the hospital. Please, Peri, you gotta help me. I didn't do it."

I sighed. "Okay. I'll see what I can do. Sit tight."

"I have no other option."

I clicked off the call. "Put the cork back in the bottle, Mel. Madder's been arrested for attempting to kill Ma. We gotta get him out of jail."

"How many times a month does she visit the jail?" Gabe asked Mel with a laugh.

I laughed, too. "How much do you think bail costs?" I asked them.

"How would I know?" Mel said.

Gabe shrugged. "I think it has to be cash or something, right? Isn't that why there are so many pawn shops near bail bond places?"

"Yuck." I sat at the table and dialed my Dad.

"How's Ma?" I asked when he picked up.

"About the same. Still sleeping. She's beautiful even when she sleeps, you know that?"

"Yes, I'm sure she is. Listen, you know Madder, right?" I almost ran my fingers through my hair. Thankfully, I remembered how loaded it was with products to keep all the curl and height in place. My hand could get stuck in there. But I needed to do something with it.

"Maurice? Yes, I met him yesterday," Dad said. "Lovely man."

"Right, um, right." Something was pressing on my leg. It was Raphael. I scratched his head. My breath came easier. I continued scratching. "Well, the thing is, Dad, he's in jail. He's been arrested for attempting to kill Ma."

"That's ridiculous! He brought her to the hospital. He's the one who called me."

"Yeah, well I guess the police are more focused on his past record. Anyway, um, he needs help with bail money."

"I'll call our attorney right away."

"Great, thanks Dad." I hung up and looked Raphael in the eyes. I think I told him *thank you*. "Actually, the wine's a go. Dad's taking care of him.

Chapter 32: Continue To Be You

Ma woke before Ezra left for school the next morning.

Dad called with the good news.

"Can I speak to her?" I asked. He put her on.

"Whoever would have thought I'd wind up in a place like this?" she asked.

"Absolutely no one, but I'm glad you did."

"It's the most ridiculous set up ever!" she laughed. "I had to rip out my own IVs because the nurses were waiting for a doctor to say I didn't need them. Now who better than I could tell you what my body needs?"

I laughed. "I'm not sure if you're insane or if you're the smartest person alive. I am sure you sound like your old self, though. Do you know what happened?"

"Not really. Madder had just come from the flower shop to work with me for the rest of the day. When he arrived at the door, there was a package on the step. A pretty white box. He brought it in and pulled the jar of honey out."

"Any note with it?"

"No. I thought it was odd, but I'd just recently joined the Philadelphia Beekeeper's Guild. I assumed it was a special induction gift. You know, like a secret message the way the Mason's work."

"Only you would think that, Ma."

"I had just made tea and thought I'd plop in a little of their honey. I was sure it was raw."

"I think that honey was poisonous."

"Really? Why would they send me poisonous honey?"

"I don't think it was from the beekeeper people, Ma." I pinched the bridge of my nose. "That honey pot was taken out of Mr. Wooley's house."

"Oh goodness."

"Yes. The police have it now. They're testing it for Grayo-something."

"Grayanotoxin, probably," she said for me. "Ha! The common name for honey poisoning is Mad Honey disease. Isn't that hilarious?" She laughed. "If I ever got angry, I guess that's what you would say was wrong with me!"

"So you know honey can be toxic?"

"Who doesn? It's actually an ancient weapon. The Turks perfected it."

"Weapon?"

"Yes. It was used with some warring faction somewhere. I can't quite recall the details. It's not the easiest way to kill someone. You really have to limit the bees' world to intentionally make the nectar, hence the honey, poisonous. It usually only makes people sick or incapacitated for a couple hours. Ordinarily, the victims live. Whoever did this was really, really good."

"I wouldn't call them that."

"Wait a minute poopsie." Ma spoke to someone else on her end. "Oh, I think I get to go home soon," she said to me. "They're letting me out of this joint!"

"Great. I'll see you later today."

I hung up and gave the good news to Ezra before he sped out the front door to go to school.

In the dining room Mel pulled a paper from the printer and handed it to me.

"Our to-do list," she said.

I glanced over it. There wasn't much on it that didn't have to do with Mr. Wooley.

"Oh crap," I said. "We should have taken a dress from his closet yesterday to give to the funeral home."

"Why not take one of those?" Mel pointed to the gowns on the table.

I looked at the list of people who had been called about the funeral.

"Can't. Marissa Slocum is probably coming on Saturday. She can't have anyone, dead or alive, wear one of those dresses until after she's seen in hers in a couple of months."

"Not even an old dude in a coffin?"

"I would think especially not even an old dude in a coffin." I sipped my coffee. "Ugh. I meant it when I said I don't want to go inside his house again. I was just going to let Noreen in and then lock up when she's done. Now not only do I have to go inside, I have to go into his bedroom." I pointed a forefinger into a nonexistent dimple, tilted my head and smiled, wide, at her. "Will you go with me? Pretty please? With a cherry on top?"

She pretended to glare at me, or maybe she really did.

"Only if you talk Gabe into being our bodyguard."

He laughed at the suggestion when I called, but quickly agreed.

"So do you think there's something wrong with him, Mel?" I asked as we drove to pick him up. "I mean, think about it. After all the craziness going on in my life this week, he's still interested in me."

"Maybe that's the thing. You're definitely different."

"So do you see what I mean? What kind of guy wants—"

"Some woman who's different from ninety-nine percent of the others out there?"

"You think I'm *that* different? I was talking about my psychotic family shenanigans."

"Peri," she turned in her seat. "Have you noticed I haven't even thought of calling Ed this week?"

"Actually, I'd been hoping you were calling him when I wasn't around."

"He's called me every day to check in on me."

"That's nice."

"It would be, except we have nothing to say to each other. I haven't begun to tell him about what's going on with Mr. Wooley, with you, or even with your mom."

"Why?"

"Because he wouldn't be so accepting of it. He'd want me to quit working with you because he'd think I couldn't handle it. Actually, he'd want me to quit because he couldn't compete with it."

"I don't understand." I pulled into the lot at It's Your Mission MMA. "Compete with what?"

"Peri, everyone likes you because you tackle life head on. Yes, you try to control it, organize it and make it go according to your master plan."

"Which is a lovely way of saying I'm a control freak, by the way." I beeped the horn.

"Perhaps, but the world needs control freaks. *Your* kind of control freakishness. My point is, that's what makes you special. Even when we all complain about it, you still continue to be you. You might grit your teeth or bite your tongue for a few minutes—and God knows you sigh all the time—but you're never apologetic about being you."

"I'm not sure if you're complimenting me or not."

"I am. What I'm saying is, I don't think my marriage is strong enough for me to find out who I really am and, let me be me, with the passion that you are you. *That's* what I want. I have no life force, or whatever you choose to call it, being Ed's wife."

"Life force? That sounds like another term from my mother."

"I think it is. Still, whatever life force I have, has to be repressed so that his is brighter, stronger, greater somehow. I'm not willing to be on the sidelines in our marriage anymore. I don't want to be a supporting role for Ed. And I don't think Ed will be able to handle that."

"Wow." I leaned back in my seat.

"So, I think if you find a guy who enjoys you being you so much, don't worry if he's crazy. Just enjoy the ride," she finished as Gabe and Raphael exited the building.

"Even if he has a dog?" I asked.

"The dog seems to like you, too."

I had insisted on meeting Noreen at the front door of Mr. Wooley's townhome. I seemed to have better luck making an entrance from that angle.

Inside I led the housecleaner directly to the pantry.

"There are some root vegetables in here that have a pretty strong odor," I said opening the door. "Other than that and the refrigerator, I got all the food out."

"Very good," she nodded as she eyed up the kitchen. I hated that I couldn't help but agree with my mother. Noreen was only probably in her early forties, yet she dressed as if she were twice her age in polyester pants and a shirt that looks remarkably like a man's bowling shirt. She had very broad shoulders, almost no chest, had a slight hump to her back, very short curly hair and unnaturally large, fleshy lips that were perpetually shiny. Shiny from spit, not gloss.

"So, uh, as you can see, there's lots of powder from all the police coming in to fingerprint the place."

"Oh yeah," she said, though it sounded as if she were surprised.

"The dining room is just as bad." I pointed.

She followed my finger and plodded into the dining room. I watched her circumnavigate the space. Her lips protruded further than normal as she nodded at whatever was going on inside her head.

"Hm," she eventually said, standing before me. "What kind of cleaning you want?"

I frowned. "Well, we're going to be putting this place up for sale, so if you could do a really good, deep cleaning, that would be great."

"That's double the money you know."

"I know."

"Be back in four hours."

"Will do."

Gabe and Melissa waited for me in the living room. She was sitting in a chair, feet propped on the coffee table, leafing through a magazine. Gabe was wrestling with Raphael on the floor. I cleared my throat, loudly.

They looked up at me.

"I'm going up to Mr. Wooley's room, now," I said. Mel waved. Gabe nodded. "I asked the two of you to come here because I didn't want to do this alone."

"Oh, right." Mel threw the magazine onto the coffee table and got up.

"Sorry." Gabe stood.

I screwed my face into a grimace. "You're acting like one of my family members," I said to him.

"Be careful," Mel added. "She'll take away your driving privileges if she gets really mad at you."

"If you hadn't snuck off twice to stake out Carolyn's building behind my back, I'd say drive my car whenever you want."

Gabe laughed. He took my hand and dragged me to the stairs. "C'mon. I'm guessing his bedroom would be up there."

He led us up the steps. They twisted around and ended in an open area. A life-size statue of Marilyn Monroe in a billowing white dress greeted us. Raphael sniffed her, his hackles raised.

"Three bedrooms?" Mel said, entering one at the end of the hall. Gabe and I waited. "This one has its own bath. Nothing in the closets, though." She went in the next as Gabe went into the one in the front of the house. I saw no reason to be the first in any of the rooms.

"This is the master!" Gabe hollered.

Mel exited the second room. "Do you realize this place has three bedrooms with private baths in each one?"

"I've never been up here." I stopped to let her enter the master ahead of me. "That is nice, though, eh?"

"You betcha." She turned, inside the door of the bedroom. "How much will this place go for?"

"Lots."

"Too many lots for us to buy?"

"Us as in?" I raised my eyebrows.

"You and me," she said. "I can't sleep on your sofa in that tiny row home for forever, you know." She turned back around and walked into the room.

I followed her. "You're seriously thinking of not going back to Ed?"

"I seriously am."

"First . . ." I blinked several times. "We gotta get through this murder investigation thing right now. I'll fix your marriage after that and then I won't have to worry about moving anywhere." I stepped around her, screamed and things went black.

Chapter 33: The Theory

When I woke, I was lying on the floor with both Gabe and Melissa bent over me.

"What happened?" I asked them.

"You passed out again," Mel said. "I think you saw that."

I slowly rotated my head to look where she was pointing. There, in the corner of Mr. Wooley's bedroom stood Mr. Wooley in a white pirate shirt, purple velvet morning coat and black satin pants.

"The wax figure!" I said. Gabe extended his hand to help me up. "I was wondering where it was."

"Is that what he looked like?" Mel asked.

We approached the figure.

"Yep. That's what he looked like," I said. "Identical. Isn't that amazing?"

"Why did he have a statue of himself?" Gabe asked.

"Remember when I said I had been planning a party for a client who was murdered?"

"Yes."

"Well, it was a funeral-themed party."

"In the springtime? Not at Halloween?"

"It wasn't to be spooky." I explained the theory behind coming out and bidding good-bye to his old self. "This wax figure was to be in the casket." I reached out to touch Mr. Wooley's cheek. It was smooth and cool.

"Is the dog wax, too?" he asked.

At the feet of the wax figure, Raphael was nose to nose with what appeared to be a sleeping dog curled up beside his master.

"Oh, um, that's Tiger."

"Tiger's a dog," Mel said.

"I see you're using your extrasensory detective abilities," I slapped her arm. "He was Mr. Wooley's pet."

"What is he now?" Mel asked.

"He's a freeze-dried dog. Oh. Yuck." I backed up until I was able to lean against Mr. Wooley's four-poster bed.

"I'm not sure if *yuck* is good enough," Mel said. She, too, backed up. "What do you mean by freeze-dried?"

"When Tiger passed away, Mr. Wooley sent him to a place where they used some kind of freeze-drying process to preserve the dog as lifelike as it could be preserved."

"Is that normal?" she asked, turning to Gabe.

"I've never heard of it," he said. "Why is it here now?"

"It was going to be put on the wax figure's chest in the coffin because Mr. Wooley had said that's what he wanted to happen to him."

"Ew. Are we going to have to take it home?" Mel asked.

"Not right now," I said. "I'll look in the stuff from the will again and make sure that's really what he wanted. Maybe he was just going for impact at the fake funeral, who knows? I mean, I don't want to have to come back here, but I also don't want to get stuck with that thing in my house if we don't need it."

Raphael pawed at Tiger's head and whined.

"Leave it," Gabe said. The dog sat, looking up at him. "So, really, I wasn't all that far off when I was confused by that 'lifestyle' title you have," he said to me. "Your Wooley guy was out there, huh?"

I laughed. "Mr. Wooley was a nice guy. He really was. He just always wanted to be a nice woman, I guess. Whew!" I shook my head. "Who'd a thunk, huh? The last thing I expected when I planned this funeral was for him to show up dead."

Mel opened a door to find a large walk-in closet and dressing room lined with red velvet. The back wall was mirrored. A red velvet chaise was in the center.

"Why would you ever need a chair in the center of your dressing room?" I asked.

"I think so you can see what you'll look like when you're sitting down," Mel offered. As if to prove her point, she reclined on the chaise, looked at herself in the mirror and fluffed out her hair.

I began perusing the racks.

"This is why I don't understand the whole transgender thing." Gabe pulled out a pair of black patent, peep-toe, platform stilettoes. "Why would anyone wear these? They look impossible to walk in."

"Sure, but they're adorable." Mel took them. "What size are they?"

"Mel! We need a black evening gown. Find. Evening. Gown," I ordered.

Eventually we settled on a sparkly one-shouldered number and the shoes Gabe had found, though I wasn't sure if shoes would even be necessary.

Out in the bedroom, Mel opened a dresser to rummage for underthings. "Think he'll need nylons?" she asked, pulling out a garter belt.

"I never met the man, but judging by what I'm seeing here today, I think he'd want the full regalia," Gabe said. He leaned against the bed. Raphael jumped up to sit by him.

"Yeah, probably so," I said to Mel. I squinted my eyes at Gabe and the dog. "Does he sleep with you?"

Gabe winked. "Maybe you'll find out one day."

Back downstairs Noreen was sitting at the kitchen table, reading a book.

"So you'll need four hours, right?" I asked her.

She nodded and waved her hand. "By two o'clock," she said. "I'll be done by two."

I glanced at the pantry and sniffed. The odor was mild. I stepped closer and sniffed again. Finally I put my head in the closet and took a long whiff.

"You all right?" Gabe asked.

"Yeah. I just thought . . . I'm not sure what I thought. C'mon, let's take these to the funeral home."

"Uh, could you drop me off first?" he asked. "I don't uh . . . I can't . . . Um, yeah. No funerals homes."

"Then I guess I'll have to find another date for Saturday," I joked.

His face went taut. "Seriously. It's okay. You don't have to go."

He nodded and scratched his neck. The dog leaned into him. I got the message: he'd been to enough funerals for a while.

Mel and I parted company with Gabe and Raphael at the studio. We left the clothes at the funeral home and then I decided to drop by Custom Floral to pick up something pretty for my mother. I made Mel stay in the Ford.

Pearl was working alone in the store. I knew she was there, because as soon as I walked in my eyes stung and watered.

"Peri!" she exclaimed from behind a display off to my right. "What are you doing here?"

I dug a tissue from my purse. "I need to get something for my mom."

"Oh, yes, I heard of her unfortunate incident."

"What?" I blew my nose.

"What about your mother?"

"She was sick. I just need something, quick and easy. I know you don't like her. I'll take something already made."

"Here." She shoved a vase of pale pink and white carnations into my hands. "Take this. On the house," she added as she removed the little Mylar balloon that read *It's a girl!* from the bouquet.

I left because she had gotten too close and I couldn't breathe, could barely see. As I walked toward my Explorer, I had a horrifying epiphany.

"Mel!" I shrieked as I ripped open the driver's door. "I think Pearl is the killer."

"No way!" she said. "Get in. Tell me."

I climbed into the driver's seat and pulled more tissues from my purse. "So, right before I was shoved into Mr. Wooley's pantry my eyes burned a little. I thought it was from the onions in there, but my eyes didn't burn when I was there today. The only time I have that problem is when I'm near her."

"Okay. And?"

"Well, she's mean and creepy, and she doesn't like my mother." I blew my nose.

"I don't think we can call Beatty with just that."

"I don't either. What do you think we should do?"

"I haven't a clue."

We sat in the truck, silently mulling over the situation. At some point I realized if I didn't leave the parking lot soon, I'd have to pay the full-day rate for parking. I started up the engine.

"You have a plan?" Mel asked.

"No. We have to check in with Ma. If we exclude her, she'll kill us with some honey or whatever else is in her collection of healthy products."

Knowing my mother's dislike of coffee, despite its being a bean from a plant as I'd pointed out to her numerous times, I knew she wouldn't have any in her house. So Mel and I loaded up with extra-large cups before we headed to my childhood home.

"You really think it would be a good idea for you to officially move in with me?" I asked.

"Not in your current home," Mel said.

"I can't leave it."

"Why?"

"It's Gram's! How would she feel?"

"Like maybe Peri's moving up in the world."

"We can't afford anything like what Mr. Wooley had."

"So you're thinking about it?"

I honked my horn at the delivery truck in front of me trying to make Fifteenth Street a three-lane road. "I don't know what happened to me. I used to be able to look at the world and say, 'This goes here. That goes there. I'll do this and that will happen.' " I shook my head and sighed. "It seems like since the day Mr. Wooley died, I haven't been able to think straight. I almost answered you with 'let me take care of this funeral and then your marriage and then I'll think about it.' What happened to me? I should be able to take care of it all at one time. *And,* I still haven't spoken to Mick since he came to see Ez in the hospital. I think Todd's leaving tomorrow or maybe Sunday. I'm running out of time to get him and Mick to talk."

The delivery truck stopped. I did, too.

"Back up," Mel ordered.

I looked in my rear view. "I can't."

"Not the car, *you!* You need to back up." She hit my arm. "I know exactly why you can't think straight. You're thinking about too many things that aren't your responsibility to think about. You're frying your brain!"

"I'm about to fry that idiot's brain! Look!" I pointed at the truck in front of me. The driver had gotten out and was opening the rear loading door. So I did put my SUV in reverse, hit the left blinker and backed up as far as I could. "He's making a delivery right here in the middle of the street. I specifically avoided Broad Street because it doesn't seem like anyone knows how to drive down that road anymore. Now I'm thinking there's something in the air around here and it's spreading. Like a virus is killing off driving brain cells."

"His truck is bigger than everyone else's. I think that gives him the right away," Mel said. "Don't change the subject."

I waved and smiled nicely to the taxi driver in the next lane to let me go ahead of him. He ignored me, but the older gentleman in the Town Car behind him let me in. "I always have better luck with old men," I said waving *thank you* to him. "Maybe that's who I should be dating."

"Again, stop changing the subject." Mel turned sideways in her seat. "It's not your job to fix my marriage or to fix Todd's relationship with Mick."

"But they both need fixing and no one else is willing to do it."

"Maybe they don't need fixing. Maybe no one else seems willing to work on them because some things aren't worth working on. Some things just need to go to the junkyard and die."

I couldn't produce a response until I turned right on Spruce Street. "You make me sound like a hoarder."

"I kinda think you are. A relationship hoarder. You have no problems letting go of old stuff and unused things in your house, but boy, once someone is in some kinda relationship you can't let it be anything other than that. You can't even call the utility companies to change the name on the bill from your grandmother's to yours because you don't want your relationship to completely end with her."

"Dammit!" I said. "Why'd you let me turn at Spruce? Now I'm going to have to go all the way around . . ." I sighed. She remained silent. After a few minutes, as I wove my way back around to where I really needed to be, I caved. "I hate it when you're right, you know that?"

Chapter 34: Literally Your Life

Eventually, I made it to my parents' place but I didn't park. I passed by and turned at the end of the block.

"We messed up," I said. "It's lunchtime."

"What are we going to do?" She gripped my arm. "I can't eat there!"

"It's okay," I said. "We can kill two birds. Let's test my idea about people recognizing Mr. Wooley. We can go up to La Colombe and nose around while we have a pastry and more coffee."

La Colombe can be confusing for first timers, which judging by the look on Mel's face, is exactly what she was.

"How do you know what to order?" she asked me in a whisper. "There are no menus. Is everyplace like this now? Suddenly, I can't remember dining anywhere except at one of Ed's pubs. I never had sushi until last night. I've never ordered without a menu. What's going on in this world?"

"It's just the way they do it here." I patted her back. "No menus. Most of the people are regulars, though, which is why I'm wondering if any of the baristas had recognized Mr. Wooley lately."

When it was our turn at the chic and modern counter, I ordered two cappuccinos and two peach tarts. We stepped aside to wait.

"I feel old here," Mel said. "Why does everyone look so young?"

"Because we're surrounded by a lot of art students," I said.

"Don't worry about it, though. Most of them smoke. In ten years, you'll look younger than they will. Oh, first cup is done." I reached for the drink. Some young guy grabbed it instead.

"Yo, dude, wrong cup." I tugged it out of his hand.

"Sorry!" He backed off.

"That's it," said the barista. "Give the hipster some Philly attitude. Maybe he'll go home." He handed me our other cup.

"Thanks," I said passing it to Mel.

"Hey, doesn't Shelby Wooley come in here all the time?" she asked him. I was impressed. She catches on and thinks fast. "I haven't seen him in, like, forever."

"Ha!" he laughed. "He still does. Just not as his usual self." He turned to take orders from the hipster crowd.

"See that?" I asked. "He *was* recognizable!"

Mel sipped her cappuccino. "Oh. My." She panted, once. "Gawd." She closed her eyes and took a longer sip. "This is the best. I could orgasm right here, right now. Why do we go to Wawa?"

"There's more of them than La Colombes." I steered her to a tiny table. We sat to eat our tarts.

"So he was recognizable even in drag," I said. "Since he was killed in the evening on Thursday, I say we go to The Franklin tonight and see if anyone remembers him leaving with someone from there."

"I've only heard about that place, never been in." Mel nibbled and swallowed harder than I thought was necessary.

"You've never been in The Franklin? It's a landmark!"

She wouldn't meet my eyes. I could tell by the set jaw she was burning inside.

"So you and Ed never went anywhere other than one of his pubs?"

"Correct." She took another bite. I watched her chew.

"So the pubs were literally your life."

"Correct," she repeated. Another bite. More chewing.

"So I think maybe you're right. Some things should be thrown in the junkyard."

She looked up and smirked. "I think I might need a croissant to go. I'll eat it on the way to your parents' place."

Once sufficiently loaded with carbs and caffeine, we made our jittery way back to beautiful, tree-lined Delancey Place. My parents were home, resting, obviously resting in their living room. We could see them and Madder through the windows.

I brought in the pink and white bouquet.

"What a charming arrangement!" Ma exclaimed as she held it aloft. "There's a sweet innocence about it. The perfect gift to balance out the negative vibe of attempted murder." She hugged me with her free arm. "You have the perfect eye poopsie." She set the flowers down on the coffee table and returned to her snuggled position in the crook of my father's arm.

Mel sat next to Madder on the love seat and I took the free chair.

"We came for your help, Ma," I said.

"What can I do for you?"

I glanced at Mel then Madder. He was the wild card in the room. I knew him only through Pearl. If I were right, there was a strong possibility he'd throw in his allegiance to her.

I guess I took too long to respond because I realized everyone in the room was staring at me, Madder included. He had a cup of my mother's tea in his hand. That's right, he was drinking tea in the home of the people who bailed him out of jail. I knew he'd side with my parents, not Pearl. I nodded to him.

"I think Pearl Slack is the murderer," I said.

"BOOM!" Madder yelled, jumping up. "Man, I knew there was something not right with her." He ripped me out of the chair. "Let's go get her."

"Wait!" I shook myself loose from him. "I don't think it's that easy. First of all, I'm not a hundred percent sure. That's why we came to you, Ma. You need to tell us how one of your TV heroes would handle it."

I explained the smell at Mr. Wooley's house thinking what I had thought was bad onions was really Pearl's perfume.

"That's all you got?" Ma asked.

"Well, yeah." I glanced at Madder. Clearly, he was disappointed.

"So we need you to help us get more," Mel said.

Ma stood and paced around the living room, tapping her chin as she walked.

"Did she know Wooley was in town?" she asked.

"Not officially. We just spoke to a coffee barista who'd clearly recognized him in his women's clothing."

"Mr. Wooley was a drag queen?" Madder asked.

"Yes. That's what the original flowers were for. His coming out party."

"It's possible he was in the shop last week," he said.

"WHAT?" I think all three women said it at the same time, maybe even my father, too.

"Yes. This older man came in wearing a red dress and shoes and a big, wide red hat. His was wearing makeup, but he was definitely a man. You could see his Adam's apple."

"Go on." I texted Jacqueline to see if she could text me a photo of her dad.

"He wanted a fresh black rose to put in his hat for the day."

"That's all?" I asked.

"Yeah. I mean, Pearl looked at him funny, but she looks at everyone funny. He said he'd wait for her to dye one, so he sat on a stool while she went in the back to dye the flower."

My phone dinged with Jacqueline's response. "Here." I showed Madder the photograph. "Did he look like this?"

He took my phone. "Exactly like that. Only with very red lips."

"How did he pay?" Ma asked. "Did he use a credit card?"

"I think so."

"Crap!" I yelled. "I should have thought of that! His credit card would have his name on it!"

"Right," Ma said, still pacing. "So Pearl knew it was him for sure. Okay, I have a plan. Let's stake out her house and wait for her to come home. Then, *before* she goes inside," she paused to nod once to me, "we'll surround her and make her confess. We won't go inside because Peri will be with us so we won't have anyone to call when we get arrested."

"Why don't we just go to the shop and do it?" I asked.

"Why do you want to ruin my fantasy?" Ma wanted to know.

"I'm not trying to ruin your fantasy. I'm just thinking she probably won't leave the shop until it closes. We have several hours between now and then. Why are we waiting?"

"I suppose we could corner her at the shop," Ma said. "You just wait outside, Peri. That way when the police come, you won't be incriminated."

"I can't get arrested again, Honey," Madder said. "Suppose we could make her confess in a way where I would stay out of jail?"

"Aren't we all kind of ignoring the obvious, here?" I said. "Why aren't we calling the police?"

"Again, why are you ruining all the fun?" Ma asked.

I sighed as I crumpled onto the sofa. "You guys go. Make her confess. I'll stay here and wait for Philly PD to show up on caller ID."

"Maybe I stay here with Peri," Madder said.

"Mel, are you in with me?" Ma asked.

"Oh why not? I've had the most exciting week of my life. Why not end it by going to jail?" She shook hands with my mom. "How will we make her confess?"

"She'll charm her into it." My father stood and kissed my mom, hard, on the mouth. He cupped her bottom with both hands. "You go get 'em girl," he said before heading toward the kitchen.

Ma went upstairs to change clothes, thankfully. She was still wearing the hospital gown with the back ties tied.

"That's the kind of relationship I want," Mel said. "Like what your parents have."

"The kind that makes everyone else uncomfortable?"

"Yeah, I think so."

"Me too," Madder added. "There's something truly beautiful about your parents."

"Then why does she take hiatuses?" I asked.

Mel and Ma left together talking about role-playing good-cop and bad-cop on the way to the flower shop. They both wanted to be the bad cop. I realized it was close to time for me to let Noreen out of Mr. Wooley's house so I hunted down my father. He was up on the third floor in his office, reading through papers in a manila file.

"Hey there, Dad," I said, rapping on the doorjamb.

"Hello my sweet," he responded, taking off his glasses.

"I just wanted to let you know I'm heading out, now. Madder is doing something in the greenhouse that he said Ma wanted him to do."

"Sounds good to me." He rounded the desk to plant a kiss on my cheek.

"Keep your phone handy," he said. "In case your mother needs you. She's never been right with any of those television mysteries, you know. I can't imagine she's on the right track now."

"What do you mean?"

"I have a client coming in soon, so I won't be able to answer my phone. You'll need to be on call in case your mom winds up in a little trouble again." He hugged me. "I love you, sweet heart. You're such a joy."

I left my father's office, taking my time going down the stairs instead of using their elevator. The weight of his words just seemed to require me to move slowly.

Ma was never right.

Did we rush to judgment?

Was Pearl the wrong person?

Was I setting that poor, over-stressed, over-worked floral designer up for a full-on Honey attack?

I may have sighed as I got in my Ford a few minutes later. I may have sighed a lot because I knew how disappointed my mother would be to find out she was wrong.

Chapter 35: Detailed Motions

I stopped by an ATM to get the cash I'd need to pay Noreen, then called Beatty when I was on my way to Wooley's.

"How are you?" I asked with too much cheerful, positive energy.

"Not good now," he responded. "What happened? Wait. Should I put this on speaker so Jameson can hear?

"That might be handy."

"You're on."

"You're going to find this funny," I said. "My mother and Melissa are on their way to Custom Floral. They may even be there now, to force Pearl Slack into confessing to Mr. Wooley's murder."

"That's not funny," Jameson said.

"Right, well, I thought I'd give you guys fair warning. Pearl isn't fond of my mom. They were once rivals in an herbology class. Things could get ugly."

Beatty burst out laughing.

"I love your mom," he said when he calmed down. "Any reason why they suspect the florist?"

I told him my story.

"So it's all your fault that things could, as you say, get ugly?" Beatty asked.

"Possibly."

He and Jameson both laughed.

"Well, it's certainly an interesting theory," Jameson said. "Interesting enough that maybe we'll stop by the florist today."

"I haven't made it out to Wooley's house yet," Beatty said. "Do you think the housecleaner is still there?"

"I'm on my way to let her out now."

"Sounds like you're talking about a dog. Keep her there for us, would ya? We'll be heading over soon."

I called Mel's cell.

"Perfect timing," she said. "Your mom just cornered Pearl."

"Oh no! Is she browbeating her?"

"I'm not sure what browbeating means," Mel whispered. "She's lecturing her on the dangers of chemicals in perfumes."

"I'm so relieved."

"Don't be. Pearl just threatened to call the cops if we don't leave. So far, your mother has destroyed three floral arrangements in an effort to make them look better, and ruined a mauve coat by trying to force Pearl to throw away all of her artificial dyes."

"Is all that part of her effort to make Pearl confess?"

"She said she was trying to butter her up. The plan was to make it look like they had a lot in common and then your mom would try to help her somehow and then . . . I don't know, Peri. I'm sure wishing I had stayed with you."

"Tell Ma that Detective Beatty has already dismissed Pearl as a suspect."

"Did he really? When did you speak to him?"

"He didn't. I just told him and Jameson our theory. They didn't think it was anything that should make them dash right over."

"Damn! I was hoping we were on to something."

"Yeah, me too." I turned down Mr. Wooley's street. "We'll regroup later and see what else we can come up with. Right now I gotta take care of Noreen."

I pulled over and parked street side behind a blue hatchback with New Jersey license plates. I figured it belonged to Noreen since it was the only car around. Suddenly, I realized that's why Beatty had been having such a tough time finding her. If he had been looking for a car licensed in Pennsylvania, or a woman living in the Philly area named Noreen Parkerson, he wouldn't find her. Noreen was a Jersey girl.

I got out of my truck and lingered, staring at the blue car. Beatty was insistent that I kept her here at the house. Was there a specific reason? Could she be the last of the nine people I'd told him about that he had yet to clear? Did that mean something?

Did it mean I had neglected to tell my mom something that maybe would have helped her solve her first case?

I leaned against my Ford and called her.

Her voice mail answered.

I called Mel, who picked up immediately. "Oh my God, Peri! She won't stop talking. Pearl is crouching under some shelves in the corner. You mom has her pinned there and she won't stop talking about plants and herbs and poisons. Come get her!"

"Make her get on the phone. Tell her it's a matter of life or death for me."

"Honey!" Mel shouted. "Peri needs to speak to you. Now! She's in danger or something."

I heard a shuffling and the sound of something breaking. I put the call on speaker so I could use the phone to send myself an e-mail reminder. I wanted to make sure I called Pearl to make arrangements to pay for whatever damage my mother had done. I heard Ma tell Mel they couldn't leave the shop but it sounded like they did anyway because suddenly there were honks and other city traffic sounds in the background.

"Poopsie!" Mom shouted into the phone. "What's wrong?"

"Who referred Noreen Parkerson to you?" I asked.

"What?"

"Who referred Noreen Parkerson to you?" I asked louder.

"Peri Mercury! I cannot believe you interrupted my interrogation! I think Pearl was about to crack!"

"Ma, she didn't do it. But I think you know who did."

"What?" she asked yet again.

"Think hard, Ma. Who referred Noreen Parkerson to you?"

"We gotta run!" Mel yelled in the background.

"I'll call ya in a minute." Ma clicked off.

I got back in my SUV so I could sit. In my mind's eye, I could picture Pearl chasing them down the street. Perfume bottle held aloft, spraying with abandon directly at my mother's dreadlocks flying behind her.

Ma called back from her cell a few minutes later.

"We're in the car, Peri. Do you need to be rescued? Where are you?"

"I'm at Mr. Wooley's house. I need to know about Noreen Parkerson. How did she get referred to you?"

"Let me think." She paused. I knew she was tapping her chin. "I believe an associate of your father's referred her to us. Why?"

"She's Mr. Wooley's housecleaner. Or she was, anyway."

"And?"

"And I just thought it was convenient. She worked for him. She didn't like you . . ."

"I'm still not understanding why this was so important that you had to interrupt me."

I sighed. "Call Dad," I said. "Ask him who referred Noreen to you. It's very important. Please do it now." I clicked off hoping she'd do it and make the same connection I was making before Beatty arrived. That is, of course, if I was making the right connection.

As I got back out of my Explorer, I remembered my dad saying he had an appointment with a client. I looked at the time on my phone. If the client came right after I left, then he or she would still be in therapy for at least another fifteen minutes. I was going to have to stall Noreen.

I tucked my phone into my back pocket as I headed up the walk to Mr. Wooley's front door.

She was waiting for me in the kitchen, in the same chair where I'd left her.

"I just want to make a quick tour of the house," I told Noreen. "Stay right there a minute." I went upstairs. Walked through each bedroom. Everything was perfect. There wasn't even dust on top of the picture frames.

I spun a circle in Mr. Wooley's bedroom wondering how long I could stall Noreen with nothing to do.

It was then when my eyes landed on Tiger, the freeze-dried dog.

I held my breath—I don't know why—and picked him up. With his body held as far away from me as possible, I took him into the red-velvet dressing room. I rubbed him all over the velvet chaise lounge. I didn't know much about dogs, but I was pretty sure they shed.

Tiger didn't.

So instead of calling Noreen up to vacuum the chaise, I took the dog to her.

"Hey there," I said as brightly as I could. Tiger was under my arm, as if that's where he belonged. I hoped she couldn't tell how stiff my torso was as I did my best to not actually let him touch me.

She eyed him up, flaring her nostrils into a snarl.

"What are you doing with that thing?" she asked, sinking her chin into her chest.

"I'm supposed to take it to the funeral home so that it can be buried with Mr. Wooley," I explained as if I were telling her it was a beautiful day outside. I think I was even smiling like an idiot.

She grunted, maybe snarled a little.

"So I was wondering if maybe you could use the brush-head on the vacuum nozzle to give him a good onceover." I shoved the dog out in front of her face.

"You're crazy." She pushed back her chair and stood.

"No, I'm not. Honest," I said, because a truly crazy person would have agreed with her. "I'm following through on the instructions he left in his will."

She shoved the chair into place at the table.

"Fifty dollars extra," I added, barely able to refrain from saying *ka-ching!*

"You hold it."

She pulled the vacuum out of the utility room off to the side of the kitchen, attached the brush to the nozzle and set to work. She had a methodical approach, making straight, barely overlapping lines from the front to the rear of the dog. I turned it over to let her do his stomach thinking it was too bad she'd spend the rest of her life in jail. I knew several other clients who could use her.

We were still alone when she finished.

"Did you sweep the back stoop and driveway?" I asked.

She glared at me with one eye almost shut. "Another fifty," she snarled.

"Absolutely." I nodded. "You do great work. I agree. Another fifty."

She replaced the vacuum and took the broom out. Once she was outside, I watched her sweep, using similar slow, systematic and detailed motions to what she used with the vacuum. I called Mel.

"Where are you guys?"

"Your parents' place."

"Did Ma ask Dad where he got Noreen yet?"

"I don't think so."

"Make her! I think Noreen is the killer but I want Ma to figure that out."

"Why do you think that?"

"No time to explain. I'm stalling Noreen at Mr. Wooley's for as long as I can. Beatty is on his way to talk to her, too. Ma needs to get her ass here and solve the mystery!"

"Okay! I'll nudge her."

We clicked off. I texted Beatty. *Where r u?* and replaced the phone in my back pocket.

I paced around the kitchen scheming for more stalling tactics. None came to me. What did come was the realization that I was petting Tiger as I carried him under my arm. He gave me something to do with my hands. I finally understood how pets could be calming. I was certain if he were alive and responding positively, I probably would have enjoyed the time we were spending together.

Noreen finished sweeping and came inside. She glanced at the microwave clock. "I have been here a half hour longer than expected."

"I'll add that to the hundred I just added to the four-hour deep-clean rate," I said.

She smacked fleshy lips as she gathered a bucket of dirty rags and a canvas bag that I assumed was her purse.

"So do you have more houses to do today?" I asked, following her to the front of the house.

"I'm done."

"You really do a great job," I said as she opened the front door. We exited together. "Really. You must really enjoy your work."

She stopped on the sidewalk to cast a wary glance my way before continuing without responding. Perhaps I used one too many *reallys*.

"So now that you're down a client, will you be taking on more?" I asked.

We stopped at the back of her car. She opened the hatch. I was surprised by the interior. It was littered to near maximum capacity.

"I don't want any more clients from you," she said as she struggled to find a place for her bucket of rags.

"You . . . why not?" I asked Noreen. "I work for some of the most prestigious and well-respected people in Philadelphia."

"And you know some crackpots," she said.

"I do not."

"I suppose with a mother like yours, you never learned to tell the difference," she mumbled. She shoved the pile of debris forward in her car to make more room.

"Excuse me?" I grabbed her arm. Only close friends and relatives get to make disparaging remarks about a Philly girl's mom. In addition to the Philly girl herself, of course. "My mother may be a bit eccentric, but she has a heart of gold. You will never find someone more understanding, more compassionate, more—"

"Whatever." She shook out of my grip. "Where's my money?"

My cell buzzed in my pocket with a text. I pulled it out and read the message from Mel: *Weissman referred Noreen!!!! We're on way!*

Chapter 36: Came To Again

I replaced the phone in my pocket.

"I don't have all the money on me right now." I crossed my arms. "I had no idea how much extra you were going to charge me."

"When will you be paying me?"

I sat on the edge of the opened hatch of Noreen's car with Tiger in my lap. "Let me see," I said and pet him while I pretended to think long and hard. "This is the first time a client of mine ever died so I'm not really sure how long it will take for his estate to be settled."

"Unless he had legal or tax problems, it shouldn't take long," Noreen said.

"By long, how long do you mean?" I asked.

"Within a month."

"Have you had experience with customers dying?" I asked her. "You could probably teach me what to do. I'm sure I'm leaving things undone."

She gave me that squinty-eyed glare again. I swallowed hard because I realized I'm probably a bad actor and she's now suspicious of my motives for talking to her.

"Though I guess every situation is different, right?" I asked. "Ahem. So, about your cash . . . or are you okay with a check? I don't think I have your mailing address."

She spit. She literally spit on the sidewalk.

"You know, I think I remember learning somewhere that it's illegal to spit on the sidewalk," I said to her. "Why would you do such a thing? That's disgusting."

Tires squealed in the distance.

She stepped to the side to look around my SUV. I stood to look, too.

"Oh, I think that's my mother," I said.

Noreen turned on her heel and shoved me into her car. Before I had a chance to respond, she slammed the back hatch shut. Next thing I know, I'm careening down the road under a pile of rags and rubble.

I wiggled my arm under me and pulled out my phone. The hatch was so overfilled with crap, I couldn't quite get the phone to the point where I could see it clearly. It took three tries before I got through to Beatty.

"You missed Noreen," I hissed into the phone. "She's kidnapped me. I'm in the back of her car. It's blue. A hatchback with Jersey plates and it's being followed by my mother's hot pink Prius."

"I'd think you were joking if it weren't for the fact that I just passed a blue hatchback with Jersey plates followed by a pink Prius."

By the time I climbed out of the debris enough to be able to see, we were on Kelly Drive heading away from the city. Ma and Mel were right on our tail. Ma waved at me and gave me the thumbs up. I heard sirens. Before I could return the thumbs-up, Noreen's car screeched to a halt and Ma crashed into us.

My head slammed into something hard and I blacked out, again.

I came to as a couple of EMTs were putting me on a stretcher. I heard my mother's voice in the background.

"As soon as Archie told me Leeann Weissman had referred Noreen to us," she was telling someone, "I knew she was the killer. I just had to rush to save my precious Peri. Oh look, she's awake!"

Ma approached my side as an EMT shone a light in my eyes.

"Your pupils are not dilating right," he said. "I think we need to take you in. You might have a concussion."

"Nonsense," Ma said. "Peri always passes out when she doesn't want to face something."

"I didn't pass out, Ma." I let my head fall back on the stretcher. "I bashed my head on something when you hit us."

"I'm so sorry Peri." She kissed my forehead. "I didn't mean for that to happen."

"That's okay," I said. "Tell him I don't want to go to the hospital. I can't take the bill."

"If I smashed you then I think my insurance should cover it," she said. "If not, Dad and I will be happy to. Well, not happy about you being in the hospital, but you know what I mean."

Beatty came over before I could respond. "You okay enough to give me a statement?" he asked.

"My head hurts to think, but I might be able to handle it." I tried to sit up. Ma grabbed my shoulder to keep me down. "Wait! The dog!" I said.

"What dog?" Beatty asked. Mel approached from behind him.

"In the back of Noreen's car, there's a freeze-dried dog. We gotta save it."

"I'll just talk to you after you're seen by the doctors," he said.

"Actually, she didn't bump her head that hard," Mel interrupted. "I know what she's talking about. Peri's just taking care of her people. I'll get it Per."

The docs at the hospital made me stay the night. I wasn't sure if it was because they were worried about my concussion or about the kind of treatment they thought I'd get from my mom. I'm still not sure how they expected me to rest and heal with all the interruptions. Between the nurses making their rounds and the beeping machines, I barely slept all night. I had a screaming headache when Gabe and Raphael brought me breakfast the next day.

"How's the head?" he asked as he handed me a pastry bag.

"It hurts." I peeked in at a croissant. "I'm a little nauseous now. My mom forced me to take an herb that's not sitting well with me."

"It's not my herb, poopsie," Ma said from the empty bed in my room. She had slept on it the night before. "It's your concussion."

"Anyway, Gabe, I appreciate it, though I think I'll eat this later." I set the bag on the tray table. "How did you know I was in here?"

"We spoke on the phone last night." He sat on the edge of the bed.

"Sorry. Things are a little hazy."

"Trust me, I understand." His dark eyes laughed into mine.

"Maybe I need to learn some self-defense moves," I said. "You know any good teachers? My cousin and I are going for our detective licenses."

"Me too!" Ma yelped. She sat up. "The three of us. We'll be the Three Musketeers of Detectivetry. Detectivery. Detectionary?" She tapped her chin. "We'll make up the right word. Right, Peri?"

"Right, Ma."

"Did she tell you how it happened?" Ma patted the space beside her and, after getting the nod from Gabe, Raphael jumped up to sit by her.

"A little." Gabe squeezed my hand.

"Well, for some reason, she became obsessed over where Archie had found Noreen and started bugging me to find out. I think that was her psychic intuition kicking in. Her inner spirit was trying to tell her. Actually, I'm wondering if she was channeling her grandmother." She pinched her chin in thought. "Anyway, I asked Archie. It turned out that Leeann Weissman, who's a fellow professor with him at Temple, recommended her. I thought it very strange that Leeann's husband had been killed by poison, Shelby Wooley had been killed by poison, and someone fed me poison and we all knew Noreen."

"So she killed Weissman, too?" I asked.

"She did. Do you know why?"

"Ma, I didn't even know she killed him."

Ma threw a dreadlock over her shoulder and leaned forward as if to be intimate. "She's a very bitter woman." She nodded. "Her husband had left her when they were very young, shortly after marrying. She never let herself heal from it so she turned into the mean-spirited person she is today. That's what I tried to help her with, you know. I wanted her to find her happiness."

"You told her she was unlayable," I said.

"I told her she'd be more relaxed if she'd have a little sex every now and then and that it's easier to do so when you look layable. Get your facts straight, poopsie."

I glanced at Gabe. He winked back.

"Okay then," I said. "She was bitter over her husband leaving her."

"Right. He'd left her over twenty years earlier."

"How do you know all this?"

"I knew her past from when she worked for me. She used to complain about me pestering her with questions. So I knew her whole past. Her hubby had been in the bee business. When he left her, he left it. So she'd been handling bees and honey in her angered state for a very long time. Few people make a living from bees, and she wasn't one of them. That's why she did housecleaning, dog sitting, and numerous other side jobs throughout the years."

"So she killed Sy Weissman because . . ."

"He was her first guinea pig. I guess she was cleaning their place one day when he had scheduled exterminators to come in and spray. They filled the indoors with that evil stuff when she was working. They even attached something to a hose and sprayed down the outside, including the driveway where her car was parked. Beekeepers don't like pesticides. So the next time she came in to clean for him, she switched out his honey with some of her own special blend."

"So she killed Sy Weissman because . . ." I repeated.

"He was a bee killer in her eyes. She got even."

"Wow."

"The same for Shelby Wooley. She came in one day when the exterminator was leaving."

"I remember that!" I said, sitting up much too quickly. I got dizzy and lay back. "She made a nasty remark about *that homicidal man.* I had no idea she who she was talking about. Now it makes sense."

"Yes. The police are now looking into more deaths here and over in Jersey that could be tied to her."

"Holy cow," I blew out a stream of air. I didn't sigh. I was just processing what my mother was telling me. "So why did she try to kill you?" I asked. "You've never used a pesticide in your life. Was it over your argument?"

"No. Actually, she wasn't trying to kill me. She was—"

"Trying to frame you for the other murders. That's what Jacqueline thought."

"Speaking of me," Jacqueline waltzed into the room. Mel followed her. Jacqueline was head-to-toe black. Black Chanel-looking suit, which probably was Chanel. Black chemise. Black pearls. A long black veil attached to a new black hat. Black gloves and black shoes. But she wore true red lipstick.

Mel, on the other hand, had on black jeans, a gray and white sweater and Coral Bombshell lipstick.

"Speaking of you," I prompted.

"I'm here."

"We're on our way to the funeral." Mel kissed my cheek. "I'm sorry you can't go."

"I'm sure you are." I pressed the button on my bed allowing me to slowly sit up more. "How's Ezra? Where's Ezra? Did I speak to him last night? How's his blood sugar?"

Mel laughed as she came around to sit opposite Gabe on the bed. "Todd brought him and Mick in last night. I guess they had spent the evening together. You told them you were glad they kissed and made up."

"Did they?"

"Apparently so."

"That sucks." I pouted.

"What's wrong?" Gabe asked.

"They didn't need me." I took a deep breath. "Though I think it might feel kind of freeing, too."

"Don't worry, Peri," Jacqueline said, putting her hand on Melissa's shoulder. "I shall always need you and your benevolent wisdom." She tilted her head and sighed then turned to my mother. "Did you make more of your tea?"

Acknowledgements

I had so much fun writing this book. Thanks to Honey, I had a chance to combine some of the unique, funny, beautiful and lovable traits of people I've been fortunate enough to meet in the course of my crazy life. This book also gave me a few challenges. I'm a girl with a squeamish stomach. For helping me with the hospital, toxin and concussion details, I thank my sister-in-law, Jennifer Shiroff, and my friend, Maureen Weiss. Their medical expertise helped me make this story possible, because believe it or not, honey (just like almost anything) can be a murder weapon. I thank Joyce Mitchell for letting me wrangle her into becoming my editor and for tolerating my quirkiness *and* for dealing with my insistence on style **and** helping with the "buts." I thank Dana Weinberg because I believe it was during one of our walks when I "met" Mr. Wooley and his story came to life. Then it was on many of our walks that we worked through issues I had with it. And I thank my many good friends— particularly the abundance of other Lisas I've been blessed with, a couple more Jens, and just one Florence—who have never doubted my ability to tell a story, who have always supported my writing efforts, and who are really just great people. I also thank my kids for tolerating the dinner table talk. I know it's not always easy when Mom gets stuck in a story and goes on and on and on about things like how rhododendrons can kill. You guys could become saints if it weren't for the fact that you're Jewish. Finally, I thank Esther and Abraham for teaching me more than I can grasp. I love you all!

About The Author

Lisa Shiroff writes because she's not sure what else she can do with herself. Oh sure, she's a wife, mom of two kids, and she manages to walk her dog every day, but as far as careers go, the only thing she knows how to do is write, cook and mix a drink. Chefs and bartenders have to work weekends, though, so she's sticking to the writing gig. She currently resides in south Jersey where she has easy access to Philadelphia and Ben Franklin's grave.

You can learn more about her books, check out photos from Philly and find the recipes to Peri's baked goods on Lisa's website at (where else?): www.lisashiroff.com.

Or you can stalk her in a non-creepy way:

Friend her on Facebook: https://www.facebook.com/lisa.shiroff.9

Follow her on Twitter: @LisaShiroff

Check Out Her Other Books
Hitting the Sauce
Revenge Café

And short Stories:
What You Tell Yourself
What Others Tell You
A Most Original Story

www.ingramcontent.com/pod-product-compliance
Lightning Source LLC
Chambersburg PA
CBHW020612110726
47899CB00002B/480